Praise for

Louise Pentland

'Gorgeously **warm and relatable** – I loved being in
Robin Wilde's world!'
PAIGE TOON

'I'd love Robin Wilde to be my new best friend. In fact, I feel
like she's become it through these pages. **Wonderfully written**
and full of humour that had me laughing along from start to
finish . . . **Funny, heartfelt, tender** and **empowering!**'
GIOVANNA FLETCHER

'Totally hilarious, this boasts a **refreshingly relatable** view
of just **how tough motherhood can be**'
HEAT MAGAZINE

'**Utterly self-assured**, so, so, so **honest and downright brave** . . .
Every page is packed with hard-earned wisdom, joy and truth'
LINDSEY KELK

'**Warm and engaging** . . . [Robin Wilde is a] chatty,
winning yet poignant heroine'
SOPHIE KINSELLA

'So much **warmth, heart** and **honesty** . . . Louise's exploration
of mental health issues is refreshingly honest. If you've ever
felt like the only person in the world who isn't perfect . . . this
is what you need to read. A fabulous mix of escapism
and relatability, **this is a hug of a book**'
DAISY BUCHANAN

LOUISE PENTLAND is the *Sunday Times* bestselling author of the Wilde novels trilogy and non-fiction book *MumLife*. She's the number one parenting vlogger in the UK, with 9 million combined followers across her social platforms. Louise is the creator and host of the podcast *Mothers' Meeting*, where she interviews fellow mums and discusses all things motherhood.

Louise featured on the '*Sunday Times* Top 100 Influencers' list and was crowned as the number one 'mumfluencer' by *Mother & Baby*. She was also a UN Global Ambassador for Gender Equality and an NSPCC Ambassador for Childhood. Louise has filmed with an array of people, from Kim Kardashian to the Pope at the Vatican. She is also involved in the support and encouragement of childhood literacy with charity Bookstart, alongside Prince Charles and the Duchess of Cornwall.

🐦 @LouisePentland
📷 @louisepentland

Also by Louise Pentland
Wilde Like Me
Wilde About the Girl
Wilde Women
MumLife

Louise Pentland

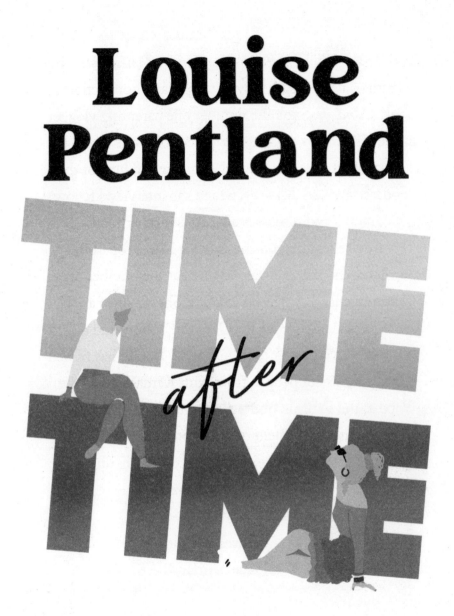

TIME after TIME

ZAFFRE

First published in the UK in 2022 by
ZAFFRE
An imprint of Bonnier Books UK
4th Floor, Victoria House, Bloomsbury Square, London, England, WC1B 4DA
Owned by Bonnier Books
Sveavägen 56, Stockholm, Sweden

This is a work of fiction. Names, places, events and
incidents are either the products of the author's
imagination or used fictitiously. Any resemblance to
actual persons, living or dead, or actual
events is purely coincidental.

A CIP catalogue record for this book is
available from the British Library.

Hardback ISBN: 978–1–83877–408–0
Trade Paperback ISBN: 978–1–83877–409–7

Also available as an ebook and an audiobook

1 3 5 7 9 10 8 6 4 2

Typeset by Envy Design Ltd
Printed and bound in Great Britain by Clays Ltd, Elcograf S.p.A.

Zaffre is an imprint of Bonnier Books UK
www.bonnierbooks.co.uk

This book is dedicated to anyone that's ever wanted
to go back and have one more moment.

Prologue

June

UNTIL ABOUT FOUR HOURS ago, my life was pretty uneventful. I have a little routine and I like it like that. I'm comfortable. Most days look like this: wake up, coffee, make and pack lunch for me and David (pasta salads, soups or pittas for me, and the exact same every day for him – ham and mustard sandwich, white bread, butter on one slice of the bread only and yes, he does notice if I don't do it exactly how he likes it), walk to Pearls and Doodles, the shop I work in – no, *manage*. My friend Vivi is always telling me not to downplay what I do, and I basically run Pearls and Doodles. Work all day (and fall into multiple scroll holes on Insta, oops), lock up, come home, make dinner for me and David, ring Mum to say hello, maybe text Vivi a bit, watch some TV and go to bed. Saturdays are usually for David's motorcross, and Sundays we go to Mum and Dad's for a roast. You might think it sounds boring, but I like it. It's quiet and predictable and filled with the people I love.

After today, I *really* like predictable!

I'm getting ahead of myself, though. Sorry. Let me tell you about my day.

Today is Sunday, and until about twenty minutes before we sat down for Mum's beef, everything was normal. Thankfully, despite being mid-June, it's not baking hot, so it doesn't feel quite as strange having the full roast shebang, even when most people would be crowded round a barbecue right now. Besides, even if we were having a freak heatwave Mum would do a roast. She's a woman of principle. 'Sundays are for roasts, it's how we like it,' she'd tell you.

Mum, every 'Fresh Honey' hair in place and wearing a smart short-sleeved wine-coloured fitted dress, had wheeled the faux-wood-clad heated hostess trolley into the dining room from the kitchen. Dad had ironed the white linen napkins earlier. I tell them every week that I don't mind eating in the kitchen with paper serviettes, but Mum insists. 'You have to have standards, Tabitha. Once

2

those slip, it all goes.' I'm not really sure what she thinks will go wrong if we don't use the 1980s hostess trolley or just grab a bit of kitchen roll for our laps, but I know not to make a fuss. If you think I'm stuck in my ways, you should meet my mum! There's no point arguing; we're having the linen. She looks forward to this all week: she takes pride in hoovering the dining room and refreshing the potpourri in the bowl on the well-dusted windowsill, so I don't want to upset the apple cart. I love my mum dearly. All the same – and I'd never say this to her (or to anyone else) – it does sometimes feel like she's stuck in the wrong decade. Picture Miranda's mum in, er, *Miranda*, and Violet Crawley from *Downton Abbey*. (But not so posh.) She's happy, though, and that's all that matters. I can cope with a bit of dated ritual for a few hours, especially if her cooking is involved.

'No David then today, love?' Mum asks in what she thinks is an oh-so-casual voice, but I know it's loaded. Mum and Dad aren't keen on David. He can be a bit mardy, but they don't see the nice moments like I do. The cups of tea brought up to bed; the fact that he always fills my car with petrol for me so I don't have to fight with the pumps; the way he always leaves me the last chocolate Hobnob in the packet. He's the best.

He's also started hinting about perhaps decorating the spare room, in preparation for, well, a baby, I guess. Just when the nappy ads come on on TV. I'm not sure how I feel about that, but I'm getting used to these sweet nudges.

I notice that Dad, equally smart in navy shirt and pressed chinos, looks up from his Yorkshire pudding batter, waiting to see how I'll react. Classic Dad. He doesn't say a lot, but I can read him like a book. He worries about me but wants me to have my own life without fussing round too much.

'Perhaps a bit busy, is he, Tabby Cat?' Dad suggests, softening Mum's tone a little, ever the peacemaker.

'He wanted to come but he's busy, yeah. Working on his car for the next race – pretty exciting,' I say, avoiding eye contact because, like Mum and Dad, I too wish David had prioritised this lunch – not that I'll admit that to them, or him. I don't want to be one of those women who doesn't let her boyfriend have fun.

'Oh dear. You'd think working in a garage he could do that during the week,' Mum says, quickly adding, 'but I do understand. We're not wild young fun things, are we, Tony?' She chuckles to Dad with a defusing laugh. Even though I know she has so much to say, she won't. No one wants to wobble that apple cart!

'Ha. No, not quite as wild or young these days.' Good old Dad. He looks back and forth to Mum and I, seemingly a bit nervous. He's not usually on edge. I don't think he's ever disagreed with her in his life. Or with anyone. He's a gentle soul, probably just over-thinking Mum's tone. She'll be fine. I brush away any concern for the perceived nerves, it'll be nothing.

I feel almost guilty about how nice they are. I wasn't really that annoyed at David, but now my parents are being so forgiving, I almost am.

'Well, he's the one missing out on Mum's beef, and now there's all the more for us!' I say, gesturing to my full plate that she's been serving up from the trolley while we've chatted.

'Quite right, lovely!' Mum jollies. Having had her little dig, she can move on. 'There might even be a few leftovers. Dad loves my beefy bits, don't you?' she adds with what I think she thinks is a flirty smile but that looks a bit odd.

She looks to Dad to back her up, and after an awkwardly long pause, he smiles and nods. I suspect he doesn't want to think too much about Mum's beefy bits during a family meal. No wonder he took his time there. Bloody hell.

Mum chatters on through the roast about all the latest gossip. I've spent my entire life with this woman, but I still can't keep up with her many friends and all the things that happen in our town of Ottleswan. Radio Barbara, she should be called. I love her weekly round-ups. Her best friend Debs is thinking of organising a fundraiser for the town. Suzanna thought her husband was having an affair, but in fact he was just secretly having scalp massages every week because he read in an online pop-up that it would help his receding hairline (she's a bit annoyed that he was doing something in secret, but mainly relieved he wasn't having it off with his colleague from Swindon). Amanda Across the Road's daughter has just had a baby (cue pang of guilt for not yet being ready to give them a grandchild, followed by another newer and rather surprising pang of baby envy). And have I seen the email she sent me about a three-week trip to Turks and Caicos that she and Dad are thinking of taking in October? She's sorry she's not got the full itinerary to share yet, but they've not booked anything so far.

'We should think about doing that soon, shouldn't we, Tony?' Mum says as she starts to clear away our plates and reaches into the hostess trolley for dessert. Mum is the queen of old-fashioned puddings. Anything stodgy and delicious you remember from your schooldays, she's a master of. Thanks to her hero, Delia, treacle tart, bread-and-butter pudding, jam roly-poly, trifle – Mum's puds are all to die for.

'Ooohh, what is it today, Mum? Pineapple upside-down cake?' I say, craning to see.

'Spotted dick today, love!' she says with great pride. 'Shouldn't we, Tony? We should book that now and get the early-bird discount. It's only a few months away.'

Dad looks at her in silence. It's a bit odd. I thought he'd say yes and reach for the custard, but he carries on just staring.

'Dad? Want some spotted dick?' I say, to nudge him out of his trance.

'Barbara, I need to talk to you,' he says solemnly. I look back and forth between the two of them trying to work out what on earth is happening.

'Oh God, Tony, what? What's happened? Is it the premium bond? Is it not worth what we thought? Because if it isn't, I've been putting some aside for a rainy day and I really don't mind using—' Mum starts gabbling.

'No! Barbara, stop! I can't – I can't keep doing this,' Dad blurts. I'm not sure I've ever heard him raise his voice. It sounds wrong.

Everyone freezes. Mum goes puce. She's not used to being interrupted. I feel a bit freaked out.

'Should I go?' I whisper, starting to move away from the table, taking my now crumpled linen napkin off my lap and placing it on the perfectly ironed tablecloth that we've had for as long as I can remember.

'No, love. Since David's not here and it's just the three of us, I think now— I think this is a good time. Well, as good a time as any. I'm not sure there is a good time for this . . .'

Honestly, my dad isn't one for drama, but the tension is worse than before they announce the winner on a reality TV show where a second feels like an hour, and I have to bite my lip to stop myself from telling him to spit it out.

'I, well, gosh, this is hard to say. I've wanted to tell you and your mum . . . Well, I've wanted to tell you, Barbara, but Tabitha will need to know as well—'

'Oh my God, Tony, is it back?' Mum grips her spoon and her knuckles whiten. 'Have you found another mole? Dr Astew said if we see any new marks on the skin, even years after, we should go back straightaway. We can sort it early. We survived last time, we can do it again. I'm not going to—'

'No, Barbara. Please! Let me just say it.' Dad looks almost grey with worry, which is odd as he's quite tanned from all

8

the time he spends in the garden. My garden, sometimes, bless him. Mum is still a firm shade of crimson. None of us does well with 'big things'. We're not 'big things' people. We're Sunday-roasts-every-week people. That's how we like it.

'All right, Tony,' Mum says, surprisingly calmly. 'If the cancer's not back, thank God, and it's not money, what is it?'

We both look at Dad, this time nobody butting in.

'It's Bernie,' Dad says simply.

'Bernie? Bernard Miles, from the pub?' Mum asks incredulously, visibly relaxing. She exhales softly and reaches for the serving spoon for the spotted dick, which I'm sure she's worried is going cold.

Dad goes to the pub every other weeknight, without fail, for an hour and a half. Mum loves it because she has a bath and watches her soaps; Dad loves it because it's his chunk of time to talk to his friends, read the paper, have a couple of shandy halves and come back home to a happy wife. It's been this way for as long as I can remember.

'Yes. I don't know if I've ever mentioned it to you but Bernie is, well, he prefers the men over the ladies,' Dad says tentatively, his hands shaking as he folds and unfolds his napkin absentmindedly. Mum looks baffled. Dad takes a big breath and exhales, looking directly at her.

'That's fine, Dad. It's 2022. Good for Bernie for being gay,' I say, eyeing the pudding. I can smell the vanilla-y custard and my mouth is watering. I know Mum and Dad's generation aren't quite as forward-thinking as mine, but I don't think we all need to be shocked by Bernie's sexual orientation. I don't know him well, but from the times I've chatted to him at functions or Christmas do's, he's seemed a nice enough man.

'Yes, good for Bernie. Why shouldn't he love whoever he likes?' agrees Mum, looking at me to give her the nod for saying the right thing. She tries her best. She's liberal and loving, but she doesn't always get it quite right, so I give her the affirmation that she needs and smile.

'Yes, I suppose so,' says Dad nervously, leaving the napkin now and picking up his dessertspoon, spinning it round in his hands, his face looking a bit peaky. 'The thing is, whoever he likes is me.'

Mum starts laughing.

'And I feel the same way for him.'

Mum stops laughing.

Chapter One

YOU KNOW THOSE PEOPLE who hate Mondays? That's not me. I'd never admit it to anyone because I don't want to seem smug, but I really, really love a Monday morning.

Driving the short distance home last night was a blur. It's like I slid in behind the steering wheel, blinked and was suddenly standing in our tiny cottage kitchen telling David what had happened.

After Mum stopped laughing, she started crying. Dad said sorry many times, to both of us, while also crying. Mum ran upstairs; I followed. I don't know what I'd planned to say to comfort her, I was in shock – I still am – and what do you say to someone who has just found out that their husband of nearly thirty years is gay? She told me to go. Is it awful that I felt relieved? I needed time to process, and just wanted to come home to David. My David. I knew I needed to talk this through with someone who would understand. Turns out he wasn't all that helpful.

When I got downstairs, I saw Dad had unplugged the hostess trolley (he's always thinking of that electricity bill, and it was oddly comforting – a reminder that he's still *my dad*. Of course he is.) and I watched him slump back down at the dining table looking exhausted and pale. In the centre of the table, untouched, sat the spotted dick.

I didn't know what to do, but I knew he wouldn't mind if I left.

I sat down at the place I'd been in, it felt like a lifetime since I'd been there, and reached out to put my hand on his, giving it a, hopefully, encouraging squeeze.

'Does he make you happy, Dad?' I whisper. I'm scared Mum will hear from upstairs but I'm concerned for Dad, feeling very torn.

Dad looked up and for the first time that day I saw a genuine smile. 'Yes, Tabby Cat, unbelievably so.'

'Then I'm glad for you Dad,' I smile back.

He nods in the way he always has, we sit in silence for a moment and then I think it's time to leave.

'Love you, Dad,' I ventured as a reassurance and a goodbye.

'Thank you, Tabs. Love you too. Ever so much,' he said with a very faint wobble in his voice. It was the 'ever so much' that got me.

I left before he saw me cry. I didn't want him to think I was crying about him; I was crying *for* him. I would hate to have to hide so much of myself for so long. I felt sad that that's been his life.

'Bloody hell, Tab, I never saw that coming!' was David's less-than-sympathetic response, with a chortle. He'd barely looked up from fixing whatever greasy bit of car engine he'd unceremoniously plonked on our kitchen table. I wish he'd keep those things in the garage – I've told him a million times, but it doesn't seem to go in.

'It's not funny, David! This is my parents' *marriage* we're talking about!' I told him.

'Well, they're still your parents,' he said matter-of-factly, not laughing now but still not looking up from the hunk of metal. He can be so black and white about things. I wish I could just switch my emotions on and off like that. It must be a man thing.

I began crying again at this point and, to give him his due, David did instantly drop whatever tool he was using and stride over and envelop me in a giant bear hug. He's built like a rugby prop, so it was a seriously breath-squishing cuddle. I was so upset I barely thought about the motor oil on my favourite cardi; I just sank into the cuddle and let it all out in big, unexpected sobs. Poor Mum. Poor Dad. Lucky Bernie, I guess.

David ran me a bubble bath while I texted my friend Vivi, who was much more understanding and said she'd try to pop in to the shop to see me tomorrow.

Right now I'm making my way down towards the main town square, to Pearls and Doodles, which is my little shop, packed from floor to ceiling with treasure. Well, I say *my* shop, I don't own it or anything, but I do work here and run it day-to-day. It was a grocery shop originally, and I remember it opening as a vintage shop when I was a teenager, and even then thinking it was magical – and that was before it was trendy to shop vintage and be sustainable. All my friends wanted to go on the bus into Swindon to try make-up samples in Superdrug or buy bangles and hairbands in Claire's Accessories, but I just wanted to stay here in my sweet, safe little market town and lose myself in Pearls and Doodles. It's in a terrace of niche shops: an old-fashioned chemist's, an estate agent's, an upmarket deli and a hardware shop, and it sells everything wonderful: trinkets, jewellery, homeware, art, stationery, candles, accessories, all the things that make life a little bit more special. And a couple of rails of vintage and second-hand clothes. Some of the items are antique, most are second-hand and a few are new, but they're all beautiful to me, everything having a story or feeling like it has meaning behind it. It's like magic.

So much more valuable than anything mass-produced or from a chain.

I've always loved knick-knacks and ornaments. When I was little, Mum would indulge me and let me have some pocket money to buy books and toys in charity shops and at church jumble sales, but she was never that keen on charity shops herself. She's more of a John Lewis kind of woman. Dad says I get my 'magpie tendencies' from my aunt, Bridget. Apparently she was really into 'all that stuff' – she loved car boot sales and flea markets and found all sorts of brilliant things.

Bridget lived with us when I was a baby, so I know Mum was really close to her younger sister. After she died in a car accident, Mum kept a lot of her things neatly packed away in the attic. I was never allowed to play with them but occasionally Mum would let me take a couple of bits out to look at. After a while I stopped asking because I could see how upset Mum would get at the memory of her poor sister.

When I was little my mum gave me a beautiful tin box covered in red roses that's full of souvenirs from when Bridget travelled around Europe. They may not seem like much, but as a kid I thought of them as treasure: shells from beaches, beaded bracelets maybe bought in town square markets, tiny little worry dolls, paper fans with beautiful illustrations, beer mats, ticket stubs to museums. I guess knowing they were important to Mum made them all the more special. Maybe that's why I love antiques and knick-knacks; they feel like much more than just 'things' – they carry people's stories with them. It's almost like they carry something of the person themselves.

I did my school work experience here, at Pearls and Doodles, when I was sixteen and loved it. I did pretty well, too, as Julia offered me a Saturday job and now, ten years on, I manage the shop. That's how I met David, when he was working at the hardware shop just down from Pearls and Doodles, before he started at the garage. And later, at the pub, when we went in groups of mates. I've never been out with anyone else, not seriously. There were dates at school, but David's the one for me.

Julia is semi-retired and moved away about three years ago, but has kept the shop open as it's making good money. She inherited the shop when her grandma died, and had it painted bright magenta pink. Very 1980s! Though she's always been fond of it, I don't think anyone has ever put as much love and care into it as I have. At least, that's what Julia tells me! I work here during the week, and either she drives over for the weekend or Sue, her friend who lives nearby, comes down and covers. It's a good set-up, and it's been smooth sailing since the start, just how I like it. Julia trusts me, I know this place like the back of my hand and I love it like my own.

Julia has her own stock that she keeps in the back room for me to top up with when needed, but most of the shop is rented out by individual vendors. Crafters or antique dealers, mainly. They rent a little nook or corner, fill it with goodies, we sell them and they post or bring more in. My favourite thing is that Julia has a few shelves near the till that she keeps for 'shop stock'. She still loves the thrill of the hunt for a special vintage piece, so if she spots something special in a charity shop or at a trade fair, she brings it down and ties a price tag on, with the price written in elegant black script. In recent years I've started buying and selling too. Nothing major, mostly silver jewellery (I can't resist something shiny), and I have a bit of a thing for vintage handbags. It's better that I buy and sell than buy and keep – David would have kittens if he knew how much I'd spent on my collection over the years! Sometimes I've even 'flipped' pieces of furniture for a profit. I buy small wooden tables, sets of drawers or handmade shelves, sand them, paint them and voila, a whole new look.

I love meeting new vendors – my favourite part of this job is the people. But seeing their wares is always exciting too. I have two new lots of stock coming in today, so it is going to be a great Monday.

One seller is a woman called Kath, who sells gorgeous clear phone cases with pressed lavender flowers embedded in them – Lavender Lovelies – who has booked the space over the phone (we have a landline, how retro!) and is bringing her items in today. I'm happy to help her. Her products are not vintage (obviously, being phone cases) but Julia loved the idea of pressed flowers so agreed to rent the space to her. I love opening the packages and seeing what's inside. Sometimes, if the shop's empty, I'll talk out loud as I tear open the boxes, as if I'm doing one of those oh-so-addictive unboxing hauls on YouTube. Ha! Maybe I should do one for my slightly secret Instagram. The other vendor, Forget-Me-Not Jewels, has also booked over the phone and is sending his pieces recorded delivery. I didn't speak to him; Julia arranged it a couple of weeks ago, but since he sells jewellery I'm excited to set that out for him.

Anyway, I walk the fifteen minutes into work, dropping Mum a quick text to see how she's doing, then I send one to Dad too. I grab a latte and croissant on the way in from Bott's Bakery, which has been there for donkey's years and is incredible. Once at Pearls and Doodles, I open the shutters to the front window displays, turn on all the lamps and fairy lights and take a deep breath in. Yes, I really do love it here. A couple of years ago Julia had the front repainted, in palest matt pink, with 'Pearls and Doodles' in dove grey retro script, with iridescent white highlights over the curves on each letter, over the wide double-fronted window and door. Sometimes this feels more like home than the cottage and David.

The morning runs smoothly. The new lady with the lavender cases is lovely. She is a vision in patchwork, pompoms and shocking-violet lipstick. Her hair is long, in two plaits, and I notice in among her cluster of beautiful vintage brass cuff bracelets (I'm like a magpie for mid-century pieces) there's also a plastic one with 'granny' spelled out in beads. Cute.

She chats for a while, buys a couple of cloth dolls with little lace dresses on for her granddaughters and great-niece (she tells me all about them with such love, which is rather endearing) and then busies herself setting up her display. It's really nice. She's added small vases of dried lavender all round her shelving unit, draped garlands of tiny purple pompoms from each shelf, and the cases are fabulous. It only takes her an hour, but as soon as she leaves a few customers begin admiring them. I put some money in the till and pick a case for my own phone. Looks good to model the shop stock, and it's so pretty. Each one is a bit different, and the one I choose has four sprigs of lavender and hundreds of tiny silver stars strewn through. I love a sprinkle of glitter, so this really appeals to my magpie-like tastes. This is turning out to be a really good Monday . . . aside from the whole Bernie, Mum and Dad fiasco. I try not to think about that.

By lunchtime I'm starting to wonder when the other new vendor's parcel will arrive. It's often a bit slow on a Monday – although that will change when the schools break up for summer – but I'm kept busy enough with a couple of customers. I keep telling Julia we should join the modern world and have a website, supported by social media channels (think how the shop would look on Insta!) but she won't entertain it. She's of an era before online shopping. She says her things are special, that customers can never really understand their beauty unless they hold them, feel them, see them in person. I don't doubt it's better to buy in person, in the shop, but then again, it's 2022. I'll keep nudging her.

I don't really tell anyone about my own Instagram account. I mean, that's an understatement – the only real-life person who knows about it is Vivienne, and I've sworn her to secrecy. I'd be mortified if anyone I knew found it.

It's not that it's anything weird, it's just, I dunno, I don't want people to think it's lame or that I'm being one of those cringy online show-offs who say things like, 'I've had so many messages asking where XYZ is from.' It's not very me. I don't even show my face on there; it's strictly business.

I know at my age it should be all grey crushed velvet interiors, perfectly contoured selfies or maybe a couple of smiling children in co-ordinating outfits, but unfortunately, that's just not who I am. My Instagram, @TabbyRoseTreasure, is just a sort of digital scrapbook of things I find that I love. Mainly little curiosities from charity shops that I'd love to have in my home (sometimes I do bring them back and David rolls his eyes, but he knows they make me so happy), or things I've made.

Oh yes, I should mention that I do a little more than 'flipping' furniture. I make things. Well, I 'tart them up', as David says. Julia has a back room and when the shop is really quiet, or sometimes after it's shut, I use it as a workshop.

Julia doesn't mind. I don't want to sound arrogant, but I'm pretty nimble with a sewing machine too, a skill I have from Mum. I often find clothes in charity shops and spend my lunchtimes altering them to fit me perfectly, adding embellishments, moving hemlines up or down, and then give them a try-on in the back room and have a twirl in the old mirror we've had here since my work experience days. I find it so soothing; my own secret world. I've altered a few bits for Vivienne and her daughter Kitty, too, and they love it. Mostly I'll keep the pieces of furniture at home, so our cottage is the epitome of shabby chic ('More shabby than chic,' David teases). For years I've posted my creations on my Instagram and people have asked to buy them. I tentatively branched out into offering some of my other finds for sale, and it worked. Last week I posted a set of Victorian lace handkerchiefs (found them at the bottom of a basket in a charity shop for £5.50, ironed them, repaired a couple of tiny tears) to a lady in Texas for £45! I thought they'd be nice display props for the shop (Julia always reimburses me when I find things like this; she gives me pretty free rein which, obviously, I love but never abuse), but then couldn't resist snapping them for Insta and voila! I've not told David or even Mum and Dad about all this. Vivi says I should stash the cash for a lavish holiday or a designer bag. Actually I have recently bought a Chanel pre-loved bag, which I haven't used yet. Where would I wear it? I don't really go out-out, or to any posh events. But it's an investment, and will only grow in value.

By early afternoon the new vendor's stock has arrived, but Vivi hasn't. I also haven't heard from Mum, and am starting to feel panicky about that again. I'm trying hard to push it out of my mind and keep focused.

Text to Vivienne: *Hey! New box of goodies just arrived! Jewellery!!! Shall I wait till you get here to open, or are you gonna be a while? Xxx*

I busy myself dusting the displays, and luckily a couple of customers come in, so that fills half an hour.

Text from Vivienne: *I'm SO sorry. Been dealing with the bloody sink all day! I'm collecting Kitty in a bit but could come in with her. Promise she'll behave Xxx*

As much as I adore Kitty, who's my goddaughter, after all, so I'm sort of spiritually obliged to love her as well, I could really do with some quiet time to chat properly with Vivi on her own today. I don't feel I've really processed what happened last night. Kitty is the most energetic six-year-old you've ever met. Vivi and her husband Neil call her 'spirited', or on bad days, 'challenging'. She's wonderful and I love having her to stay or taking her to the park or for an ice cream, but that much 'spirit' in a shop full of delicate antiques has never been a good idea. Plus, the Mum and Dad stuff is really starting to sink in, and I just know I'm going to cry when I next talk about it. Pushing my disappointment down, I reply to her text to put her off and turn my attention to the package of jewellery I need to display before home time.

The shop is pretty quiet, so now seems as good a time as any to set up. Forget-Me-Not Jewels has hired a full display unit with lighting, right at the back of the shop. In the package are about fifty different pieces including floral brooches, engraved brass hand mirrors, strings of aged-looking pearls, iridescent Czech bead necklaces, the old-fashioned screw-on earrings that you rarely see these days, and lots of twinkling gemstone rings. All are wrapped in crumpled brown tissue paper, and some come in worn little boxes that no doubt have been part of some stories in their time. I love to imagine who once owned these things, or where they came from.

Once I've unwrapped everything, written a stock list and attached the allotted price tags, all beautifully handwritten by Julia, I take them over to the display unit and carefully put them all in. With the lights shining down, it looks stunning, flecks of light from the beads and gems reflecting over each other. One ring catches my eye. Nestled in a tiny maroon box with a minuscule gold hook-and-eye catch, it looks like it's got quite a history. The gold band is inlaid with three stones, clear, purple, clear. I'm fairly sure the middle one is an amethyst, but I don't think the clear ones are diamonds. It'd be in a dedicated jeweller's if they were. Slightly frustratingly, it was the only piece that didn't have a price tag for it, so I'll have to clarify the amount with Julia or ask her to contact the seller. It's so pretty in its simplicity, and I've always been a sucker for crystals.

Looking around the shop, I can see nobody's here. If anyone did come in and start perusing the new jewellery display, I reason, I'd dash straight over and pop the ring in its case. Until then, I can have a little try-on. It slides on easily and fits my middle finger perfectly! I feel a little buzz of joy at adorning myself with something so pretty, and head back to the old till (something else Julia isn't ready to bring into the modern world, but I don't really mind, it's very quaint) to check on my Instagram and greet any new customers.

Before I've even had time to find my phone, the door ding-a-lings as a new customer comes in. Usually I'll just give them a polite 'hello' and leave them to mooch (I hate going into shops and the assistant constantly asking you what you're looking for – makes me all edgy), but this woman looks incredible. She's in retro acid-wash jeans, silver flats with a pointed toe, a ruffle-collar shirt tucked in at the waist, and she must own one of those GHD air diffuser things because her hair has some serious volume. It's like she's walked straight out of a vintage clothing shop after the most incredible haul ever. Even her belt and earrings are in keeping with the whole look. I'm not one to speak up, but if this customer knew how much I love vintage finds too, I think she'd be impressed. I'm constantly on at myself to wear more of my own vintage clothing collection, currently sitting in the wardrobe in the guest room at home. Today I'm wearing wide-leg jeans and a tight black tee from H&M. A beautiful vintage silk scarf by Jacqmar in blues and greens on a cream background is holding up my hair, which would be a halo of wild dark-blonde curls if I just left it.

'Love your outfit,' I call over to her. Now she's browsing a selection of floral china candlesticks. 'Where did you find it all?' I ask with a smile.

'Thanks!' she says, delighted. 'Just standard places, really. Woolworths, C&A, and I often find some OK bits in Littlewoods.'

'Oh, wow! Classic pieces then,' I say.

'Ummm, if you think so . . .' she tails off, looking somewhat less delighted. Hope I haven't offended her by calling them 'classic'. Maybe she thinks they're a bit more niche. Now I wish I hadn't said anything!

'Anyway,' I try and recover, 'I think it looks fab. Definitely one for an OOTD!' I try to laugh to show her how chill I am about the awkward air.

'Er, OK,' she says, looking baffled. Wow. This has not gone how I thought it would.

Probably best not to try and explain myself or harass her more, I think as I finally find my phone.

Text to Mum: *I've been thinking of you all day, I hope you're OK. Hope Dad's OK too. I'm here for you both, love you both so much. Shall I pop in tonight? David's working late so won't mind Xxxxxxx*

As I'd expect, my phone vibrates less than a minute later, but instead of her reply it says 'message not sent'. Weird. I put my phone on airplane mode, thinking it just needs reconnecting.

'Whoa! That is so rad,' says the customer I've just ballsed up with, looking at my still-not-connecting-to-4G phone, and who is now standing by the till on her way out. She's even got the lingo to match her outfit!

'Oh!' I respond, surprised by her enthusiasm after

she'd shown so little of it when I praised her outfit. 'It's one of our new cases. They just came in today.' Secretly I'm pleased I bought one earlier. I knew it was a good idea to model the stock!

'Aha! Never knew you could get calculator cases, but they've got everything these days, haven't they?' She laughs. 'Saw a few bits that I might come back for, but I've left my chequebook at home.'

OK, this woman is a little odd – she's not just dressing vintage, but living it! Still, I don't want to be rude; you meet all sorts when you work with the public.

'Right. Well, we're always here, and if there's anything you want to reserve, just give us a call and I can sort that for you.'

'Thank you,' she trills, much warmer now, and off she goes out of the shop.

Naturally I overanalyse every step of the interaction. If it were me and I'd made the effort to go full vintage, or some sort of retro cosplay, I'd love a compliment. Thank God she saw my new phone case and the situation was defused. I've never considered calculator covers, but that's a really good idea. Stationery is big business. I make a note to mention it to Kath when she comes in to restock.

It's nearly five o'clock although it doesn't feel like it

as it is still so sunny outside, but for once, I'm happy the working day is over as I start to pack up. I open the till to cash up and the ring catches the light – I nearly forgot I was wearing it! I slip it from my finger and put it back in its special box.

Remembering Mum, I pick up my phone and turn off airplane mode. This time my message sends straightaway, and her reply comes through quickly.

Text from Mum: *Oh love. It's all a mess. I love him, he says he loves me, just not in 'that way'. Loves Bernie in that way. Feel so confused. Has everything been for nothing? Sorry to dump on you. Debs says I should see a counsellor. Dad's talking about moving out! He says he's sorry but it really is over. Can't imagine it. Don't want Dad to live a lie but don't want to lose my husband. My Tony. Come over if you like but don't think I can do a full dinner tonight. Will just put a quick lasagne and garlic bread in. You'll have to chop a salad. Make sure you check on Dad. So worried about him but so cross, conflicted. All very uncertain.* ☹ *xxxx*

My heart squeezes at the thought of them being sad, and it all being such a muddle. I half don't want to go over because I don't really know what to say for the best, but I can't leave her like this. Plus, Mum's 'quick lasagne' is pretty appealing. I send her a message saying I'll be over soon, another to Dad to let him know I'm here for him and another to David letting him know he'll have to pick up a microwave meal or fish and chips. I remember he's working late tonight, so I don't think he'll mind.

I finish cashing up, and going into the back to the safe I glance at the stock, thinking how calming it would be to just set up in here for the evening. I know there's a box of vintage clothes that need attention before I can hang them out; I could put on a podcast and get out my sewing kit and the steamer . . . I wonder if there are any pieces in here that the customer from earlier would like? Maybe I should take a leaf out of her book and pull a few of my special vintage items out of the wardrobe. Not sure I could be as bold as her, but maybe a hint of a 1980s vibe wouldn't cause too much of a stir?

Chapter Two

I THINK IF I'D JUST found out that my husband of thirty-two years was in love with a man called Bernard, I'd spend a few days crying, eating, wallowing in baths, eating more, crying on the phone to Vivi as she persuades me to sign up to Tinder (to be fair, she does this every time I have a tiff with David) and eating some more again. I'm not saying I'd eat my feelings or anything, but perhaps eat till I felt so sick my feelings weren't really a concern. Nice and healthy, you know? My house would be a tip, my hair would look like a nest (although that's kind of standard – I don't need a marital bombshell to achieve the 'is that a style or is that bedhead' look), and I'd be a pale, wobbly wreck . . . but not Mum. Never one to let standards slip, the house is exactly as it always is. If there were a medal to be awarded for comforting consistency, she'd smash it. Or polish it and display it carefully somewhere she knows every visitor would see it, but then say, thrilled but coy, 'Oh *that*? Ha ha, I'm surprised you noticed. I need to put it away.'

The half-moon table in the hallway still has the same pad of paper 'borrowed' from their last cruise; the lounge still has its green velvet sofas with matching cushions plumped and placed; the flowers in the front window have been diligently replaced and refreshed (though I wonder if Dad will continue his weekly tradition of buying them, or if Mum will just pick some up with the weekly shop). I breathe in the room's familiar scent and feel a wave of calm wash over me. Perhaps everything is all right and back to normal. Maybe I had some sort of fever dream and imagined it all, like the time I thought I'd met Adele and we were close friends when in fact I'd just had a really vivid daytime nap dream. Vivi still calls her 'your mate Adele'. In fairness, I think Adele and I would have a brilliant time. I snap back to reality, noticing Mum talking.

'He's packed a bag and says he's staying with a friend for a few days,' Mum begins bitterly as she walks into the lounge with a floral tray of tea and half a packet of biscuits. I wonder if he's just gone straight to Bernard's. 'He won't say which *friend*,' she almost spits, as she stands in front of the TV, tray in her arms. I don't want to confirm her suspicions, but all of their friends are couples they've known forever; why wouldn't Dad share where he is? I am fleetingly angry at his secrecy, but then just as quickly I'm sorry that he's felt he has had to lie. He must be so afraid. Or maybe ashamed. I hate thinking about all of these huge emotions. I'd just like to be back with my mate Adele in our little dreamworld.

I can't bear hearing her so angry, especially when it's about Dad. I have no idea who I'm supposed to be loyal to here. It doesn't matter how old you are, it's horrible being the 'child' in the middle.

'I don't know what's more worrying, that Dad's packed his own bag or that you've not shaken the biscuits out onto a plate!' I try and lighten the tense mood with my winning comedy skills (that have never won anything, I might add). I gaze over at the mantelpiece to all the family photos. To look at them you'd think we were perfect. Me on Dad's shoulders with Mum looking up, laughing; us all together under some palm trees on our annual trip to Spain; four-year-old me on my first day of school. The ideal happy family.

'The biscuits are the least of my concerns,' she says three octaves higher than usual, not really paying attention as she sets down the tray on the polished mahogany coffee table and takes coasters from the designated coaster caddy, laying them out to place the teacups on.

'I know, sorry, it was a stupid joke. So, Dad's packed a bag,' I repeat to show I was listening. 'You've no idea where he's gone?' I add. I'm scared to ask bigger questions. It's so rare to see Mum angry, I don't know how best to approach things. She seems to be trying to carry on as normal. I think she's put some mascara on (albeit smudged), along with a smart jade-green skirt and pretty white top. If David left me, I think I'd just pull my hair up into a bun, take off my bra and accept my fate, living as a fleshy blob sack forever more, never seeing a structured waistband again as long as I lived. Good on her for being fully dressed, let alone the mascara.

'Bernard. He's gone to stay with him. Obviously,' she says simply, the anger completely dropping away, staring sadly into her teacup.

'Oh, Mum. I'm so sorry. It'll be OK,' I suggest, not really believing it myself but hoping I've said the right thing.

Mum sighs, taking a sip. 'I feel so up and down with it all. It's such a lot to take in.'

I nod sagely, hoping she'll just carry on because I have no idea what I can say to help. I don't want to upset her, and I don't want to say anything negative about Dad.

'My husband has left me. My marriage that I worked so hard for is over. I wanted this so much, always wanted a nice husband and a baby.' She smiles weakly at me, the baby she still has, I suppose.

'He's my best friend, *was* my best friend. He's lived a lie, and maybe he lived it for me, maybe he felt he had to. He said maybe he'd always known, deep down, but that he'd tried so hard to think it away, to push it all down. I'm cross at him for not telling me sooner, and sorry for him for not feeling able to, terrible that he was trapped in something that wasn't true, stupid for not realising and then cross all over again that he's left. It really is just so much, Tabitha!' It all starts tumbling out quicker and quicker, and I see her eyes fill with tears. My heart breaks for her and her mascara. She barely ever cries. I sit still, trying to give her 'space' to talk it all out. I want to say something funny to cheer her up – my go-to approach when someone's upset – but I don't think it's time to joke about her make-up running.

I wish I was one of those people who had the right words, who could solve things. I feel almost pained at how horrible all this is, and then guilty for thinking of my own feelings.

'I'm so sorry all this has happened, Mum. I wish I could wave a magic wand to make it all OK. I wish I could time-travel back and sort it all out somehow.'

I expect her to burst into big, heavy, tearful sobs, but she takes a long breath in. She has a sip of her tea and I can almost see the cogs turning in her brain, control coming back to her.

'I'm scared, Tabitha,' she says, much more calmly now, which is almost worse.

'Of what, Mum? I'm here for you. So is David.' Not sure how much David is, but I want her to feel loved.

'Of all of it. Scared none of it was true, him loving me. He said he did love me and that he loved the family side of life but just, he needs to live authentically. I want him to too but I'm scared I'll be so alone now. I'm scared people will gossip about him. I still love the man, I don't want him to have a terrible time, even if he has left me! You know what people are like round here, they'll love this.' Her face is calm but her eyes dart between me, the teacup and the mantelpiece pictures.

'You can't worry about all of that right now. He did love you. I'm sure he still does,' I offer with as much optimism as I can muster.

We talk for a little while longer. Mum says the same

things in new ways and I offer the same answers in vaguely different ways. I'm not sure she's really taking it in; I think she simply needs to get it all out and feel like someone is listening. I'm a woman of very few skills, but listening is definitely one of them so I don't stop her. Our tea goes cold and neither of us touches the biscuits, but by the end, I can see Mum is relieved, as though all the thoughts that were swirling around her brain have left for the day. No doubt she'll revisit them all over again but for now, she's vented and I am glad I was there to listen. Though I'd rather not have listened to 'I suppose we didn't do a lot of lovemaking. It always seemed to be me who tried to keep things interesting, you know, get him moving. Now and again it worked, sort of.'

'There's no point wallowing in all this. We've both made our mistakes. He's made his, in whatever way that was, and I've made mine. I can't live in this horrid state of upset forever, can I?' she says, her voice rising at the end in a sort of panic.

'Mum, this isn't anyone's "mistake". You weren't to know. If he's always been interested in men, deep down, like he told you last night, then how could you have helped? Also – and I'm not saying leaving you is OK – Dad didn't choose to love a man, it's just who he is.' I don't know how to tell her how sorry I feel for Dad, for keeping this a secret all these years and never living 'his truth', as the youth would say.

'I don't mean with Dad. Maybe I should never have married him! Maybe I should have stuck with what I had.'

I don't want to make this about me, but if Mum hadn't married Dad . . . 'You mean, stayed single?' I resist the urge to add 'and child-free'.

'No! Your dad wasn't my first.' OK, good for Mum for having a great time before Dad. But honestly, she doesn't mention sex for my entire life (her attempt at teaching me about the birds and the bees was leaving a book in my bedroom titled *Growing Up* and that was that), and now I've heard about her love action – or lack of – with Dad, and fear I'm going to hear how she lost her virginity. Bloody hell.

'I was steady with someone else. Michael. He was gorgeous. Very tall, dark hair down to his shoulders, always wore so many rings, I remember. Granny hated him, I think. Bridget thought he was brilliant. But he wanted a big, exciting life. He wanted to travel, or live in a city, going to all the flashy clubs and concerts, and I started to want a home and a family and that was the life your dad – Tony – was offering. He was, I thought, the best option. Times were different then, you married for life and you had to make a good choice, you know? Your dad offered me that. Michael didn't take it well. He wanted me to wait for him while he went off exploring a bigger, brighter life but I couldn't. I wanted to settle down. I don't think he was the sort that girls like me turned down, so he broke it all off and I married Dad.'

'Mum! What do you mean, "girls like me"? You were a catch, I've seen photos. You're still a catch. You're kind and beautiful and funny, and a snappy dresser – look at that skirt!' I say, smiling and shaking my head at her. Bless her.

Saying that though, the thought of Mum in 'flashy clubs' is almost more shocking than everything else we've had this week. This is Mum, who used to think the music at the PTA school discos were 'a bit much', so Mum having a wild boyfriend who lived the high life is more than a surprise.

It's a whole week of revelations, it seems. First, Dad liking Bernie, and now Mum telling me she went to 'flashy clubs'. Seems like even Mum is cooler than me.

'I didn't know there was someone else. You didn't tell me that.' There's a theme here, and I'm totally starting to feel frustrated by it. Nobody seems to tell anybody anything. We're all so caught up in not wanting to create a fuss, myself included, that I'm starting to think we're just living a weird double life – who we really are underneath, and then a cool, calm, collected facade on top. All I do is go to work, try not to wind David up, think about getting married and having a baby, which I know David would love – the baby bit, anyway – and that's it. Should I be doing more? Be more open with myself? Bloody hell, I don't want to just pick 'the best option', wind up never living the life I love, never wearing all my vintage clothes, never managing to do the things I dream of (even if they are daft little things), and then David running off with some man from the pub when I suggest a three-week holiday to the Caribbean. Though that's a really niche situation, right?

'Did you hear any of that? You've gone off somewhere into one of your daydreams,' Mum says. 'You always were away somewhere else, on your adventures.' While I'm starting to think I should go on some actual bloody adventures. Maybe *I'll* go to the sodding Turks and Caicos!

'Sorry,' I say, shifting on the sofa, my bum going numb and my jeans digging into my hips. This is a wake-up call: it's time to start living, time to be bold. Instantly I push it all down again. 'You were saying about your life? There was someone else. You must be devastated. I'm here for you, Mum.' Hopefully that was the right reply. I don't want to have to admit that I know deep down I'm wasting my life. Who wants to add that to the mix today?

'Devastated? No. Severely miffed? Very much so,' she says resolutely. 'He's told me what's happened. He's not done . . . anything. He's just worked it out in his mind. Or accepted it and communicated it, I mean. He said he really does love me, thinks so highly of me. At least I've got that. That was decent of him. But yes, severely, severely miffed, Tabitha.' Mum looks at me matter-of-factly as though she's just read the email to say there's been a replacement in the food shop order. She really is coming round to this quickly. I feel like I'm on an emotional roller coaster!

Sensing my bewilderment, she carries on. 'Look, I'm not saying I'm not upset, of course I am, I love your dad very much, always will, but maybe things weren't as perfect as you thought. After all the initial excitement, which was fantastic and no complaints from either party, he did seem to love it when I—'

'Yep, OK, yep, yep.' I don't know what she is about to say, but I'm not going to find out. There are things a daughter shouldn't know.

'Sorry. Yes, for many years we were more companions than married in *that* way . . . if you know what I'm saying here. I suppose now I know why.' She trails off. I want her to let it all out but I really don't want her to go into any more detail about her and Dad's sex life. Though she either doesn't note my uncomfortable shift on the sofa opposite, or chooses to ignore it.

'I have needs and urges too. I'm not all dried up, you know. Maybe it's time for me to find myself, as you young ones say.' She reaches for a biscuit and takes a bite, pondering this notion.

As much as I don't want to hear how 'dried up' she isn't, I have to admit it, I'm beyond impressed with Mum's resolve. It's almost inspiring. If she can weather this absolute mess of a storm, maybe I can figure out what I'm supposed to be doing. I know this much: I need to do SOMETHING. I can't just be the unmarried girl who works in the knick-knack shop forever.

I pick up a biscuit too.

'Mum, you're a good woman. You're going to be OK. One day you're going to meet someone lovely, if you want, and you're going to have a full relationship. With all the . . . trimmings. You're not ready right at this moment, but one day you'll find you want to get up and get out there!' I say, jumping up a bit, flinging crumbs everywhere but surprising the both of us with my uncharacteristic oomph.

'Yes! Yes, I will. I'm going to have a GREAT time, Tabs!'

Then she lowers her head and dissolves into noisy, grief-filled tears.

Chapter Three

July

As the summer evenings linger on and the sun begins to shine, time goes by in a bit of a. blur. I absolutely love the early-morning light streaming in through our thin curtains; it's so much easier to jump out of bed and seize the day. Except I'm not super-seizing it. The only thing I'm really seizing is work, because I love it. If I'm honest, everything else just feels messy. Hard to seize that, isn't it?

The old bronze bell on the shop door tinkles as Vivienne strides in with her trademark confidence.

'You're a sight for sore eyes!' she says, coming round behind the counter and plopping herself on a stool beside me. I can't think why she'd say that: I'm just in cropped jeans and a loose, paisley-print blouse in pale green and purple. A jumble of bead necklaces, vintage. My curly hair is shiny but its usual untameable self, pushed up into a messy bun. Though I am wearing a pair of lilac second-hand Mary Janes by Carel, a huge bargain that I sat up half the night bidding for on eBay.

Vivi is gorgeous. Jet-black hair that tumbles all the way down to her lower back; huge almond-shaped brown eyes; full lips and curvy hips. Vivienne likes to make an entrance wherever she goes. She's easily the best-dressed at any occasion, but she's the sort of woman who could wear a four-year-old Primark sundress and look effortlessly chic. Today she's wafted in wearing a bright cotton midi skirt with a print that looks like violet paint strokes over a burnt-orange background, with a little white camisole top tucked in. Her décolletage and arms are glowing with some lovely highlighter and her gold jewellery twinkles under our shop lights. You see? Even on a casual drop-in she fills the whole room. I can see why Neil dotes on her.

But then, she was in adverts on TV as a kid, in all the school plays and did a fair bit of catalogue modelling. She's had ambitions to be in a West End show – she's certainly got the star wattage, the skills and the devotion to succeed.

And an agent, though I've no idea when she was last in touch with him.

'Oh my God, what a relief to see you! Please take over my liiife,' I laugh, mock-shaking her bare shoulders in desperation.

'Still all weird then?' she says without a hint of judgement at my somewhat pathetic greeting.

'Yep. More than weird. Mum's trying to work up a whole new lease of life and to "find her second wave". She's watching a lot of YouTube videos about middle-aged women who have completely changed their lives, and the other day she referred to Ruth Langsford as her "hashtag style queen". She actually spelled out "hashtag", though, bless her,' I sigh, smiling. Mum loves a bit of *This Morning* and is scandalised if anyone calls it 'daytime TV', despite it being just that, and my favourite sort of TV. She always watches when Ruth or Eamonn are on, and I know I can make her cry with laughter by showing her Ruth's funny Insta reels – in fairness, I laugh, too.

'I saw her the other day with Debs. Both in skinny jeans. I'm not sure I've ever seen your mum in trousers before. Gotta admire them though, Tabs. Why shouldn't she have a go at feeling great? Ruth's a hottie!' She laughs, which sets me off, and instantly I feel the heavy anvil on my chest lifting.

45

Vivi has a way of making you feel like everything will be OK. She's confident in herself, always has been, ever since we were primary school mortal enemies.

I went to the local school and it was all very 'small town'. I'd been to nursery with most of the children in my class, Mum knew most of their mums, we all lived nearby, you get the drift. Then one day in Year 3, Miss Berlow introduced us to a new girl we were all 'to make feel really at home', Vivienne Patel. Vivienne had moved to the area from London and seemed to ooze style and sophistication, even in her grey school pinafore. Everybody wanted to be her friend, including me.

At home time, her mum would come to collect her in a rainbow of beautiful saris, their gold thread sparkling in the sunlight. Vivi would tell us how her mum, Nishma, had been a real princess in India, with pet monkeys and rubies and diamonds as toys, before she moved over here to study at a top London university and won the 'Cleverest Person in England Award'. Nishma had met Vivi's dad, Gordon, at university and they'd fallen wildly in love. So much so that Nishma gave up all her riches to live over here and have a family. They'd lived in London, where Vivi was born, in a mansion, but Gordon had taken a new job here in the West Country, so they were just renting the bungalow until he found another suitable mansion. She didn't want to tell us but her dad was a spy on a secret mission, that's why he drove the old battered car. It was part of the job, you see.

I remember being in total awe. I couldn't believe a princess and an undercover spy would be at our boring old school gates, and couldn't wait to see what mansion my friend would move into. I'd never really known glamour like this, so Vivi was a shining beacon of excitement in my very ordinary life. Vivi told us how on her summer holidays they went to stay in her grandad's palace that was made of gold, and we were all enthralled.

Miss Berlow sat her next to me and I felt almost star-struck. I was honoured that Miss Berlow thought highly enough of me for this privilege – the new girl looker-after. I strutted round the playground with my head held high, showing Vivi all the sights we had to offer, which were few, but I didn't care. I was just so dazzled by her.

We made friends quickly and Nishma asked my mum if I'd like to come over for tea. I desperately wanted to have dinner with Indian princesses and a secret agent, and I felt thrilled to have been invited. Obviously Vivi really liked me if she wanted to show me her awesome life!

While we were sitting round the table having the

most delicious Indian food that my mum would never have cooked, I asked about the pet monkeys. Nishma laughed. 'Has Vivi been making up tall tales again?' Gordon chuckled.

'No, I haven't! Tabitha is a liar,' she shouted, banging her little fist on the table.

She was instantly told off by her mum and I began to cry. Mum was called to come and collect me. Nishma and Gordon very gently told me they weren't a princess and a spy. Nishma worked for the council and Gordon at the local supermarket. I never asked if Nishma had won 'Cleverest Person in England'.

The next day at school Vivienne cornered me in the cloakroom. 'Tabitha Burnley. If you tell ANYONE about my mum and dad, I will get you,' she said, menacingly pointing her compass at me.

But her ability to work a story and have everyone eating out of her hand earned her a lead role in the school productions, and from primary school on, she fell in love with musical theatre and spent every Saturday morning at dance or drama classes, paid for by her TV work that she sometimes booked through her children's talent agency. And of course she was always hugely popular.

We spent the rest of primary school staying as far

away from each other as possible, she afraid I'd ruin her mysterious and lavish image, me afraid of her compass-point rage.

It wasn't until secondary school when we found ourselves partnered up again that things improved. When One Direction got huge, we were both fans, her of Harry Styles, me of Liam Payne. We both found creative ways of getting out of hockey – eugh! – inventing bruised ankles, complete with bandages and painted-on bruises in vivid colours (I've always been good with make-up!). Or explaining that we'd been told to clean up the art room cupboard by the art teacher and so were not available for games and backing up each other's stories.

By this time, Vivi was acting in local productions and going for theatre auditions in London, earning a bit of cash and fuelling her ambitions to make it on the London stage.

Now marriage and motherhood take up the lion's share of her time.

'Well, it might all turn out to be the best thing ever,' Vivi muses from her stool as she picks up a Jiffy bag full of miniature doilies ready to be displayed and twiddles them round between her thumb and forefinger.

'You think it might be the *best thing ever* that my dad is looking to buy a flat with Bernard and that my mum is having some sort of midlife crisis in a pleather pencil skirt? Oh yes, absolutely fantastic.'

'Bernie's nice. My dad knows him,' she carries on, missing my point. 'Be grateful your life is so interesting. I'm literally just living MumLife Groundhog Day. You're like the star of a soap opera!'

'First off, your life is bloody lovely. Secondly, I'm not sure how I'm the "star" of a soap opera, but I love you for trying there. Thirdly, it's not about Bernie. I'm sure he's lovely. It's really not because he's a he either – I'm so unbothered by that side of it. Surprised but not bothered. It's that however you look at it, he's left Mum. My parents are splitting up. I'm from a broken home, aren't I?' I say, flopping my arms onto the counter so hard the old till rattles. I half hope it breaks so we can join the twenty-first century and have a computerised one. This one is beautiful, but doing all the maths in my head during a sales rush is tough. This must have been here since the shop opened. You have to push really hard on the top left-hand corner just to release the drawer, and it doesn't even tell you how much change to give – you have to tot it up yourself!

'You're not from a broken home! It's called a "blended" home now. Also, I don't know if you've noticed but you're twenty-six! You live in a cottage up the road with your boyfriend of nearly ten years, Tabs. You're an adult, remember?' She laughs, pretending to flick my forehead and then instantly flipping into sweet-young-lady mode when somebody comes in to browse.

'I *know!*' I laugh very quietly, aware that the customer might overhear. 'But it's still hard. Mum is distraught underneath all her "new me" efforting, Dad's in bits, feels so guilty for leaving, yet wants to start his new life but it's just really difficult. I'd like you to know I'm only laughing because you're laughing. Not because I'm happy about any of this,' I add petulantly, giving her a look but noting she's still smiling.

'Yeah, but your mum is dealing with it, strutting around town in a skintight pencil skirt and her shirt unbuttoned for once, and your dad is finally free to stand in his truth and live a love-filled life with Bernie. The only person I'm seriously worried about is you. Is everything OK?' she says, at first adamant and then softening. Sometimes I think she knows me better than I know myself.

'Mmmm . . . yes. No. I think so.' I watch the customer pick up an antique sterling silver photo frame and put it down again.

'Oh, that sounded very convincing,' Vivi says.

'I just feel a bit meh. I'm worried about my parents, of course, but it's more than that. I feel like my dad is about to start his second life and I've barely started my first one . . . Like everyone around me is doing brilliantly and I'm not.' Suddenly the secret niggling sensation I've had for a while feels very real, and a little part of me wants to run home and cry under my duvet.

'*What*? Who on earth around here is smashing it? I'm still not on in the West End, I spend my days ferrying Kitty back and forth on the school run, always being nagged by Mum for not giving Neil more kids, and God knows how I'm meant to do that when he's at sea six months of the year, a-ha ha! You're smashing it. Your cottage is gorg, you run this place practically by yourself, *aaand* I've been watching your Insta. That's going mad, isn't it?'

'Bye. Thank you!' I smile as the customer decides against the frame and leaves. 'Anyway, I wouldn't call five thousand followers mad,' I protest, blushing. 'I just like posting my finds and—'

'And selling them for a profit. You're not daft. I bet you've got a stash of cash.' She laughs loudly now the customer has left.

'Well, maybe a little bit put by,' I say, smiling wryly.

'Right, so, you love your job, you're smashing your

secret side hustle, your home should be in *Elle Decoration*, what else? Is it David?' She pauses, knowing of course it's David.

I pause too. It's like all my thoughts are a big scribble and I don't know how to make them into nice orderly lines.

'I love David. He's a good man,' I start flatly. Vivi nods, encouraging me to go on. 'It's just . . . I'm not sure he's that bothered.'

'Bothered by what?'

'Bothered by me. Bothered by life! I think he just wants me to be this nice girlfriend, have an easy life, have kids, and that's it. I'm not sure he wants big things, or adventure. To be honest, I didn't think I did until Dad left Mum. Life's short, isn't it? She spent all that time with Dad, and now look at her. Skinny jeans or not, she built a life around me and Dad, and it's over in a moment. Do I want that? *Buuut* I really am quiet and mild, aren't I? That's what David signed up for. Can't change his order now,' I half joke, because things got a bit serious there.

'Aha! Well, he wouldn't cope with someone wild like me,' Vivi says, throwing her arms up in the air and spinning on her stool.

'Viv, be serious a minute. I'm pouring my heart out here.' I laugh; her energy is infectious.

'OK, yes, sorry, David wants a really bloody boring life, yep, go on,' she teases.

'Well, yes, he wants a simple life. I live a simple life. Should I want more? Should he want more? I don't know why we're not married with babies like you and Neil, although David has been looking at me longingly every time we pass the kids' clothes section in the big Sainsbury's. At least going *somewhere*, you know? Mum says just tell him to propose – apparently she did that with Dad. And look how that turned out! I don't know, something's holding me back. Probably me, ha ha,' I manage weakly, to offset how sad that is to admit. 'I know I should do something but, ugghhh, I don't *knooowww*!' I whine, and this time it's my turn to spin round dramatically on my stool. Very glad it's a slow customer day.

'Look. You're worrying over nothing. Stop comparing! Neil and I are only married because he's in the forces and we wanted the house together. You know this. You also know that Kitty, God love her, was a surprise. What twenty-year-old plans to get pregnant and then walks down the aisle with a giant bump? Not many! I'm glad it all went as it did, I love Neil and Kitty is my world, but if I could be on stage, living my dream life, you know I would. You're fine. Your parents are fine! If you don't want to get married, don't. It's 2022, for God's sake.'

'Yes, you're right. Everything will be fine. I'm fine. I'm not stuck in my life, I'm not boring, I don't need to do all that,' I exclaim. 'I've got some exciting things about me, haven't I? Like my vintage wardrobe bits, maybe?' I falter, waiting for her to convince me.

'Yes, you're stupendous! Wear the vintage clothes, please. Just put them on and rock it! You've got this, and I've got to go and get Kitty from school. I love you, and I'm always here. BFFs,' she assures me.

'BFFs,' I reply as she struts out the door, her sleek black hair swishing behind her.

Chapter Four

A FEW DAYS LATER, AND I'm back to square one. Dad has found a flat with Bernie and has asked if I want to go and have a look. Mum is in full agreement that I should carry on loving and supporting Dad and to be honest, even if she wasn't, I'd still want to. I mentioned it to David last night over my home-cooked shepherd's pie.

'Are you wanting me to come?' he asked straightaway.

'Well, yes, it'd be nice to go as a couple,' I say, a little irked that he's not more interested in this whole new chapter of our family life.

'Of course I don't mind, if that's what you really, *really* want,' he says, smiling.

'Um, OK, good.' I can't put my finger on why I'm feeling put out. We carry on eating dinner and talk about the garage, my day in the shop, the car boot sale I want to go to this weekend at Eastings Field, just outside of town.

'You love buying up old junk!' He laughs. 'Hey, why not buy one of those old wooden cribs, and do it up? I can see myself watching telly and rocking it with my foot. Lovely. Tabs?'

I ignore that last comment. 'Says you, who spends all weekend fixing up old car parts,' I jokily retort.

'Yeah, but at least I sell those on and make something. What do you do with all your old clothes and junk? Stash it around the house, I bet, thinking I don't notice. It's nice that you have your hobby, sewing bits to things, but then you just shove it all in the spare room wardrobe! Don't think I don't see it.' He carries on laughing.

Inwardly I laugh too. Joke's on him because I don't stash it; I've been selling it, more and more successfully. I have a real eye for finding little treasures that I know are worth a lot, especially once I've worked my magic on them. But something holds me back from divulging that to him.

'I know, I know, I just love them. Summer is such a great time to get winter coats for a bargain, and I want to see what they have. Besides, it's a 7 a.m. start, so you can have a lie-in by yourself and fully starfish in the bed,' I say, smiling.

'I'd rather you were in the bed with me,' he teases.

'Aha, I'm sure! Anyway, Dad's said in the text to come over on Friday at six. OK?'

David pretends to be eating and not able to talk. I go on.

'So shall I walk down from the shop, and you can meet me from the garage, yes?'

'Ohhh do you reaaally want me to go, Tabs?' He's still smiling his disarmingly charming smile.

'Yes!' I force myself not to let his grin get him off the hook. 'Why wouldn't you want to? My dad has made a massive change in his life, his family are important to him, I want us to be there. Why are you being obstructive about this?'

'Look, I like Tony, he's a good guy, but I just feel a bit ... odd.' He's stopped smiling now.

'Why?' I ask. He's always got on well with my dad. They've not been matey-matey, but Dad takes an interest in David's racing and they find common ground there.

'You know why.' He pushes the last of his dinner round his plate.

'No, I really don't. You'll have to tell me.' Though I suspect I do know why.

'Because I don't want to give him the wrong idea.' He looks up at me sheepishly. He knows this is so wrong.

'I'm still not with you, but I'm getting a better picture.' I just know he doesn't have the balls to actually say what he means so I'll spell it out for him. 'Are you suggesting that because my dad has come out as a gay man, you are now worried that you are in some kind of danger of him being attracted to you?' It takes everything in me not to raise my voice.

'Well, I'm not saying he definitely would, but he could, couldn't he?'

At that, all my resolve to stay calm is lost. How dare he! We end up having a massive row. I don't usually argue, but this has just pushed me too far. There is so much behind his comment: the insult to my dad, the blatant homophobia – not to mention the narcissism. I can't believe it.

We end it badly. I go up for a bath and sleep in the spare room, leaving him alone with his ego. I tell him not to bother coming on Friday. I know it's not his fault he's like this; his parents were close-minded and he doesn't really know anyone in the LGBTQIA+ community and he's not big into social media, so I suppose he can't help it. I'm still angry though. This is my dad we're talking about.

As you'd imagine, by the time I open up the shop the next morning I'm still mulling it all over. Nothing changes the next day or the day after that.

The end of the week rolls around, and although David's apologised, bought me a giant bag of Minstrels, sat with me through two episodes of *Antiques Roadshow* (don't judge me, I love seeing the shock or disappointment on people's faces when they're told the prices of things) and assured me he has no issues at all with Dad or Bernie, I still can't shake feeling cross.

I mellowed a bit when he came home with a cut-glass vase and a bunch of flowers. I thought they'd be for me, to say sorry, but they weren't. 'A house-warming for your dad and Bernie. To show I care,' he said. They say actions speak louder than words, and I was really touched, so forgave him, glad he'd learnt his lesson and turned over a new leaf. I know he can be an absolute arse sometimes, but he always sorts it out eventually.

Fridays are mostly fairly busy in the shop. Vendors pop in or post goodies to restock, custom picks up and today was no exception. The door didn't stop ding-a-linging and I hardly had any time away from the till. I love days like that. I love seeing other people enjoy vintage bits and bobs.

I'd displayed a little 1960s beaded bag that I found on

eBay for £15. I popped it near the new jewellery and let myself try that ring on again. It's a Friday, after all. The bag was missing a line of iridescent beads, but I had near-identical ones in my stash and I sewed them on really carefully so that the bag looks perfect now. I'm tempted to keep it, but I thought I'd display it to see what sort of interest it attracted. At least four people have admired it, even with a £35 price ticket.

With all the buzz in the shop, I'm feeling a lot better and really looking forward to seeing Dad's new place. I was having guilt pangs for Mum, but apparently Debs has encouraged her to sign up to a dating app so she's 'getting back on the horse', and then Mum joked that maybe she'd find a 'stallion', so I think she's OK. I shudder somewhat at the thought of Mum and Debs's stallion. He'll be eaten alive by the sounds of it.

The till is running low on change, so while the shop is empty, with still no sale on my little beaded bag, I grab my cat-eye vintage sunglasses (I might not be up to wearing full vintage outfits yet, but I'm sneaking in accessories and feel amazing for it), step into the sunshine and dash across the road to the newsagent. They never mind swapping a twenty for some coins.

So strange. I open the door to the shop and although

it's the same layout, it's different. There are spinny display holders of video cases right by the till. Such a novel idea to sell those. I bet if I looked on eBay I could buy some and upcycle them into retro jewellery boxes or stationery containers.

'Cool idea on the video boxes!' I say to the guy behind the till, pushing my sunglasses onto my head. He's not the regular man but seems really smiley.

'Yep, £2.50 for three nights, or £3 for the whole week,' he replies.

'Er, cool. Do you mind if I just swap a twenty for some pound coins, please? The other guy is fine about it,' I say, holding out a crisp note. Love it when you get a new fresh one.

'I'm not taking that, love,' he says, holding the twenty up to his fluorescent strip lights. 'At least try a decent fake. This isn't even paper. Feels a bit plasticky!'

Instantly I flush red. I don't know why because rationally I haven't done anything wrong. I didn't know it was a fake, but I just can't bear things like this. I can feel the eyes of the woman behind me boring into my head. She's wearing some fantastic 1980s vintage, I note: a denim rara skirt, flat white pointy boots, a white crop top with 'RollerQueen' written across it in orange. Her hair is up in an incredible firework ponytail with a deep pink scrunchie that matches her lipstick.

I take the twenty back.

'Oh my God. Sorry. I, er, I didn't know that was a fake,' I say, trying desperately to save face.

'Course not, but I'm not changing it,' he says. He doesn't believe me.

'I'll come back with another one. It's from my till over the road. I always come in here,' I say, trying to sound convincing and confident.

'I'm in here five days a week and I've never seen you.' He shrugs.

It's too much. I know people are listening and I can't stand it, so I mutter something about someone having obviously given me a fake and walk out, red-faced and almost shaking.

God, I'm so rubbish. If that were Vivi she'd have shown him who's boss. Outside the shop I stand in some shade and try to call her for a vent but my phone is doing that annoying thing where it doesn't even make the dialling tone. This is so not my moment!

Feeling embarrassed and rather deflated, I head back to Pearls and Doodles, chuck my shades back into my bag and flick the electric fan switch, sighing when it doesn't come on.

What's with today? The store is quiet, so I spend a happier hour editing pictures of a few of my recent finds. Wi-Fi is still down so I'll upload them to my Instagram later today and see if there are any bites for sales over the weekend.

I feel a little stab of alarm when I realise I still have that amethyst and crystal ring on and that I accidentally wore it out of the shop on the failed till float run. I know Julia wouldn't mind, but it still somehow feels naughty. I pop it back in the box and make a mental note to be more careful next time.

Dad's flat is lovely. It's completely different to his and Mum's house, but maybe that's what he wants. He says it's just a temporary place until Bernie sorts his 'stuff' out (I don't like to ask what his 'stuff' involves) and they can find a 'proper house'.

It's a two-bedroomed modern place with a lot of glass and steel. The kitchen is all gloss cupboards, very different to the oak doors and cream tiles in the kitchen at home – Mum's home, I suppose I should say now. The sofas are navy leather with a glass coffee table between them and I notice some travel magazines nestled on top. Maybe he and Bernie are going to take a trip somewhere. I feel glad that he's planning a nice future.

Dad makes me a sweet, milky coffee, just how I like it, and we sit down on the sofas. They're a world away from Mum's velvet ones covered with scatter cushions and blankets, but still surprisingly comfy. I hope he adds a little blanket or two in the winter. I don't like to think of him not being cosy.

'Thanks for the vase and flowers, Tabby Cat. Bernie will like those when he's back,' Dad says kindly.

'Ahhh, that's OK. David bought them, though. He's sorry he's not here. He's just really busy,' I add, not wanting Dad to know that my boyfriend is plain ignorant.

'With his cars for the racing?' Bernie asks, entering the room with a smile, picking up a bottle of beer from the side and sitting on the empty matching leather armchair next to Dad. 'Your dad told me he's into that sort of thing. I used to go down to the races myself in my younger days,' he adds warmly.

'Yep. You know David. Devoted to them!' I smile, taking a sip of my drink. 'You might have seen him down there? Maybe you could come to his next race. I sometimes go, Dad could come too'. I hope he feels welcomed by the invitation. If he's important to Dad, he's important to me.

We sit in silence for a moment or two and then Dad starts, gently, 'Shall we get it all out then, Tabs?'

I nod and we sit for at least an hour, talking about every-thing that's happened over the last few weeks and, well, years. I can't remember the last time we had a heart-to-heart like this. I'm not sure we've ever really been candid with our feelings, or gone into any great depth. It's cathartic. It's like letting all the air out of a huge hot-air balloon and then just coming down to rest.

Dad, with Bernie, explains that he never fully realised who he was until about three years ago, although, he said, 'Looking back it all makes a lot of sense. I've started to wonder if I did truly know but was suppressing it very, very much.'

I must let my sadness show on my face because Bernie adds, 'It wasn't always like it is now. It wasn't the done thing. People like us were shunned. There was the AIDS epidemic. We were made to feel wrong and shameful. For most of us,' he says reaching across the arm of his chair to squeeze Dad's resting forearm, 'it wasn't an option to come out. You just had to push it down and carry on'.

'And that's what I did, Tabby Cat. Any time I thought about, about all of this sort of thing, I just brushed it off as a fleeting thought and focused on your mum. For the first few years, it worked! I was so happy with her, loved her to bits. Still do love her to bits really,' Dad says, glancing over at Bernie.

'Course you do, Tony, she's a good woman. She'll come round, she'll understand,' he reassures.

'I'm happy for you both. I want you to be happy, you deserve that.' We sit in silence for a moment and then Dad slaps both his thighs, gets up and takes a beer out of the little fridge.

'Time for something stronger than coffee, I think!' he laughs. 'Do you want anything, Tabby? Didn't get any rosé in but you're welcome to a beer?' I laugh back, 'No thanks, Dad, nobody makes coffee as good as you so I'll stick with it.'

We spend an hour or so, the three of us, chatting on the sofas and enjoying each other's company.

Dad's vibrant and animated, which seems so unlike him. He's always been a 'yes dear, no dear' kind of husband, but for the first time ever it's like he's really alive and I can't help but love it. It can't have been easy to do what he did and although I'm – selfishly – heartbroken Mum and Dad have separated, seeing him like this makes it feel better. The phrase 'live your best life' has never seemed more apt. Here is my dad, sixty-two years old, finally really living his. If only I could figure out what exactly I need to do to live mine.

Chapter Five

JULY IS EVERYTHING YOU'D want it to be. The sun is shining, and every time I go outside I breathe in the delicious scent of cut grass; I've even treated myself to a pedi so I can feel confident in my sandals.

Dad and Bernie have fully settled into their flat and seem really happy. I've dropped a few bits of my vintage furniture round to jazz up the place. Just a little brown leather magazine rack that I restained the legs of and a small plant stand that I painted black, but Bernie seemed really pleased and I welcomed the appreciation. They're going to look for a more permanent place next year, but for now I'm glad they have a base to start this next chapter. I've been over a few times for meals or just a quick visit, although David's been busy every time. I try not to take it personally. Mum says she's pleased for Dad and that it was a long time coming. She's focusing on her new situation and says 'I'm a hashtag new woman!' a lot. I'm not sure she fully grasps the hashtag thing, or that she is a new woman yet, but I'm not going to stop her when she seems to want to get hold of life too.

I don't know whether it's the summer sun, or the fact that I stood my ground and slept in the spare room for a couple of nights after that row last week, but David is being particularly sweet. Meanwhile Vivi has been busying along with MumLife, school runs, PTA duties (which she says she hates but I know she loves really) and encouraging me to do more on my Instagram, which is booming at the moment. I'm up to nearly eight thousand followers now.

Essentially, everything is ticking along really nicely.

Something, though, has been playing on my mind. I've tried not to think about it too much because it's the most ludicrous thought you can imagine. But just to air it, I'm spending the night at Vivi's house and I'm going to talk it through.

Most people grow out of loving sleepovers, but not Vivi and I. With Neil away on duty so often, Vivi is always glad of the company and David never minds a night with a few cans and the TV all to himself. I've taken a bag to work so I can go straight from there, and at lunchtime I popped out for the essentials.

The shop didn't have the video cases in anymore, but that only further cements the ridiculous notion that I'm planning on talking to Vivi about. While in there, I picked up biscuits (Time Outs for me and caramel digestives for her), jam doughnuts, a couple of tubes of Pringles, a bottle of sparkling rosé (Happy Friday to us!) and a cute biscuit-decorating pack for Kitty. I love buying her little treats.

Settling down on the sofa surrounded by snacks, we raise our wine glasses with ice chinking in them (I know, classy), while Kitty gets stuck into the biscuit-decorating, eating more icing than makes it onto the biscuit.

'OK, so what's all this about?' Vivienne asks excitedly. 'Please tell me you're ditching David and have found your knight in shining armour to whisk you away for a life of fame and fortune!' She's joking, I hope.

'No, Viv, that's your dream, not mine,' I say, biffing her with a cushion and nearly sloshing my wine on the blanket-covered sofa. Oops.

'Aha, yes, but I could live it vicariously through you, couldn't I? I could be your travelling PA and Kitty could be your mascot.' She laughs as Kitty jumps up from the fold-out kiddie table she's been working at on hearing her name.

'I don't think celebrities have mascots,' I laugh. 'Although this mascot would be the greatest the world has ever seen!' I grab Kitty onto my lap and start tickling her until she giggles and wriggles free.

'I'm not your manscot, I'm your bakery lady! Here you go,' she proclaims, handing out the dodgiest-looking cookies you've ever seen. They're more icing than biscuit at this point, and, I suspect, have been licked many times.

'I know, but you're not tied down,' Vivi says, giving a loving but firm look in Kitty's direction. 'You still could do all the things on your bucket list. I'm not sure I could live a glamorous Hollywood life now, but you could.' She flings herself dramatically back into the sofa, deftly grabbing the Pringles as she goes.

'Yeaaah, I guess. I mean, I sort of am living my bucket list dreams,' I say, staring into my wine glass. Maybe there's a better dream in there somewhere.

'No, you're not! What are your big dreams? Like the big, *big* ones.'

'Just carrying on at Pearls and Doodles. David being a bit more involved in family stuff. Perhaps having a couple of children one day,' I say, shrugging.

'They *can't* be your big dreams!' Vivi exclaims incredulously.

'Mummy, I want Auntie Tabitha to have babies!' Kitty jumps on her, putting her face super-close to her mum's. 'And if that's what her dreams are then you're not the boss of big dreams,' she says, her hands squishing Vivienne's cheeks inwards. I smile at the act of protection there.

'Yes, you're right, a dream is a dream, and Auntie Tabby can have whatever she wants.'

While Vivi wrestles Kitty off her I think about my 'big' dreams. Why do we have to have giant dreams? Why can't the little, 'normal' dreams be enough? Maybe because that's too flipping boring! I shake myself out of it.

We spend a while talking about how marvellous the dribbly biscuits are and how there aren't enough neon and black iced flowers. It is probably going to be a trend soon and she's just ahead of her time.

Once Kitty has settled from all the excitement and is zoned out in front of Disney+, I take a deep breath and start.

'Look, Vivi, I know this will sound utterly insane, but you're my best friend and if there's anyone I can tell, it's you,' I say gravely.

Vivienne has the same look of focus on her face she has

when she's filling out the school disco health and safety forms. Suddenly I feel quite on edge. She nods, encouraging me silently to continue.

'At work, there's this ring . . .'

'I can't condone anything illegal, but I'm never going to snitch on you,' she says, putting her hand on my knee across the sofa.

'OK, that's appreciated, I think, but this isn't illegal.'

'Well, thank God, because I'm not entirely sure I did mean that. I'm not putting mine and Kitty's lives on the line for a ring,' she gabbles in relief.

'Right. Good to know. Nobody has anyone's lives on any lines. Just listen.'

'OK. Listening.' She takes a big sip of wine.

'Right, so, there's this ring. It came in a few weeks ago and I tried it on,' I begin.

'Yep, that's OK, that's normal, I think,' she nods, invested in the story.

'It is. I try on lots of the little bits of jewellery; they're nice, I put them back, I sell them. Cool. Fine. OK. This ring though, and I know it sounds crazy, is . . . well, it's magic.'

'Magic?' Vivi repeats, waving her wine glass like a wand, swishing the fizzy rosé once again very dangerously.

'I know! I know this sounds mad, but it's WEIRD! I put it on and weird shit happens. When I put it on,' I lower my voice to a whisper, 'I have powers.'

'I'm just going to go with this, Tabitha, because I love you, not because it sounds reasonable. What . . . powers . . . do you have when you wear it?' Vivienne has narrowed her eyes as though she's trying to work out my dastardly plot to trick her somehow.

'I promise you I know how nuts this sounds. I've been thinking it over all week. I've been too scared to wear it, knowing what it can do.' I down the last of my wine ready to pour it all out (the weirdness, not the precious wine).

'When I put the ring on, I instantly have this little buzz go through my body. Like when you're a kid and you're waiting for a friend to come over for a slumber party. Or when you check your bank account and there's a tiny bit more than you thought there would be in there. Like a little jolt of energy.'

'So you really like the ring? That's OK. Why not buy it?' She nods slowly as if I'm not quite all there.

'No, there's more. When I wear it, people are different. Like, they're still people and still the same, but . . . different,' I finish, not losing eye contact.

'I'm sorry, I'm now officially lost.' She shakes her head.

'So am I,' I wail in despair. 'I don't get it either! Things are just a tiny bit off-kilter, a bit ... peculiar.'

'Give me an example. A mad, mad example.' I love her for sticking with me on this.

'OK! Two weeks ago, I'm wearing the ring and this girl comes in. She's wearing jeans, trainers and a really cool vintage Michael Jackson T-shirt. You know how I feel about vintage so I said, "Love your tee!" and she started telling me about how she bought it at his Wembley tour date last year!' I open my eyes wide, willing her to understand how impossible that would be.

'OK, so maybe she's really confused,' she tries.

'Yes, maybe. But how about this? Whenever I wear the ring, I can't get on the Wi-Fi.'

'So your Wi-Fi signal is a bit crap?' I can see I'm starting to lose her now.

'No! I tested it. Ring on, no Wi-Fi, ring off, instant Wi-Fi. Ring on, no Wi-Fi, ring off—'

'Yep! OK, bit peculiar. So what are you saying?'

'I don't know ... that the ring has energy? Maybe it's the crystals in it. Like it's emitting radons or electrons, or something?' I start to feel a bit panicked by the whole thing. 'It's not just in the shop. I accidentally wore it out about a week ago and went to the newsagent's. It was laid out differently. Like they'd rearranged the whole shop overnight with video cases and everything all different, and then the next day, without the ring, they'd put it all back to the way it always is!'

Something is scratching away at the back of my mind now.

No – it's gone.

'And what happens when you don't go near the ring?' Vivi is smiling now as if I'm telling her a really elaborate joke with a punchline on the way.

'Nothing. Everything's normal. I miss it, like, I crave it. I like wearing it for that buzz, but I'm starting to feel like something seriously strange is happening. I promise you I know how ridiculous this all sounds. You know me, I'm not the sort to want weird shit happening. I'm the most boring person in the world. I do absolutely nothing, with, as if we could forget, no big goals at all!'

'Don't say that. You do have goals and do things! Your Insta is fantastic.' Vivienne is a good friend.

We sit and think for a while, both completely baffled. Vivi puts Kitty to bed around eight o'clock (after she'd watched *Frozen 2* for perhaps the ninetieth time, which I was grateful for as I was telling my absolutely barking-mad ring story) and we order a Chinese from the takeaway restaurant in town. As we're dishing it up, Vivienne having some of my sweet and sour balls, me having some of her sweet chilli beef, she suddenly jumps to life.

'I've got it!' She flings her fork and grains of egg fried rice sprinkle all over the carpet behind her.

'Argh!' I nearly choke. 'Bloody hell! What?' I say, reaching for my can of Tango (again, classy lady).

'We need to be scientific about the ring. We should test it.'

'What, like in a lab? I don't know anyone with a bloody lab.'

'No, you div, just test it out. Try it on and make a note of what happens. Wear it out and about, take it home and wear it. Bring it here and wear it. Then we can see what's really going on.' She's so pleased with her foolproof plan.

'I can't wear it out and about or at home, I don't own it. It hasn't even been priced up. I'm not in touch with the vendor as it's Julia who runs that side of things and she's got all the details, so I can't ask. I can't even buy it. Julia would be seething if she knew I'd taken stock home!' I feel a bit queasy at the thought of making Julia cross. I never make anyone cross.

'You wore it to the newsagent's,' Vivi points out, as if to justify her new idea.

'Yes, but that was an accident,' I remind her.

'Have more accidents then,' she says, taking a bite of prawn toast as though this is the most unremarkable thing in the world.

This is why Vivienne is my best friend.

Chapter Six

B Y THE TIME MONDAY comes around, I've thought and rethought about what's going on with the crystal ring a thousand times. By the end of Friday night, Vivi was quite into the idea of it being magic. I'm not sure if it was the fizzy rosé, the desperation for excitement in this little town or genuine belief, but it was fun nonetheless.

We talked about every possibility. Am I imagining the ring even exists? Maybe. To counter this, I'm going to take a picture and send it to her. Am I misreading the details around me? Maybe. Vivi has supplied a clipboard (bit cringey that it's Kitty's LOL Doll-emblazoned one, but needs must, as Vivi says) that I'll have with me at all times to jot down any observations. I might jettison that accessory and just take my own notebook, but I didn't want to scupper her enthusiasm. As well as observing, I should apparently ask those around me for as many details as possible. I did point out that asking strangers 'What year is it?' 'Where am I?' might make me sound a *bit* odd, but Vivi waved away this notion with a top-up of my drink.

I considered talking to David about it, but thought better of it. It's tricky enough trying to get him to understand my PMT, so I doubt he's going to get on board with a mystical amethyst ring that makes people appear from the olden days. Bloody hell, it sounds so insane, doesn't it? Maybe the pressure of Mum and Dad's split has affected me more than I thought.

Insanity or magic, I'm going to find out today.

I marched down the high street with real purpose in a deliberately vintage-looking outfit. This is the most thought I've ever put into an outfit, and I feel pretty great about it. Initially it was nerve-racking stepping outside in something that isn't jeans or a print smock dress and tan ballet flats, but as soon as I realised the sky wasn't going to cave in on me wearing what I wanted, I felt so good. I should do this more often, mad/magic ring or not. I decided that if I was right about the ring and I was going to mingle, I didn't want to stick out!

I didn't actually have a vintage coat, so my standard M&S cotton jacket would have to do. Not vintage, but more shabby than chic. I gave David a peck on the cheek as I left this morning and he said, 'Where are you off to, all dolled up? You look gorgeous.' I reminded him that I was going to work, same as every day. Bless him.

Julia is in this morning for a paperwork session (looking incredible – bouncy blonde blow-dry, Versace sunglasses, immaculate sand-coloured linen shirt dress), and to inspect the little flat above the shop that she rents out. It's leased by Trevor, who commutes into Swindon during the week. At the weekends he usually goes to visit his family. He just uses the flat as somewhere to sleep, really. Last year was so . . . how do you even describe 2021? . . . that he ended up working from his family home so much he was barely in the flat. I don't think Julia minds. She's being paid rent, she says, and despite him being there so rarely, she still has to carry out the inspection.

Thinking of flat inspections makes me wonder when David and I might see our landlord; we've been in our cottage years and he's only been round twice, I swear. But perhaps I should be thankful for small mercies. He hasn't put the rent up in ages.

With Julia bustling around, I don't feel like I can test the ring. I don't think she'd mind if I tried it on quickly, but I can't imagine she'd be thrilled to hear I'm constantly wearing the stock.

The shop is unusually busy for a Monday morning, so Julia comes down to help me on the till.

'Someone I follow on Instagram recommended the shop,' one customer mentions as she pays for two china trios and a brushed-felt robin ornament. 'You should have your own account! I searched for it but couldn't find it. Just a girl I follow saying she loved it in here. Had to pop in.'

The customer and Julia chat for a while and I lose myself in dreams of setting up social media for the shop. I'd love that. My own account is doing really well; 240 more followers this weekend because I shared how to turn a vintage necklace into a light catcher.

After a deluge of custom, a stack of paperwork, an uneventful flat inspection and a chat about me maybe doing some social media work 'in the future' (why wait, I don't know, but I didn't like to push), Julia heads off home and I have a moment to sneakily check my phone.

Text from Vivienne: *Any luck, time traveller? Will pop by in my TARDIS after school run.*

Text to Vivienne: *No luck yet. Been busy. Operation Photo first!*

Did Vivi just write *time traveller* . . . ? A flush of heat rises from the pit of my stomach and floods my face and the rest of my body.

Unhooking the key from its little spot underneath the giant old till, I dart over to the jewellery case, unlock it, feel a wave of anticipation at wearing the ring and snap a picture of it in its tiny leather box.

Text photo.

Text from Vivienne: *Ohh pretty. Now put it on and FaceTime me. I dare you!*

Excited to have an accomplice, I take the dazzling ring out of its box, slide it onto my finger and instantly feel the jolt of energy I was telling her about. I'm shaking as I reach back onto the display shelf to pick up my phone.

No signal. *See!* I smile to myself because I want to call her smugly and say, 'I told you so! No Wi-Fi with the ring on,' but just to test it, I grab my jacket, switch the 'open' sign to 'closed' and head out down the high street to see if my phone has better luck with signal.

Having never gone beyond the newsagent's, I feel a

bubble of dismay at my act of rebellion but force myself to put one foot in front of the other. So far, everything just looks like a typical Monday morning. Trees look the same, and it's definitely summer. It is so crazy how it looks completely different but also, oddly, the same. The buildings look the same too, which isn't a surprise since it's a really old market town and nothing has changed for about two hundred years. But then the shops all have such different signs. Wow, the 1980s really was – is? – a different time when it comes to design. It is like *everything* was made using WordArt. I sort of love it. I head towards the green, which is surrounded by a cluster of shops, but something stops me before I reach it. I'm sure I've never seen a travel agency here.

On the left side of the road, maybe three hundred yards down from Pearls and Doodles, there's a glass-fronted terraced shop with a huge grey sign at the top of the window with 'Global Voyage' emblazoned in orange. Pictures in the window depict permed women sipping cocktails on beaches while men with hairy chests and thick moustaches stand smiling nearby. 'Best Package Deals' and 'Malta and More' are written on neon circles and stuck to the glass. If ever I needed proof that I was in a different time, this is surely it. I've never seen a more dated depiction of a holiday. Who even books a holiday face to face? That's what the internet is for!

I grab my phone out of my pocket to take a picture, but it doesn't work. Every time I tap in my PIN code, the screen freezes. No signal, no Wi-Fi, it's not even opening now! This is beyond bizarre. I'm starting to feel so alarmed that I turn on my heel to dash back to my shop. This isn't fun, this is scaring me. I'm just Tabitha from real life. Maybe I'm having some sort of awful episode and need medical help?

'Don't let the Malta deal lure you in. Costa Brava is much more fun!' calls a voice from the shop door.

My tongue feels thick and my chest is tight. I look in the direction of Pearls and Doodles and consider running back as fast as I humanly can, but the woman carries on. 'You OK? Didn't mean to make you jump. Just bored in here, my boss is off and I've had no customers all day. I guess everyone's away on their summer holidays, rather than booking them, eh?' She smiles, gesturing at the clear blue sky.

'Er . . . yes . . . me . . . ha ha . . . as in . . . yeah,' I stutter, turning round to face her and trying to regain my composure, instinctively twisting the ring round on my finger.

The woman in the shop looks so cool. She has curly

hair, but cut in a short bob – she's definitely a volume-over-definition kinda gal because it is sort of . . . everywhere, but it really suits her. She has similar colouring to me, though maybe faintly lighter eyes, and her features are much daintier. She's around my height – five foot four. She's in an orange knee-length pencil skirt with a casual black T-shirt tucked in and is wearing a bunch of bright fabric-y bracelets along with a few plastic wristbands like you get on an all-inclusive holiday, but I reckon they're probably from something much cooler, like a festival or gig. I spy a matching orange blazer hung on the back of her chair, which looks sort of like a human, because now the chair has huge shoulders. If I weren't freaking out so much, I think I would laugh. I wish I could pinpoint one single emotion and deal with it, but right now I'm flashing between fear, excitement and panic so quickly I've no idea where one ends and the other starts. I just stand there blinking uselessly in the direction of my shop.

'You wanna book something?' she asks earnestly.

'Um, I didn't know this was here,' I say, gesturing to the shop and taking a tiny step forward.

'Come in and sit down!' she says, stepping back inside, me following her. 'It's been here ages. Are you new around here?'

'Er, yes. Is this not new then?' It's new to my bloody reality! If this even is reality.

'No. My sister's friends with the owner, that's how I got this gig. Think it opened just as I started secondary, so it's been here nearly a decade. I'm twenty-one next month. Gonna see the world!' she exclaims excitedly, gesturing with her arm round the shop.

I stand there in disbelief. The Formica desks are littered with booking forms, brochures and promotional leaflets. The walls have huge posters showing exotic-looking destinations. One desk at the back has a huge ancient beige computer on it with a massive kind of printer to the side which I think might be a fax machine.

'Wow. This place is so . . .' I don't know what to say. I want to say 'old' or 'retro', but is it? Is this just 'now'?

The girl takes a second to really look at me.

'Don't wanna pry, but are you OK?'

'Huh?' I say, tearing my eyes away from all the things I can't quite believe I'm seeing.

'You seem really spaced out.' I can tell she's being polite and is worried for my sanity. 'Have you got anyone with you, or are you out shopping on your own?' she asks tenderly, bringing me back to the moment.

I need to pull myself together. What would Vivi do?

Where's that bloody clipboard when you need it? She'd go into one of her roles. I need to channel that and stop sounding so confused. 'Yes. Sorry. I do feel a bit spooked. It's been one of those days, you know?' I say, trying to sound more balanced and less like a woman about to have a panic attack because she thinks she has literally freaking . . . yes . . . *time-travelled*!

The niggling at the back of my mind explodes to fill the rest of my brain and it all clicks into place.

I've only gone and travelled back to the 1980s!

Even thinking it sounds insane, but it's the only way I can explain what's been going on.

'Tell me about it! I have one of those days every day.' She laughs. She's so young but so personable and chatty. I was so timid at twenty. In fairness, I'm pretty timid at twenty-six. I push forward with the conversation.

'Well, I've had one of those months.' My voice breaks. This is so unlike me, but suddenly I can feel everything bubbling up, and tears sting my eyes. What the hell am I doing?

'That's OK, let it out,' she soothes maternally.

'I don't really like change, but my parents have just split up after years and years together. My dad came out to us between a roast and a spotted dick, and nothing's been the same since.' Wow, I didn't realise this was affecting me so much. Why on earth am I sharing it now? Whenever or whatever 'now' is!

'Ohhh God, what? I'm so sorry . . .' she trails off. 'I think I know someone who's gay. Well, Elton John is, we know that now, hey? People don't like to admit it though, do they? That "Don't Die of Ignorance" poster was all over the place, wasn't it? Your dad did well to tell you at all. Got over the stigma, I mean.'

I nod silently, thinking how different things were in those days for people, but how unprejudiced she seems.

'I don't know why I'm telling you all this. But I've just been keeping it in for weeks. Well, I've told Vivienne and David bits,' I say, trying to compose myself.

'Vivienne and David?' she asks.

'Sorry! My best friend and my boyfriend. Bloody hell, we don't even know each other's names and I'm just blurting out all my problems. I can't tell you how unlike me this is! I'm having a REALLY strange day.' I force a laugh.

'Well, I'm Bea, and I'm happy to listen. Mrs Fletcher, the boss, is off sick at the moment, so I'm here alone a lot. I'm living at my sister's and she's got a steady boyfriend, so hasn't got a lot of time for me, and all my friends are either setting up home with *their* boyfriends, or the really clever ones are off to university. I'm just stuck here,' she says, slumping into the orange swivel chair behind the desk and flopping her arms down in front of her.

'I'm Tabitha Rose. Most people just go for Tabby or Tabs or whatever,' I say. I don't know why, but I hate introducing myself. I always go in strong and then feel so awkward. Why did I give my full name, like it's my first day at nursery?

'Oh my God, I absolutely love that name! Tabitha Rose. It sounds like something out of a fairy tale, doesn't it?' Bea perks up.

'Ha, I suppose so. I hadn't really thought of it before, but yeah, it's nice!' I can't help but warm to Bea.

'So why don't you book a holiday for you and David? Would he like the Costa Brava? Guaranteed sunshine,' she says, pushing a brochure across the desk.

'Mmmm, maybe,' I say, flicking through, pretending I'm Vivi in one of her productions. I need to find a way to work out what the hell is going on.

'Does he like to travel?' She carries on with her sales patter.

'He's travelled a bit. But not really, not at the moment,' I reply, deflated. 'He doesn't see why he should spend all that money on a week away when he could spend it on motorcross.' I smile at her.

'Wow.' She raises her eyebrows.

'Yeah, he really loves cars.' I force a little laugh.

'Why don't you look into a solo trip?' Bea suggests with rising excitement in her voice.

'Umm, I'm not sure I'd be very good at that. Probably a bit out of my comfort zone. I'd want David to come with me.'

'No! It'd be fab. That's what I'm doing at the end of the summer, or end of the year. Or new year. Whenever I can get the money sorted really. My sister's not keen on the idea, but I've told her I've got to spread my wings. I need to see the world!' She's fully animated now, and it's almost infectious. I wish I'd been that adventurous when I was her age.

'That sounds so fun for you! Where are you going? My friend Vivienne toured all round Asia on her honeymoon.'

'Oh, cool! I want to travel around Europe for six months. I've put a deposit on the first flights. Nineteen ninety is going to be my year!' she cheers.

I reel in shock.

She didn't say that . . . did she? *Nineteen ninety?* No. I'm hearing things. It can't be. If it was, that would mean . . . Well, I don't want to think about what that would mean.

'Nineteen ninety,' I repeat in a whisper. I know this is what I came here to confirm, but hearing it has shaken me.

I'm in the actual past.

'Yep. Got a nice ring to it, hasn't it? Nineteen ninety! Whole new decade. Or, if I can sort it all out, I'll go in a few months, in nineteen eighty-nine and then THAT will be my year, ha ha!'

This is too eerie for me. The alarm is rising in my throat again. I need to say or do something, but I'm starting to worry that I won't be able to 'go back to normal', or I won't see Mum again, or Julia will notice I'm missing from the shop and sound the alarm.

'Yeah, ha ha, 1990, woo-woo,' I muster. 'I've got to go. Really. Gotta get back to my shop,' I say, standing up and leaving the brochure on the desk.

'Ahh, bummer, I was going to sell you the trip of a lifetime!' Bea jokily complains, gesturing at all her brochures, still full of beans. 'Do you wanna go home and think about it?'

'Yes. Yes, that's exactly what I'll do. Lots to think about. See you!' I say as I leave the travel agent's and hurry back down the street. All I want to do is get back to Pearls and Doodles, get this ring off my finger and never put it on again. That was strange as fuck, and I'm not up for it. I thought I liked the buzz and the adventure, but I don't. Never again. Never, ever again.

Chapter Seven

'YOU DON'T MIND VIVI and Kitty stopping over tonight do you, gorg?' I ask David on the phone as I walk home from the shop that evening, still shaky from my afternoon. You know that feeling you have when you come off a big funfair ride? Like, 'wow, that was so fun!' mixed with 'but I'm almost certain that rickety old thing wasn't safe, so thank goodness I'm alive', mixed with 'screw it, though – let's go on again!' That's how I am now. With maybe a rather large dollop of wondering if I'm losing my mind stirred in for good measure. I need a BFF debrief and I need it stat.

'On a Monday? Don't you have work tomorrow?' he asks, confused.

'Yeah, but they'll just walk in with me in the morning and head to school. It's not that big a deal. Just fancy some company,' I say, trying to remain calm and not like I need to tell my best friend that I'm having a mental breakdown because I've potentially just hallucinated an afternoon of time travel. The familiar wave of panic floods in again. Am I going mad?

'I know, but what will we do for dinner?' he asks, still concerned. 'Are you OK?'

'Yes! I'm just walking really fast, so a bit out of breath. I could cook for us all, or we could order in,' I say as cheerily as possible but willing him to just accept the plans.

'On a Monday? Takeaway on a Monday?' Acceptance isn't going to come easy here.

'Oh my God, David! I'm not asking you to change your whole life, I'm just asking if you fancy a takeaway so my friend and I can chat. If it's that big of an issue you could bloody cook for us!' I snap, losing my patience.

'Calm down! It's just different, isn't it? I don't mind cooking or a takeaway, I just don't understand what's going on. I'm happy with whatever. I could do my famous spaghetti bolognese,' he says softly, making me feel a bit bad for snapping.

'Sorry. It's women's things,' I offer in a stroke of genius.

David is absolutely not a modern man and 'women's things' are a total no-go for him. God knows how he'll cope if we have a baby – he won't want to be anywhere near the business end. Obviously I'd rather he get a grip, but for now, I'm going to use it to my advantage. I don't have time to change his deep-rooted foibles at this moment.

'Riiight, OK, yep, roger that, you have your friend round, I'll do dinner and then head out to my engines,' he says in what he thinks is the most loving way possible.

'Thanks, gorg,' I say, putting the key in the lock of our little sage-green front door. I love this cottage; how close it is to everything, even if it's old and rickety and we only rent it, and the wind blows under every single door, rattling the entire house if you don't use a draught excluder (David hates that ours are all pink and floral, ha!). All the same, it's perfect to me.

I pop my keys on the little hall table that I upcycled last year (found it in a skip on someone's drive, took it home, added barley-twist legs instead of the boring boxy ones, painted it cream and voila! A masterpiece. They went wild on Instagram for that), kick my ballet flats off, hang my jacket under the stairs and put the kettle on.

I'd actually already invited Vivi before I checked with David if he minded (bit naughty, but it's been SUCH a day), so she's packing a bag for Kitty and heading over. I move into the lounge and pull out the old Quality Street tin stashed full of little toys that I've collected for my goddaughter over the years from charity shops and car boot sales. There's nothing particularly special in there: marbles, Shopkins, a few old Sylvanians, sheets of stickers, mini notepads, prizes from Christmas crackers and ball bearing puzzles, but every time she's here, she loves it. It's nice having a child in the house. I stop and wonder for a moment, again, what it might be like to have my own. I do want to be a mum, but I should probably have my life together a bit more before I get pregnant. Mum says I should be married first. I have these thoughts so often I'm almost bored with them.

I hear the old brass knocker go on the front door and I open it to find Vivi and Kitty smiling at me.

'We've bought unicorn cakes!' Kitty shouts, holding out a box of mini cupcakes from the corner shop. She's wearing her pyjamas and school shoes.

'Ohhh, my favourite!' I say, reaching out to take them. 'And you've come ready for bed.'

'I know! I'm having a sleepover,' she says into my stomach as I give her the squishiest cuddle.

Vivienne leans on the wall to take her shoes off, detangle herself from two rucksacks and a carrier bag full of what I hope are more snacks, and a school book bag. Her long black hair is getting caught in the book bag Velcro as she leans down, and all her gold bangles are being crushed by the heavy plastic bag.

'Oh my God, are you all right there?' I laugh.

'Oh yeah, just the epitome of yummy mummy, don't mind me.' She bends to let everything fall unceremoniously to the floor just as David opens the front door and crashes into her.

'Bloody hell! Decided to stand right there, did you?' he says, frustrated at Vivi.

'Oh, hello, David! Lovely to see you too. Thank you so much for welcoming me into your delightful home. I'm so very sorry to have inconvenienced you with my existence.' Vivienne Hawkins née Patel takes absolutely no prisoners, and I love it.

'Here we go,' David says, brushing past to drop his shopping bags in the kitchen.

'Only joking, David, love you really,' she calls, rolling her eyes and smiling.

'Yep, love you too, Vivienne. Is Neil still on tour then?'

Everyone traipses through to the kitchen, which only takes about four nanoseconds because our cottage is exceptionally teeny with just hallway, lounge and kitchen downstairs and then two bedrooms and a bathroom upstairs. The kitchen leads out to a long, walled garden which smells incredible in the summer. Dad loves the roses, and always spends time each week making sure it's all shipshape; or rather, he used to. I feel a little pang of longing for Dad, and for that cosy little world that has gone now. Me and Dad haven't talked as much as I'd have liked since our big heart-to-heart, I must call in soon, but since Mum's swapped her weekly roasts for trying her hand at Facebook ('I've been catching up with all the old gang, and they haven't changed a bit! It's quite fun to be at home in your scruffies, having a riveting conversation with someone you wouldn't have dreamed of letting see you that way! It's the beauty of the internet, isn't it, darling?'), I've missed our usual routine and his regular presence in my life. Also, maybe selfishly, I hope he'll still come and help me with the cottage garden through the summer when everything's settled down. I know he's just busy finding his feet for the first time in decades, bless him.

'You look away with the fairies, Tabs!' David says as he pops back into the hall to kick his shoes off, looking me up and down. 'Yep, ten out of ten for the outfit, Tabs, like I said. Bit different.'

'Mmm? Sorry, I was thinking about Dad,' I muse. If he

just mentions an outfit I'm wearing, it's a compliment. I should probably change out of my vintage look. What if it has time travel dust on it, or maybe radiation? OK, yep, going properly mad now.

'Why don't you have him round soon? Or visit him again?' David says, giving me a little cuddle, bringing me back to the present. He does have his sweet moments. I nuzzle into him and feel OK again, before heading into the kitchen to listen to Kitty tell me all about her day at school. There's talk of a big town Christmas play, with all the local schools taking part, that Vivienne's been asked to advise on, and Kitty is beside herself with excitement. 'My mum is the boss of it!' she announces, holding out a preliminary letter from her school.

Vivi rolls her eyes. 'I'm not the boss, I'm just helping out because I have expertise in that field,' she says in what I think she assumes is a humble fashion. 'Anyway, it's months away yet, but they want everyone on board, it'll need a tonne of organisation.'

'Expertise?' David scoffs.

'Yes, David, I have professional acting experience, and now I'm passing my skills down to the next generation, thank you.' I can almost see her extend her neck to stand half a centimetre taller.

'You were in an insurance advert when you were a kid and now you do am-dram, don't you?' He smiles, enjoying the goading. My boyfriend is the king of banter, but he forgets that Vivi is sharp as a tack and will wipe the floor with him if pushed. I hold my breath, silently looking forward to her reply.

'David. I featured in FOUR television ads, spanning an array of industries, and did more catalogue modelling than I can remember. For many of those jobs I was the first child actor of Indian heritage they'd ever used. Now I am the vice chair of the Ottleswan Drama Society, and the school have asked me to come on board and lend a hand for a community Christmas play.' I don't like him poking at her in this way, but I do like it when she's on her high horse. She rides it so well.

'Oh, right. Hollywood next then,' David laughs, trying to be playful but skating on pretty thin ice.

'Excuse me, but my mum is a star. She's an actress AND a model. You are just a man!' Kitty says, climbing and standing up on one of the chairs we have tucked round our kitchen table.

'Aha, you're right!' David says, tickling Kitty's sides, picking her up and swinging her round. 'I'm sure your mum is very clever, and I'm just a silly old man!' Kitty giggles away, completely oblivious to any friction there. I lean back on the kitchen worktop, watching him play with her so happily. Uh-oh: it's like a space suddenly opens up inside me as I watch them, making everything feel intensely present, something I've felt before but don't want to name. It makes me feel out of control, but I don't want it to stop; like when you know you've fallen in love, I guess.

Pushing that right down, I focus on the now, glad the tension is broken, and everyone seems jovial again. Vivi has a lot of fight in her and you never know when she'll set that free.

'And David, do you know what I can see?' Kitty says from high in the air where she's being swung round like a rocket.

'What? The ceiling?' he asks.

'Nope. Your hair is running out!' She giggles hysterically, setting us all off.

Chapter Eight

DAVID SKULKS OFF TO his 'workshop' (a summer house) at the bottom of the garden, near the big old fir tree, to work on a new engine (and lick his wounds from the hair comment, I imagine), Vivi and I end up cooking his 'famous spaghetti bolognese' and Kitty goes through to the lounge to watch TV.

I take a bowl of pasta, some salad and a few slices of garlic bread down to the workshop, tell David I love him and that his hair is as thick and full as the day I met him (he seems soothed by this and tells me he loves me too), and head back in to eat with Vivi and Kitty.

Squished round the table that takes up almost all of the kitchen floor space, the windows open letting the summer air in, with Kitty regaling us with tales from school performances past, as though I haven't been to every single one: ('One time I was the star. The actual star. I wore all gold and Mummy plaited gold ribbons into my hair and I was the BEST"), I feel a huge wave of emotion wash over me. David has been hinting heavily for a few months now that we start trying for a baby, and I realise I need to look this in the face and accept that it's a reality. I've been putting the brakes on because I want to do things in a specific order: ring, wedding, baby. That's how I've thought it should be.

Maybe he's right; maybe I should put those niggles to one side and do it because this, having so much life in the cottage, *this* is lovely. I realise this is the happiest I've been in weeks. Including the strange joy I get from the ring.

Oh God, the *ring*.

'Is David coming in, or does he live in the shed now?' Kitty giggles, spooning a big helping of bolognese into her orange-stained mouth.

'I think he's going to eat out there in case you tell him he's got no hair again!' I giggle with her.

'I was only joking!' Kitty protests, laughing mischievously, reaching out for another slice of garlic bread.

After twenty more minutes of picture-perfect dinner time loveliness, I offer to clear away so that Vivienne can read to

Kitty and put her to bed. David comes in and parks himself in front of the TV with a beer and a grumble about 'you girls gassing away about my hair', so Vivi and I head upstairs too.

We take half a bottle of white wine (essential), a bag of salty crisps and two packets of Maltesers so we have all the food groups covered.

'God, I love your room,' Vivi says, fluffing up one of the many cushions I have at the top of the bed, while I drag a few down and lean them up against the bed frame at the foot. 'You've always been good at making everywhere feel homey.'

'Ahhh, thanks, Viv. I just like things cosy. Always keeping an eye out for treasure or a bargain, you know?' I smile.

'I know, I saw your latest Insta. Can't believe you found all that!' Vivienne is referring to a little collection of sterling silver I'd shared on my Stories and offered for sale. A few months ago I'd popped into a town hall jumble sale in the next town over, and a woman was selling a carrier bag, literally a Tesco carrier bag, of 'old jewellery'. It was a bit of a gamble because I couldn't see everything, but I'd spotted some art nouveau pieces, so figured it might be worth it. I paid £50 for the lot, took it home, untangled everything (took me days), cleaned it all, identified what was what (80 per cent tangled costume jewellery, but some was real silver), polished the special items and then photographed them. Julia has a tonne of spare velvet displays for jewellery, so I made them look really professional and thought I'd see if anyone wanted to buy. A lady in America bought the charm bracelet for £280, a man in Scotland took the cufflinks for £135 and the little art nouveau figure pendant went for £177 to an antique collector in Bath. I couldn't believe it. A few other little bits sold for a grand total of £90, but altogether I made over £680.

'Shhh! I've not told David. It's my little nest egg,' I giggle, making a mental note to delete the post now that it's all sold.

'That's some nest egg! You ought to share your Insta more. You could do something with that,' Vivi says excitedly.

'Nooo, I don't want to. It's just my sort of people that like it, but nobody else would. Besides, I don't think David would approve,' I admit.

'Oh, sod him!' Vivi says, chucking one of my many cushions over. 'Right, let's pour this medicinal wine, ha ha, and you can tell me all about your absolutely normal day.'

A few minutes later, wine in hand, bras unhooked and hair in scrunchies, I'm ready to share.

'I'm more than aware this sounds insane,' I state, looking at her very seriously.

'Good, because it really does,' Vivi replies, as though she's just humouring me.

'Yes. But I do need to tell someone the latest.' I remain serious, hoping she'll mirror my tone.

'And I'm your only friend,' she says rather than asks. Sort of offensive.

'Not my only, but my best,' I correct, then wonder who else I would say is my friend. Must work on expanding my social circle at some point.

'Carry on then.'

'So, I tested it.' I take a sharp inhale to brace myself.

'The ring?' Vivi asks, as though we're not here specifically to talk about the magical time-travelling ring. I resist the urge to roll my eyes.

'Yes. Put it on, felt that buzz I told you about, tried to call you but couldn't. My phone was just unresponsive.' I can feel excitement bubble in me as I start describing the day.

'Hmmm. Bit freaky, I'll give you that,' Vivi replies, squinting and looking at me sideways. But she's serious now.

'I even tried it a couple of times. Just like before: ring off, phone works, ring on, phone doesn't work.'

'Yeah, that's really weird then.' She sounds a bit spooked, and I'm glad. Mostly because I want company in my freaked-out space, too.

'That's not the creepiest. I went outside, for a little walk,' I continue, energy rising, which isn't like me.

'OK . . .' She smiles, eager to hear the rest.

'And I went into the travel agent's on the high street, near the green—'

'There isn't a travel agent's around here,' she interrupts knowledgeably, as if trying to catch me out.

'There is! It's called Global Voyage. Full window of posters, desks inside, it's there, on the high street. Our normal high street!' I bounce up and down on my bum, wobbling the bed, wishing I could show her a photo of the place.

'Hmmm, OK, maybe I've not seen it,' she says kindly, but we both know every shop in this town.

'Anyway, I went inside and chatted to a woman, and I swear to God she said it was 1989.' I widen my eyes dramatically at the date.

'What? A woman in a travel agent's said it was 1989?' I can see Vivi isn't with me anymore and thinks I'm having her on.

'Yes! Well, she said next year would be 1990, but . . . yeah.'

'Tabitha, are you super-stressed at the moment?' She passes one of the bags of Maltesers over to me.

'I TOLD you this sounds mad! I know it does,' I say, downing my wine, moving the chocolates to one side and flumping my arms onto my lap. 'I don't want to be saying all this either. It's so freaking weird!'

'OK. OK. Look, OK,' Vivienne repeats, trying to make sense of things and failing.

'Stop saying OK,' I demand, now picking up on her stressed vibe.

'Yep, sorry, OK. Let's just say that you, Tabitha Rose Burnley, have truly found a magical time-travelling ring. And let's just say you went to 1989. Why would that *happen*? What's so special about 1989? Other than it being an epic T-Swizzle album?'

'I don't bloody know, Vivienne, I didn't choose this! What if I accidentally do something that kills Churchill or ruins the whole world? Aren't there rules to this kind of thing? Mathematical, quantum physics rules?'

'First off, Churchill was already dead by 1989, so I don't think we need worry about that,' Vivi reassures me.

'Oh yeah. Well, someone that's not dead then. You know what I mean. Butterfly effect stuff!'

'And secondly, how can there be rules to something that nobody understands and maybe, just maybe, is a bit just in your head?' she offers as gently as she possibly can.

'Oh *God*!' I say, flailing my arms so hard this time that my crisps clatter to the floor. 'Oh God again!' I shout, this time in response to the crunchy mess I'm going to have to sweep up before David sees and moans.

'Look, this is a win-win. If it's all in your head, what a fantastic imagination you have. If it's not, shit me, you've just discovered time travel. Why don't you do it again tomorrow and see what happens?' My best friend is the eternal optimist. She makes it all sound so easy.

'It's scary, Vivi! I'm going through time or space or something!' I exclaim, eating my snacks to distract myself from near hysteria.

'You're always saying you want to have a bigger life. Maybe this is it! Maybe time travel will be your "thing".' With that, we both burst into uncontrollable giggles.

You know when something is so ludicrous but also so stressful but also so exciting and you're with your BFF and there's nothing else to say so you just laugh and laugh until you can hardly breathe? Well, it's like that, and it's the best.

Once we've calmed down, Vivienne raises both her hands as if she's about to make an announcement.

'Now! Aside from your new-found ability to travel through time,' we nearly explode all over again but I manage to nod and hold it in, 'I have a rather exciting thing going on as well.'

'Ooohhh, let's open the Maltesers, this sounds good!'

'As well as my continued charity efforts for the Navy—' she goes on.

'You literally once held a bucket at the church fete and talked about Neil all day,' I interject.

'It was a long day, and we raised over two hundred quid in that bucket!'

'Only because Kitty looked so adorable in her daddy's captain hat, but yes, carry on.'

'As I was saying, as well as my *continued* efforts there, my planning with the school for the community Christmas production and my vice-chairing of the amateur dramatics society, I've decided to pour myself into yet another . . . venture,' she finishes grandly, picking a Malteser out of the bag, swirling it in front of me in a very theatrical fashion and popping it in her mouth.

'Ooohhh, a *venture*,' I coo, playing along, shovelling two Maltesers at once into my own mouth.

'Yes! A charity fashion show at the community centre. End of August. It'll be something nice before school starts again. Just what we all need.'

'Is it?' I ask instinctively.

'Of course it is! Something we can all enjoy, raise a bit of money for whatever charity the parish votes on, a bit of glam, a bit of glitz, everyone together, some nibbles, wine, maybe even sangria! I know it's not *time travel*, but it will be fun. All the local boutiques can get involved and showcase their clothes. You could even showcase some of your bits!'

'Aha-ha, I'm not sure I want to showcase my bits on stage, but thank you anyway,' I giggle childishly.

'Oh shut *up*, you know what I mean, those clothes you've upcycled, the jewellery you find for Instagram. Or see if Julia wants to show off some of the pieces from the shop. Maybe even the Magic Ring.' She can't help but giggle too.

I feel a stab of protectiveness over the ring. I don't want anyone else to have it or wear it. Not for my sake, obviously, but it belongs to the vendor. It wouldn't be responsible to bring it out without his say-so, and I've still got no idea about the price. I'm just being a good shop manager. Plus – not that I'll admit it to anyone – I don't want to share it.

We chat for a bit longer about the fashion show, how the town committee (which, of course, Vivienne's on) are going to advertise for models on Facebook, and how I could help with styling the hall since 'you're so good at making rooms look great', and then we wind down for bed. I've cleared all my clothes off the spare room bed, put fresh sheets on (my favourite white cotton ones with the tiny pink rosebuds) and folded towels for them like they do in nice hotels. I smile at my efforts and leave them to settle in.

As I lie next to David, his light snoring oddly comforting, I struggle to sleep. My brain feels like it's a thousand wires in a box all jumbled up and you have no idea which wire is for which appliance. Maybe you don't even need that charger anymore; maybe you should keep that funny-looking orange cord; best just jam the lot in a box and shove it away to deal with another time. Except I can't seem to shove my thoughts away.

Mum seems to be fine. But I think deep down she must be really struggling. Dad's left her. I know she has her friends (and her blossoming Facebook account), but she doesn't have much family to lean on except me. After all, Mum's sister died in a car accident when I was only a baby. At times like these you need your girl gang. I'm going to make more time for her this week.

Then there's this constant niggling feeling that I should be doing more. It's not very severe, but like a dull ache I carry with me everywhere, in every area. Maybe I should be excelling more at work; maybe I should make more of my antiques and vintage clothes sales; maybe I should be pushing David to propose, maybe *I* should propose; maybe I should be starting my journey to motherhood, or maybe I should see some of the world. It's exhausting, running through all the things I think I should maybe do, when all I really want is a simple life, to go to sleep and to work out what on earth this crazy ring is.

'Babe, if you toss and turn any more you're going to fall out of bed,' David whispers. I hadn't even noticed I was moving, or that he'd stopped snoring.

'Come here,' he says, and I cuddle into him, comforted. Tomorrow is a new day.

Chapter Nine

AFTER MY BROKEN NIGHT, I decided that life in 2022 is complex enough for me. I'm not going to wear my ring again, I'm not even going to think about it. *The* ring. It's not mine. Mustn't start thinking like that. Not that I have been thinking like that, because I'm not thinking *the* ring. Obvs.

A few days go by and I don't wear the ring. I spend my time updating my Instagram with lovely little pieces I've been squirrelling away; visiting Mum; having a good phone chat with Dad and a nice evening with David in front of the TV. He can be lovely when he wants to be.

Mum insists she's fine. I noticed she'd added some silk fuchsia cushions to the bottle-green sofa. 'Just a bit of fun,' she trilled when I asked her about them. Mum is the last person on earth to do something just for the fun of it, so this out-of-character behaviour piques my interest.

'That's . . . good,' I say as she serves me a plate of coq au vin. 'I'm glad you're having a bit of fun with decor.'

'Not just decor, Tabitha, I'm having fun in general.' She smiles, taking a sip of icy water and cutting into a slice of chicken. I notice her skin looks smoother, really radiant, like in an advert for moisturiser.

'Oh. Er . . . great!' I pause, watching her, assessing her to work out exactly what's different. 'You look so well. It's . . . also good. Different. Yeah, different,' I trail off, unsure.

'Goodness me, Tabitha! You needn't seem so perturbed. Debbie arranged for me to have some highlights, and I've had a tiny bit of Botox around the eyes. I've not taken my head off and switched it!'

I've never been so stunned in all my life. Although when Dad came out as gay over the Sunday roast, and when I accidentally travelled through time, those events were quite shocking, but I can't believe Mum's had Botox. This is a woman who overthinks every single thing. I've had phone calls before about the perils of using false eyelashes ('But do they test the glue thoroughly, Tabitha? Sticky liquid near the naked eye could do you an injury!'), so I can't get over the fact that she's been having a treatment like Botox without several lengthy calls to me first. I almost feel put out. Redundant.

'I know, but Dad left you. Your husband of thirty-two years. For Bernard. I thought you'd be . . . Well, I didn't think *this* would be your reaction!' I say, completely baffled by this new woman in front of me.

'I am devastated, darling, but it has also been a bit of a wake-up call for me. I wasn't blind, but I'd been turning a blind eye. I knew things weren't what they should be. They hadn't been for a long time. Maybe never. We weren't really the . . . intimate type. Certainly not on a regular basis.'

'You had me!' I say, not really knowing how to respond to the sex thing.

'Well, the thing is—'

'No, it's all right, Mum, honestly.' I cut her off, desperate not to hear any more details about my parents' physical relationship, whatever it featured. 'I get it, things haven't been as good as they looked to be. I do understand. I just thought everything was perfect. You seemed so happy.' I push my carrots round my plate, maybe more upset about this than she is, and I'm not sure it's just the Botox. I'm glad she's loving her appearance. She looks gorgeous.

'We *were* happy! Tony . . . your dad . . . he was my best friend, hopefully still will be. I was happy to have you, and happy to have a stable relationship, and happy to have a nice home.'

'You make it sound so simple. Like that's all you needed,' I say, feeling like a small child for not understanding my mum more now that I'm an adult. I really will make more effort to know her on an equal level.

'That *was* all I needed. I'm not a whizz-bang-wow sort of person. I walked into it all knowing what I needed, happy with my lot. I'd been so heartbroken and messed around before, I was glad of some stability.'

'Ah yes, Michael. You told me about him. You were engaged, weren't you, but broke up because he wanted to go travelling?' I add, more gently.

'It was all for the best,' Mum says, finishing the last of the new potatoes on her plate.

'Well, I know that, because you got *moi*,' I say, flourishing my hands around my face, 'but you must have loved him if you were going to marry him?' I'm so staggered I've never known this story till a few weeks ago.

'I did love him. I was ready to give my whole life to him. He wasn't right, though. He wanted very different things to me.'

'Like what?'

'He was always disappearing. He wanted to be a nomad, for a start.'

'A nomad? Isn't that someone who lives in the desert with sheep?' I say, completely baffled now, remembering the nomads we'd learnt about in our human geography lessons. I couldn't picture Mum in her casual trousers and twinset, wandering the desert with a big stick, herding livestock.

'No, darling! You've gone off into one of your little worlds again, I see.'

'I am listening,' I say, not liking being caught out. 'Tell me about the nomad.'

'Right. Michael wanted to spend his life travelling from country to country, living in temporary accommodation, crashing on sofas and the like, finding bits of work here and there. I wanted to settle down and have some lovely children, live a respectable life.'

'Is travelling not respectable?' I ask, genuinely interested.

'Don't be contrary, Tabitha, you know what I mean. It was time for me to grow up, stop dilly-dallying around and establish myself. I thought that if I married Tony, a nice, kind man, had some children and kept my head down, I'd have ticked everything off my list.'

'And did you?' I ask, not fazed at being called contrary.

'Did I what?' She blinks at me.

'Tick everything off your list?' I nudge.

'In a way. It wasn't always easy, but yes: I had you, a fixed address, a stable husband – it was all I'd wanted.' She pauses thoughtfully. 'And I'm glad I had all that, but now I know life isn't about lists. You can't control your life, you just have to seize each day, each opportunity. As you young ones say, "You've got to YOLO"!'

Oh God, I love Mum. I cheer in agreement and decide not to correct her on the grammatical correctness of, 'You've got to you only live once'. She understands the gist and that's all she needs. More power to her, I say.

We ate our coq au vin, Mum served home-made apple and blackberry crumble, and then we spent the evening in the lounge watching her soaps and keeping conversation considerably lighter in tone.

Mum's really loving Facebook. She's reconnected with old friends, bought a full China dinner service on Facebook Marketplace and has seen the town committee's advert for fashion show models. To top it all off, she's applied to be part of the 'Overs' category.

'That's fantastic!' I say, stunned; she's never done anything like that before – she's not one to make a spectacle of herself.

'Tabitha, I loved my quiet life, and there's nothing wrong in wanting to keep it simple. Now, though, I'm going to live it up and, dare I say it, sex it up!'

'OK. Hurray for you! A sexed-up Mum. Lucky me.' I smile.

And then secretly shudder.

Chapter Ten

I'M GLAD MUM'S DOING OK (though I'm not a hundred per cent convinced, and resolve to keep an eye on her), but it's unreal seeing this new version of her. It feels like everyone's lives are moving forward except mine. I'm stuck, going nowhere. But then there's the ring . . . It's been about two weeks since I last wore it. Still nobody has bought it; nobody even asks to try it on. I've mentioned it a couple more times to Vivi, and she just says to have fun with it. 'If I had a magic ring I'd be going all over the place!' Maybe she's right. I can't stop thinking about it now, but I'm not sure I'm brave enough to try it on again.

For a Friday, it's very quiet in the shop. Most of the town are over at the park, where there's a food festival. Julia said

I could close at lunchtime and go if I wanted, but I didn't really want to go on my own, so I decide to stay and update my Instagram. I've had a couple more sales this week, and I'm bidding on eBay for a chair to upcycle into a photo shoot prop. I've seen them on Pinterest and they look fun.

A few minutes in, and my attention is waning. It's so silent, and all I can think about is wanting to try the ring on. You know when you sense someone is looking at you? It feels like the ring is doing that from across the room. I've been resisting it, and now I feel like I deserve a reward. Vivienne would. Crikey, even Mum would these days.

I take the little brass key from the hook under the desk, walk over to the glass cabinet and see the ring. It twinkles at me under the lights.

Hello, friend.

I unlock the cabinet, pick up the dainty leather case, slide the ring onto my finger and that familiar rush of energy sweeps over me. Like the first moment you sink into a warm bath, or the heat of a liquor shot at the back of your throat. I feel incredible. I feel alive.

Without hesitating this time, I grab my sunglasses, flip the 'open' sign to 'closed' and head out into the muggy summer air.

Everything is like it was last time. Buildings look the

same, trees look the same, cars look like they're from an old-fashioned TV show and people are wearing vintage. Hairstyles are very Charles and Diana, and the travel agent's is in my sight further up the high street.

With much more confidence than before, I start walking directly towards it. That previous feeling of panic has been replaced with anticipation and I am loving this new sense of adventure. The ring makes me so fun! Wish I was like this in real life.

Before I know it, I've arrived at the travel agent's and I'm delighted to see nobody is in there except Bea. I'd have thought a Friday afternoon would be the perfect time to book an exotic trip, but perhaps not.

Pushing open the door and taking a deep breath, I go in.

'Ding-a-ling! Only me,' I call over to her desk.

I'm relieved to see Bea smiles with recognition. 'Hello! I thought you were my sister. She's the only other person I know who says "ding-a-ling",' Bea laughs as she stands up from her desk.

'Don't get up, I just popped in to say hello and see how you are,' I say, taking a seat opposite her desk which, like last time, is strewn with brochures and booking forms.

'Ahhh, that's so rad of you.'

'I was a bit . . . off last time,' I admit.

'That's OK, I was worried about you. You seemed a bit . . . unwell. Were you coming down with something? There's always a nasty cold going round, isn't there?'

Ha! Just you wait till 2020, I think to myself, grimacing.

'Yeah, no, I'm fine. A funny time. Anyway . . .' I realise I should have thought about what I might say.

'So, how have you been? Persuaded the old man to go on holiday yet?' Bea picks up the conversation, better at the patter than I am.

'Aha, I wish! He's building cars at the moment, ready for a big motorcross rally he's got in a couple of months. Can't think of much else!'

'What about a girls' trip? Something cheap and cheerful.' She smiles, well-trained in sales it seems. 'We can do a lot cheaper than the teletext deals.'

'I think Mum might be up for a break.' I play along, wondering if we could somehow share the ring, if it would work with foreign travel, and then catching myself and realising how ridiculous all of this is. Although I bet trips back then really were cheap!

'Ohhh lovely! A mother and daughter trip would be SO nice. Is she a coast or a city woman?' Bea asks, moving brochures around her desk looking for the right one.

'Ummm, I don't really know. I should know, shouldn't I?

We used to go on really fantastic holidays. Save all year and then splash out.' I pause, feeling sad. 'Not anymore though, not now Dad's gone.'

I don't know what it is about this place but I seem to be able to share so much with Bea. Ordinarily I'd never let my guard down in front of a stranger, or even my family, to be honest. But now I can feel tears prickling behind my eyes. Stepping out of one reality and into another opens you up, apparently, especially when the new version might not even be real.

'Oh, I'm so sorry,' she says, reaching out a hand to put on mine, and I have to blink hard to fight back any leakage now. Then I realise she must think Dad has died.

'No . . . sorry! I'm being so silly about this.' I try to force a laugh as if to balance out the pain I've let show. I take my hand from under hers and wave my arms in a comedy way as if I'm just being dippy. Which, I have to say, I feel like I am. I need to get a grip. Bea has this lovely kind energy to her, dammit.

'He's alive. Just not with my mum anymore. Bit of a break-up. A huge break-up.'

'Oh God, yeah, I remember you saying now. He's gay, isn't he? How's it all going? Hope he's OK?' she asks. 'Is your mum heartbroken?'

'Well, she's had her moments, but she's getting there. Making the best of her situation. All over Facebook now!' I say, rolling my eyes.

'I don't think I've read that one.' Bea nods supportively.

Shit! Must remember when I am!

'No, don't worry, nor have I. I just mean she's really preoccupied and distracted,' I stutter, trying to cover my gaff.

'That's good, isn't it? Stops her being too down, doesn't it?' she encourages me, oblivious.

'Mmm, yes, I suppose so, but it's my dad, you know? Love of her life, and all that!' What's this? Am I angry about this? What the hell is it about this ring that makes me want to share everything with this complete bloody stranger?

'Think yourself lucky! My sister's just broken up with her boyfriend, Mike, the love of *her* life. She's done nothing but cry for weeks.'

'Oh, God. Your poor sister,' I muse, reflecting on Mum's roller coaster of emotions and then feeling selfish for not being more involved in Bea's problems. 'Were they together long?'

'Since leaving school. She's twenty-seven now. Not married, no kids. She thinks it's all looking a bit bleak,' Bea says with a sigh. 'Those things matter such a lot to her.'

'Twenty-seven isn't bleak! I'm twenty-six, and I'm not married with kids,' I say, rather offended.

'I didn't say *I* thought it was bleak, just that *she* does,' Bea says more animatedly. 'I hate all that sort of worry! Timelines and relationships and setting up home. No thanks. No, I don't think she needs to worry at twenty-seven, not at all,' Bea says with a happy confidence that I wish I had more of.

'Oh good,' I laugh.

'She's just miserable. Only wants to hide away at home and rent videos. Her friend tried to set her up with her brother, but she said she'd never love again. Bit dramatic, especially for someone desperate to be married!' She smiles, obviously having a good grasp of the priorities.

'Well, marriage isn't everything,' I say, more defending my own unmarried status than quibbling with hers.

'No way! I don't think anyone should tie themselves down if they don't want to. I certainly won't. I'm going to travel the world, see everything that's out there and then, if I want to, I'll settle down. Handsome chap, town house in London, parties every night and then we'll have a baby, three dogs and live happily ever after,' she says with a flourish.

'The dream!' I say, feeling excited for her. She has such an infectious energy!

'First stop, Sorrento, Italy,' Bea announces, picking up one of the many brochures off her desk.

'Ooohhh, lovely! I just watched someone who went there,' I join in, pleased to have something to say for once.

'Eh? Watched them go, like, went to the airport with them?' She cocks her head to one side, confused.

Shit, shit. I realise I've watched someone I follow on YouTube vlog the trip, but I can't say that. How the hell would I explain vlogging to someone like Bea?

'No, sorry, d'uh, I meant I saw her holiday photos,' I say, thinking fast. 'Watched her show me them.'

'Oh, like a slide show?' Bea says, nodding.

'Yes! She did a slide show. I watched that. Was so good. Looks lovely! I'd love to go,' I gabble.

'You should, I'm going to. I know everyone tells me I should find a man or maybe get a career, but I just can't think of anything I want more than a bit of adventure. That's why I agreed to work here – feels a bit closer to it all.' She gestures with her hand outstretched to the posters on the walls.

I nod and smile, marvelling at how different Bea and I are – literally from different periods of time – and yet I can't help but like her. I look at all the posters curling at the corners. For a second, I imagine Bea in 2022 and how she'd love travel influencers. Maybe she'd be one; she's certainly nailed the enthusiasm.

I stay a happy hour and we chat about Sorrento, Pearls and Doodles, holidays we've taken, a bit more about her sister's heartbreak. Bea has a way of making me feel like we've known each other our whole lives. This ring clearly has unique properties, because it's not like me to feel so chilled.

'Right, well, the weather is gorgeous, so I've made up my mind to get my sister out into the park to enjoy the long evening. Might do her good to have a break from the VHS player and see some actual other humans, you know?' Bea says, laughing.

I agree, take the social cue and make my way out.

'Pop in soon, won't you?' Bea calls.

'Definitely! I'll need to hear where you're going after Sorrento,' I say, leaving with a smile and a little pep in my step.

I walk back to the shop feeling wonderful, as though I've had an afternoon with an old friend. I head in, put the ring back in its place, log back into Instagram and smile – a rather upmarket vintage interiors shop in London has shared my latest post and tagged me, so I've had an influx of followers. Plus, to be recognised by such an influential account is a real buzz. This is turning out to be an excellent Friday.

Chapter Eleven

I DON'T WANT TO LET any part of my body out from under the duvet the next morning, but I have to. I'd agreed to meet Mum at 8 a.m. for the town's big summer sale, but now I'm having serious regrets.

After work last night, David and I wandered down to the fair that's come to town and let loose a bit. I'm not a huge fan of the rides, but I love the atmosphere and snacks. I was on a high from my secret afternoon with Bea and my little Instagram buzz, David was happy he'd finished some old engine, and we felt like this was reason enough (I didn't share the details of my reasoning; I suspect he's got a hunch about my Instagram account, but he hasn't pushed it. I just said I'd had a great day and met some nice people at work, and that was enough for him. Sometimes it's handy having a boyfriend who doesn't pay as much interest as he should, ha ha) to treat ourselves to a few drinks and a hog roast bun.

I'd previously moaned about standing in a crowded field, but after three Pimm's and my delicious roll, it didn't matter. We played some of the games, and David won me a cuddly panda. I cheered as he won and threw my arms around him even though I'm not usually one for PDA, but I felt so joy-filled in the moment. My new friend, a sliver of online success, a bellyful of warm booze and a kind boyfriend lit by the waltzer – that'll do it.

Back home, we finished off a bottle of wine we had in the fridge, went upstairs and made the most of the night. That felt like an amazing choice at 2 a.m. but now, at 7 a.m., naked and dreading stepping into the early-morning chill, I have regrets.

Text from Mum: *Looking forward to seeing you, Tabitha. Why don't you wear the lovely straw sun hat with the red ribbon on it? Feels like we're having a cooler day today but it's going to be sunny Xxx*

Good old Mum: even when her life's fallen apart, she has space to mother. She bought me the hat last year and in fairness, I've barely worn it. It's felt 'too good' to on a typical day out, and I'm worried the thick red ribbon will make me look a bit OTT.

Taking a very bracing breath in, I rip the cover off myself, ignore David's grumbling as the cool air hits him too and scurry across the landing into the bathroom, turning the shower on as quickly as is humanly possible. There should be medals for how fast you can do that, because if there were, I'd be winning. I've had plenty of practice, as our bathroom can be freezing even in summer. Must get David to fix the heated towel rail.

Warmed by the shower, excitement for the morning starts to blossom. Today's sale is one of the biggest car boot sales around. Personally, I'd go to a car boot every week of the year if I could, but I appreciate that not everyone is as keen on second-hand bargains as I am.

While I'm brushing my hair and swiping a bit of foundation on in the mirror, I notice a couple of old lipsticks in my make-up bag that I haven't worn for ages. If I'm going to wear a bold hat, I may as well push myself out there with the beauty regime too. Bea would!

I walk out of the bathroom in just a towel but with a full face of make-up on and hair looking pleasantly volumised, thanks to a mixture of dry shampoo and last night's bedhead situation. Given that it was a good night, and the extra TLC in the mirror, I expect David's going to love this glam version of myself.

'Bloody hell, babe, are you going clubbing or out with your mum?' he says, laughing as I jump onto the bed to show him. Fuck's sake. Instantly regret the bright pink lipstick, and I think he sees it instantly too.

'I'm only joking, you look gorgeous! You should make an effort more often, it looks good on you,' he says, reaching his arm out from under the duvet to pull me into a cuddle. I let him hold me for a second and then wriggle away.

'Mum will be cross if I'm late,' I say, still feeling a little bit stung but brushing it off because he did say I was gorgeous . . . even if it was a bit of a backhanded compliment.

'Ooohhh, straw hat *and* bright lipstick! You look fantastic, Tabitha!' Mum trills as I meet her by Eastings Field for the sale.

I love my mum. She's not a naturally mumsy mum, but she's always on my side and always champions me. Any weight I was carrying from David's disapproval vanishes, and that pep in my step I caught from Bea yesterday is back. I note how nice it is to feel it on my own, without using the ring, but before I have a chance to let that idea linger, Mum chips in again.

'Right, I've brought a few shopper bags, and I've got the box on wheels in the boot if we spot anything big. Have you got everything? Small change, a fold-up bag?'

As well as cheerleading my lipstick, she's also very practical. All the more to love her for, I guess.

'Yes, yes and yes. This isn't my first rodeo, Mum! I'm on the hunt for high-value vintage clothes I can fix up, small gilded mirrors, anything pretty with precious stones, little items of wood furniture I can paint, and if we see any Sylvanians, I'll scoop those up for Kitty.'

'OK, got it. I'll put my hunting glasses on,' Mum says, nudging me in anticipation, holding her hands up to her eyes like spectacles.

'Muuum,' I protest, though I secretly love it.

'You're never too old to have your mum help you treasure-hunt. Are you going to present them on your Instant-gram site?' she says, reaching up to tilt my hat ever so slightly to the left.

Ignoring her fiddling, I reply, 'Post them on Instagram, yes. That's the plan. I've had people buying some of the bits I've found,' I say, trying not to make eye contact because I don't want to sound like I'm bragging. I do want to tell Mum, though. It's nice to show her that I really do have stuff going on, even if I'm not following the path I think she wants for me right now.

'Oohhh, well, I'll have to put on my extra-strong hunting glasses,' Mum says happily.

'Ha, thanks, Mum,' I smile, looping my arm through hers as we set off.

'Good for you for selling some stuff. Debs sells on eBay and does very well. You could ask her for some tips.'

I decide not to tell Mum I've made over a grand now from my sales, and instead just murmur about that being a good idea. Just mentioning it in the first place was a big step. I'll leave it there for now. One small step for conversation, one not-quite-giant-but-still-significant step for Tabitha.

'Right, I need you to put your hunting glasses on too, please, Tabitha,' Mum announces, jolting me back from my little daydream.

'Why? You don't like second-hand stuff, do you? You like M&S and John Lewis.' I'm stunned. First Facebook, now this!

'I know, but I'm on the lookout for a Ruth Langsford-style pencil skirt,' she says matter-of-factly.

'Oh. OK.' This is so unlike Mum that I don't know what more to say.

'Going to sex things up a bit,' she says, giving her hips a wiggle as I watch on, horrified.

I'll never get used to her saying things like that. 'OK ...'

'Can't a woman in her late fifties—'

'You were sixty in June.'

'Shh, can't a lady of sixty be sexy?' she asks, unlinking arms and looking at me, really making a point.

'Yes, of course she can. I'm all for women of any age being as sexy as they like, but I'm not OK for YOU to be sexy!' I say, feeling like a small child but still saying it.

'Well, I'm sorry, Tabitha, but I am. In fact, I've never felt so sexy,' she says, wiggling again. I'm not sure I've ever seen her wiggle in my entire life. I don't know what's got into her and I'm not sure I want to find out.

'Right, well, OK, that's good, I'm glad,' I say as we arrive at the gate to pay our £1 entry fee.

'I've reconnected with an old friend on Facebook,' Mum calls as she follows a pace or two behind me. I was hoping if I marched off a bit she'd stop.

'Have you?' I say, suspecting this is the reason for the wiggle.

And is it me, or does Mum have a guilty look on her face? Why should she feel guilty? If anything, chatting with an old friend should make her feel better.

'Yes. Parker. He's very refined these days, just using his surname as his first name, very debonair now,' she says, as though justifying herself.

'Oh good. Didn't he used to be?' I say, playing along as we walk into the field that's set up with lines of tables full of bric-a-brac and happy vendors clutching hot cups of coffee to keep warm at this early hour.

'He was more of a free spirit back then,' Mum says, reaching the first stall and thumbing through a tray of old metal military buttons.

'OK, well, you be sensible,' I say, distracted by a table of goodies and rather selfishly wanting to shut the conversation down. I'm here to find good treasure, and not to imagine my mum in a sexy pencil skirt with the debonair Parker. It's enough to make me shiver.

Thankfully the sale is bustling, so it's hard to stand next to each other the entire time, and I don't need to push for any information on her new beau. Instead I can lose myself in the exquisite joy that is flipping through boxes of tat in search of something spectacular. Some people want soft white sand beaches and whirlwind adventures. I'm happiest in a field of junk and a morning to sift through it all. Perhaps I need to get a life! Ha.

The morning is a success. We bumped into a few friends as we meandered round the stalls, either people I went to school with, friends Mum has worked with or knows from the town, or a couple of Dad's friends' wives, who gave Mum pitying looks as they asked how she was. She brushed it off and said she was 'very well, enjoying being by myself and getting to know myself', which sounded very Pinterest, and I loved it. It's a small town, so news travels fast, but Mum was keen to let everyone who asked know that she was on good form and that she's happy for Dad now he's living an authentic life. I spoke to him a couple of days ago. He popped into Pearls and Doodles to drop off an old pot he'd bought to live in my garden (more roses for next year will go in, yay!) and he seemed really chipper. I hope that news travels fast, too.

By the end of our session, Mum lucked out with a 'Ruth Langsford-style blazer', a 'Ruth Langsford-style satin shirt' and a 'Ruth Langsford-style pair of never-worn, with tags (she's a new woman, but she has her second-hand limits) black patent heels'. Sadly, no luck on the pencil skirt.

'Why is everything "Ruth Langsford-style", Mum?' I ask as I help her load her finds into her car.

'She's my new style icon. Debs and I made a vision

board. We printed out inspirational people, wrote quotes, the lot,' she says with a sparkle in her eye.

'Wow! That's so unlike you. You said "manifesting your life" was hippy-dippy when I told you about *The Secret*,' I point out.

'I did, but Debs is keen and I didn't like to be rude. She's fragile since Malcom left,' she says, avoiding eye contact.

I don't point out that Malcom left when I was still at school and that I know she really did enjoy making a vision board.

'Mum, it's so nice to see you so . . . cheery. You seem so much more free.' I smile, giving her a hug at the door of her car, trying not to bash my own bags of treasure into her.

'Ahhh. Love you, Tabitha, you're a good girl. Life is looking up again,' she says back, squeezing hard.

We part ways with another hug (weird for us to be so open with our emotions, but I kind of like it), she drives off down the track and onto the main road to go home while I take the cut through and down the bridleway and back into my part of town.

It was a successful hunt; Mum's extra-strong 'glasses' were obviously on top form because I came away £40 poorer but the proud owner of four vintage glass perfume bottles, all different colours, sizes and patterns but beautiful together as a set; three little metal brooches (one the shape of a moth, one a beetle and one a spider, all with delicate gemstone eyes); a set of Victorian kitchen jars with the faded writing which is so trendy right now; and although no Sylvanians, I did manage to score a heavy Roses tub full to the brim with Shopkins for only a fiver.

The best bits were found about three-quarters through, when we arrived at a stall heaped with crumpled clothes. The lady said they'd been in her attic for years and used to belong to her daughter, but she didn't want them anymore. Some of it was the usual boring fare, but after a good rummage I scored some absolute gems: two pairs of Levi's jeans, five real leather belts with solid buckles in different metals, a bottle-green taffeta party dress that I think I can customise into something incredible, ten old band T-shirts ('They're really old, let's say ten for £2 on those, I just want to clear them out,' the seller had offered), and a beige frilly satin shirt. I'm not sure if I can do anything with it, but when she said, 'Let's say £15 for all of that,' I couldn't resist.

Oh, and I bagged a bashed-looking but very redeemable set of nesting tables.

I can't wait to take it all home, freshen it up and see what's what.

All of it will look fantastic on my Insta (maybe not the

lurid plastic Shopkins), and I reckon I can fix everything up well for potential resale.

I feel so buzzy, I almost skip back to show David my delights.

As soon as I've opened the door and chucked my keys in the white wicker 'odds and sods' basket I upcycled last year (was £1 from the charity shop and brown; now farmcore and fabulous), I bound upstairs two at a time with my bag of goodies.

'Wakey-wakey!' I call to David, who is still sprawled in bed, enjoying all the extra space. 'Move up, matey!'

'Uurrghhh-ggghh ... this better be worth it,' he grumbles, rubbing sleepy-dust out of his eyes.

'Er, yes, obviously it will, I've found amazing treasure to astound you with!' I say, full of glee.

'Amazing crap to clutter us up with, you mean,' he retorts playfully. I try not to let it dampen my enthusiasm but somehow it does.

'Don't be like that, I'm going to put this on my Instagram.'

OK, there, I've said it.

'Your *Instagram*?' He chuckles. 'Since when have you had an *Instagram*? I'm sure all three followers will be thrilled.'

'Well, I sometimes put a few pictures on Instagram.

It's actually gained quite a lot of followers. I use it for the vintage stuff I find.' I'm feeling bolder and bolder telling people about this. I think Mum and Bea's positive energy is rubbing off on me.

'You've got *so much* vintage stuff!' he groans, not really listening to the Instagram part. 'There's a wardrobe full of it that you never wear, you just photograph it!'

'Well, maybe I will start wearing it. Everyone loved my hat,' I fire back. I mean, two people, including Mum, complimented me on it, so that's basically everyone.

'The hat's nice,' he says, giving up the fight. 'Tell me about your finds then.'

But I've lost a bit of mojo and don't want to show him my new purchases, so I quickly say, 'Bought some clothes, perfume bottles, couple of brooches, couple of jars and some toys for Kitty,' and head off downstairs to make a cup of tea. In a pathetic display of passive-aggression, I decide not to make him one. There, that'll show him.

Chapter Twelve

August

'DO YOU EVER FEEL a bit stuck?' Bea asks as I lean back in my not-that-comfortable brown chair opposite her desk in the travel agent's. I've been in a few times on my lunch break or in quiet moments during the day this week. I told Julia I had a thirty-minute doctor's appointment. I don't like lying, but I really felt like being with Bea. Only I would have a time-travelling ring but stick to just one place every time I used it. The thought of venturing any further makes me 90 per cent terrified but 10 per cent intrigued. This is a new 10 per cent. Look out world!

I'm starting to question how the place makes any

money since there's barely ever anyone here, and obviously they're not taking online bookings. I guess that's why it's not here now – well, in 2022 – you know what I mean. A couple of times someone has popped in for a brochure, but that's about the sum of it. Maybe it was different in those days. Bea says weekends are chock-a-block, but someone else takes those shifts and handles the paperwork. I still can't get my head around booking a holiday like this. I'm grateful, though. Talking to Bea is really comforting. I don't think I realised how turbulent these past few weeks have been, with Mum and Dad separating, David's little moods and feeling lacklustre. Coming here is soothing, and I'm starting to be addicted to that. I should probably explain all this to Vivi, but she's been super-busy with the fashion show and I've been busy, well, coming here.

I snap back into reality. If 1989 thanks to a weird crystal ring can be classed as reality.

'Um, no, not stuck, exactly. My friend Vivienne does. She wanted to be an actress but she fell pregnant really young and then married her boyfriend. He's in the Navy, and now she's sort of . . . living her dream differently,' I trail off.

'What does she do? Is she local?' Bea asks enthusiastically.

'Yep, lives on Dusten Way. Not far from the square. She does a lot of am-dram stuff,' I say, thinking about how much Vivi squeezes around full-time motherhood. It's impressive.

'Oh, I might know her! I've done some am-dram, did loads at school, centre stage, me.' She laughs. I smile with her. I can totally imagine Bea on a stage, singing, acting or dancing her heart out. 'Don't remember a Vivienne though,' she continues.

Argh, I've done it again! It's so easy to feel like this is all so everyday and forget to censor what I say.

'She only recently moved here, so you probably wouldn't.' I need to change the subject. 'Anyway, I don't feel stuck, but I do worry that other people think I am and that I should do more. I've always secretly quite liked that I know everyone in town. Bit lame,' I add, now worrying about what she must think. And hope she doesn't ask me who I know! Do other people question every single thing they say?

'You didn't know me!' Bea smiles encouragingly.

'Yes, but I do now. It's so odd, I feel like I've known you forever.' Even saying that shows how at ease I feel here because it's quite bold. What if Bea completely cringes? I start to feel awkward, but thankfully she responds.

'Ahhh, me too!' Bea's smile is so warm, you can't not relax around her.

'So you want to escape, do you? Go off on your big adventure?' I say, before I embarrass myself with slushy friendship feelings.

'Yep! Just waiting for the right time.' She shrugs, looking out of the window at a couple of people perusing the posters and then walking on.

I nod, thinking she'll elaborate on that.

'You shouldn't secretly like something, by the way,' she says, looking back at me.

'Huh?' I've lost her. I thought we were talking about her adventure.

'You said you secretly like that you know everyone. Why is that a secret?' She tilts her head kindly.

'Oh! Ha! OK, I mean I like my comfort zone and I don't really want to step beyond it too much,' I laugh nervously.

'So you feel safe here, you mean?' she says happily.

Nobody has ever suggested that it's a good thing to want to stay put, and this change in tone is a revelation. I've always felt like a bit of a loser for not taking huge leaps into the big wide world like everyone else who's seemingly winning at life.

'Well...yes,' I say, as though I'd just discovered something miraculous. 'Yes, I bloody do!' I give a teeny little fist pump in the air. From pathetic to positively maybe OK in under five seconds. Way to go.

'You're so funny,' Bea laughs. 'Wanna get out of here?'

For the first time in weeks I feel that ripple of panic. I feel OK in here, within the four walls (well, three walls and a giant window) of the orange and brown travel agent's, but out there is different. What if I make the old 'changing the course of history forever' mistake? I absent-mindedly twist the ring round my finger while I think. Maybe this is the time to explore that 10 per cent in me that might be adventurous!

'You don't have to.' Bea must be able to sense my concern. 'It's just, I'm starving and I was thinking we could walk down to Jane's.'

'Jane's?' I say, even more agitated at the idea of meeting someone new, that 10 per cent adventure plummeting right down to zero.

'The bakery? I only want a sandwich or something,' she explains, taking her navy polyester shoulder-padded jacket off the back of the swivel chair and putting it on over the rest of her uniform. I'd never have paired a shiny navy suit with a tangerine-orange shirt and a grey neckerchief, but with her permed hair and completely disarming smile, it all works. Same with the orange and black combo she had the first time I came in. My mind wizzes to think about what Bea wears outside of work. If she makes travel agent work uniforms look this effortlessly cool, what must she do with all her regular 80s garb? I snap back to Bea in real life who is blinking at me, waiting for a response.

'Oh. Yes. Me too. Yes, lovely,' I say, trying to regain my composure. A bakery will be fine. Can't imagine bakeries were much different in 1989 to now.

'Didn't you say you'd lived here forever? And you don't know Jane's?' Bea says, looking at me like I've just had a lobotomy.

'No, I do, I thought you said something else. I used to know the other bakery. Also, I thought you meant a person, a friend, Jane,' I say, laughing it off as I stand up, pick my bag up off the floor and head to the door.

As we're walking towards the centre of town, away from the travel agent's and even further away from where my shop is, I swing my handbag by my side, half terrified, half exhilarated.

'That bag, by the way, is so fresh,' Bea says, wide-eyed.

'Oohhh, thank you!' I say, grinning, assuming 'fresh' means 'fabulous', judging by her admiring smile. 'I've had it in my wardrobe for aaages but never been brave enough to wear it.' I swing it with a little more gusto to show it off.

About three years ago I bought this 1950s Lucite pearl-finish bag at an auction with Vivienne. We'd seen it online, and Vivi convinced me we should drive an hour out of town to attend the auction. Kitty was in her car seat, snoozing away, and we drove down the motorway singing to all our favourite songs on the radio, found the auction rooms, engaged in a frenzied bidding war (in fact there was only one other person interested and nothing was frenzied, but that's never how Vivi tells the tale), jumped back in the car and were home in time to hide it before David saw and complained how much it had cost (nearly a hundred quid, oops). Vivienne had pointed out that it was probably an investment and that I'd wear it every day.

While the investment part might have been right, the wearing it part wasn't. It's quite an unusual piece, and I've always worried I'll look like a bit of a div, wandering around my little town with a real vintage bag. I've wanted to but I've not had the confidence. This week, though, I thought, *why not?* If Vivienne can pull off an entire fashion show, if Mum can overcome her husband leaving her, or if Bea can set off on a solo tour of the world, I can surely use my bag? It's just a bag.

'It's awesome! You're so cool with your style,' Bea muses as we walk.

'What? Literally nobody has ever said that to me!' I laugh, flabbergasted. Half at the compliment, half at how different my little town looks. Every single view is the same but not the same. As though I'm seeing familiar people in fancy dress. The cars are all a bit different; window displays stock nostalgic items, all gleaming new, and there seem to be so many more people out and about. I feel myself drifting into my daydreams but quickly snap out of my observations when Bea responds enthusiastically.

'Really? You're SO cool! Every time I see you you've done something else quirky. Those jeans that were as tight as leggings. The way you sometimes make your curly hair smooth. I'd love to be that brave with my style!'

'Hang on. Are you telling me that you're happy to jet off solo round the globe, but you can't rock a small vintage handbag?' It's my turn to laugh now.

'Er, yes. Suppose I am! But I think there's another big question we need to ask ourselves.' A serious expression washes over Bea's dewy skin.

'Oh God, what?' I dart my eyes around as if I'm going to see something very dangerous any second now.

'Sandwich or toastie?' Bea laughs as she points to the bakery about a hundred yards in front of us.

Thank God. A 'big question' I can handle.

Unsurprisingly, the bakery is what I would call 'wonderfully old-fashioned'. A huge glass shopfront faces on to the street with white frilly net curtains cradling the edges. Three huge gold pendant lights swing near the top of the window, and on the shelves, displayed to tempt passers-by, is every kind of cake, treat and pastry you could imagine. Bakewell tarts, jam sponge, cream horns, trays of well-stuffed rolls, all sitting on scalloped-edge paper doilies. Beyond the delicious window display, a bustle of ladies in buttercup-yellow dresses and white cotton aprons are all working at lighting speed to serve the crowd of customers on the other side of the display casing.

'Are you coming in, or have you frozen?' Bea asks cheerily, nudging me with her elbow.

'Yes! Coming in,' I say, trying to act like I've been here a hundred times. I wish Ottleswan had more of these old-fashioned, homey places. Now they've been replaced with chain sandwich shops or the mini supermarket that sells pre-packaged meal deals and sad-looking croissants. This is like heaven. I wish I could snap a few pictures for my Instagram, but as I instinctively reach for my phone I remember where I am . . . or when I am . . . and stop.

Inside is even better than outside. The smells are heavenly and the atmosphere is welcoming.

'What'll you have, ducks?' an older lady trills from behind the glass counters.

'I'll have a can of Appletize and a cheese and tomato toastie, and she'll have . . .' Bea trails off, waiting for me to reply.

'The same, please,' I say, not wanting to rock the boat.

'Three pound then, please, ducks,' the lady says without missing a beat.

'For both?' I say, astounded.

'That all right, duck?' the keeper of the cakes asks, slightly less friendly this time, maybe frustrated by how slow we are when she is moving the stream of hungry customers along with such rhythm.

'Yes! Absolutely.' I open my bag and take my card out, excited that you can buy two drinks and two toasted sandwiches for so little. You almost have to take out a second mortgage when you buy a coffee and a panini these days, so this is very refreshing.

'Oh, it's cash only here,' Bea says.

'Oh, right. Erm, I think I have some at the bottom . . .' I say, scrabbling for some coins at the base of my bag. It doesn't have any mini pockets or dividers, and my coin purse is always coming open, so it's kind of a jumbled mess in there.

'It's all right, I'll get these and you can get the next,' Bea offers, counting out three of the old pound coins I remember from a while back. Hmm, even if I had been able to sort my cash out quick enough it wouldn't have been right. Paying next time is going to be a bit tricky.

Sitting down on a bench overlooking the square, not far from Jane's, we tear open our toasties to cool them down. As the steam rises out of them, we watch it for a moment in comfortable silence, a moment I use to really notice the world around me. I've been so focused on going to the travel agent's, I finally really look. The outfits are my favourite thing. They don't seem 'vintage' here because they just meld in with the time-appropriate surroundings. I wonder if I could find some old money and go shopping? I wonder if the ring allows you to take things back and forth like that, or will it all disintegrate to space dust back in 2022? The fact that I just genuinely considered 'space dust' as a thing I might encounter is enough to startle me back to reality. Or at least to 1989, whatever reality that is.

'When's the right time to see the world then?' I ask, taking a tentative but excited bite of melted cheese. I've never eaten in 1989. I hope this doesn't do anything nasty to my 2022 tummy. I'm not good with too much dairy at the best of times.

'I dunno. Soon, I think.' She sighs, as if holding back. I half consider mentioning the dairy issue, but as comfortable as I feel with Bea, I don't think we're there yet.

'Are you waiting for something specific?' I probe, keeping the conversation on-topic at the same time as noticing a woman with the most beautiful cream leather loafers walk past our bench. Such pretty gold hardware glinting on the top of them, with two little tan contrast leather tassels bobbing about as she struts on.

Oblivious to only having half my attention, Bea answers earnestly, 'Um, not really. I had to save a bit of money, which I have now, but I don't want to leave my sister in a state. She's usually the responsible one, but I dunno, I feel like she needs me.' Bea pulls at her toastie some more to help it cool.

'How is she now? Still heartbroken over . . . was it Paul?' I ask, trying to remember and keep focused, which is so hard now we're out and about. My family have lived round here for decades – I wonder if I might see Mum walking past!

'Mike. She's less heartbroken now. She's had her hair permed, a bit like mine, but tighter curls. Looks great. Plus she's giving her friend's brother a go, and she seems to like him. I've met him a few times. Couple of years older than her, never married, no kids. He seems really nice. Very stable, which I think is what she wants.' She shrugs, taking a bite and adding an 'mmm' with a satisfied smile. So nice that she can simply enjoy a cheese toastie without all the usual guilt or 'will have to work this off later' rubbish you hear. I don't think Jane's bakery would know a superfood salad if the quinoa exploded all over them, and I love that. No offence to quinoa.

'That's good then. Nice that you like him too. Vivi, my best friend, who's basically like a sister to me, I'm not sure she likes my boyfriend,' I say, staring off towards the road beyond the square, suddenly thinking about whether I could bring Vivi here one day.

'David?' Bea checks, taking another huge bite of her sandwich.

'Yep,' I answer, thinking of David right now, well, thirty-three years into the future – oh, that's spooky – leaning over an engine, in his happy place. I miss him. I feel really far away from him, and not just in the time sense. I should make more of an effort.

'Did you say you were going to marry him?' she says through a mouthful of sandwich as she pulls the tab on her fizzy drink to have a sip.

'I said I thought I *ought* to marry him,' I correct her. 'He wants to have kids, and I had it in my head that it's the right thing to do, get married first, but now I'm starting to wonder if just following the so-called normal path is the way to go, especially with everything that's been going on lately. But yeah, I think I ought to.' I take a sip of my own drink after that rousing speech. I've surprised myself with my new, somewhat radical thinking there.

'That's not really the same, is it? "Going to" and "ought to",' Bea says gently.

'It's not, but I'm twenty-six and I feel like it's expected, you know? I'm not exactly a "big personality", but don't worry, I won't walk down the aisle just because other people think I should. I've got more about me than that.' I take a deep slug of my Appletize and the fizz tingles my mouth, as I feel rather proud for being so resolute on something so big.

'I think you should do what makes you MOST happy,' Bea says with renewed enthusiasm, waving her half-eaten toastie in the air as if she is addressing a huge crowd with her empowering notion.

'That's what I think *you* should do!' I laugh, pushing my shoulder over to hers. Deflecting is my superpower.

'Well, I want to travel all of Europe and meet a handsome stranger.' She laughs, pushing me back playfully.

'And I want to . . . hmmm . . . I don't know . . . run a little shop and make enough for a few more vintage bags? Maybe just have a bit more confidence in myself. Is that a bit wishy-washy?' I laugh nervously at the vulnerability of it.

'Finish that toastie and walk me back to work before I get completely fired for not selling holidays and just dreaming of mine on a bench,' Bea offers helpfully, kindly stepping over my awkwardness. 'Wish I'd bought a pudding now. It's not really a full meal without a pudding.'

'Yes! That's it. My life goal, right there. Toastie-eating is a great goal,' I say, finishing up and leaping to my feet, quietly glad I don't have to truly face what I want in life. Or, face the fact that I don't know what I want and that that in itself makes me feel less than. Deep breaths!

We link arms walking back, and I'm content. I don't have a solid life plan like Bea, but right now, in this moment, whenever this really is, that's OK because I have what I need. A happy home, a job I love and now, a new friend. I mentally note the other day when Vivi said I had no other friends. Ha! Look at me now, Vivienne Hawkins née Patel. I smile all the way back up the high street, the sun beaming down on my face, the world seeming very good for once.

'Same time next week?' says Bea, a hopeful look on her face as she stands outside the glass door to her work.

'Yep, it's a date!' I smile as I turn and walk back up to Pearls and Doodles, feeling that delicious buzz the ring gives me. I don't know how or why this is happening, but I know that, more and more, I love it.

Chapter Thirteen

'DID YOU PLAN ON being home so late?' David greets me the nanosecond I open the front door, an hour and a half later than I usually do.

Since I'd used my lunch break to see Bea, I'd not painted the little wooden nest of tables I'd bought at the Eastings Field summer sale, and I wanted to finish them up before I came home. It's easier at Julia's because there's more space. And less machinery.

'And hello to you too,' I say, slipping off my scarf and hanging it on the hooks by the door, followed by my jacket.

I walk into the lounge and notice the tray on the floor beside him.

'I've had to eat on my own,' he says, pointing at his dirty plates.

'OK,' I say. It's not as though I've forced him to face a great crisis alone. I can feel my neck stiffening with frustration but hold my tongue because I don't want to bicker, not after such a lovely day.

'Not ideal, is it?' he asks me patronisingly. I won't be drawn into this game.

'David, it's dinner in front of the TV, it's not the end of the world. I'm sorry, but I was busy,' I respond calmly and matter-of-factly, putting my bag down on the armchair to my right. It's such a tatty old chair, but I rescued it from a skip in the next town over and now, nestled by the fire (and cleaned up a bit), it's perfect for a book and a massive glass of iced peach tea. I look back to David, thinking he'll drop it, but I can see from his taut face and the way the vein on his forehead is all bulgy that he's really het up.

'Busy in a shop that has four customers a day?' he says smarmily. I will not, *will* not, will *not* rise to his bait. Bea certainly wouldn't.

'Er, it has more customers than that, and yes, I was working on something,' I shrug, as though he isn't angling for a fight. I will not join in this idiotic little charade.

'Were you?' he says, as I carry on standing there, wishing he'd just get over it.

'Yes, I was! I was prepping those tables I bought the other week. The ones I'm thinking about selling,' I say, leaning on the door frame but wishing we weren't having this pathetic conversation.

'I don't know bloody why. You never seem to make any money, but you spend all your bloody time sanding and painting and God knows what else,' he says, his stubbled cheeks flushing.

The downside to not telling him how much money I'm making from my efforts is this. Rage starts to flicker, but as ever, I stay calm.

'I do make money from them, and also I enjoy doing it. It's calming for me, thank you very much.' I try saying this with more authority, blagging some much-needed confidence, but he carries on.

'I know why you really do them, I'm not daft.' I look away into the hall so I can roll my eyes without him seeing.

'I can't believe we're having a row about some second-hand tables, David, this is stupid,' I say, not really wanting to go further, now curiously vulnerable about him finding out how much I earn or what I'm hiding.

'You just do it so all your little fans will tell you how brilliant you are,' he spits.

'What?' I say, incredulous.

'I've seen your photo-sharing account. Your Instagram. Every time you post a picture you have all your little cronies fawning over it. "Oohhh, I love this!" "Wow, so talented",' he mocks in a high-pitched voice, waving his hands around.

I can feel anger bubbling inside me and my cheeks burning, but I'm *not* going to let him rile me.

'David, stop it!' I demand, a lot more firmly than I was expecting to. 'I'm sorry you've had dinner on your own, but you're being really cruel. This isn't a big deal.' We're both startled by my tone and stay there like two deer in the headlights for a moment.

'I know it's not, but I like you being home when I get in,' he says more gently this time. From where I'm standing in the doorway I can see into the kitchen. He's dished me up a plate of mash and chicken, laid it all out on a tray with a knife and fork and I'm struck with guilt for not being home to enjoy it with him.

'I'm sorry,' I say, walking in to give him a hug, just wanting to defuse the situation and make the day nice again. I can see it all came from a place of hurt.

'I'm sorry too. I didn't mean to be cross,' he replies, eyes full of remorse.

I sit down half next to him, half on him and go in for a cuddle. I love calming him down and making things better again. I try and tell myself it's not his fault he gets a bit heated. I love him really. It's nice that he missed me.

'It's just that I'm the man, so I shouldn't have to keep making dinners like this,' he whispers as he nuzzles into my neck.

I sit up. Oh, no. Absolutely not.

'Are you fucking *joking* me?' Vivienne booms down the phone after I've told her what just happened.

'No! We had a blazing row and now he's in the summer house with his engines,' I say, trying not to cry. I'll be damned if he makes me shed even one tear. I hate being too emotional. Mum was all about 'not making a fuss' when I was younger, and my God it's stuck with me.

'His penis extenders,' Vivi says, as enraged, if not more, as I am.

'His engines,' I correct because despite his behaviour, I still feel guilty insulting his manhood. 'Probably seething over what a shit wife I'll make.'

'Well, yes, Tabs. How dare you take an extra couple

of hours to do something for yourself, eh?' Vivi says incredulously.

'I know! I'd have done it this lunchtime, but I popped in on Bea,' I confess.

'Again?' I'm not sure why she's surprised by this. Why wouldn't I pop in on her? Now's not the time to ask though. I feel so wounded by my row with David that I don't have the capacity for much else.

'I know, I know. I sort of want to call her now and tell her about this,' I say, almost awkward at suggesting I need her.

'Oh thanks,' Vivi says in a mocking way, but it feels like one of those jokes you sort of mean.

'Nooo, *after* you. You know what I mean.' I don't need more guilt added on top of my misery. I daren't tell Vivi what a connection I feel with Bea. She's so confident and optimistic. Vivi is too, of course, but there's something about Bea that brings me up. I really admire Vivienne, she's amazing, the best there is, but I aspire to be like Bea. Plus, you can have more than one friend. It's not cheating to have two friends you adore, is it? My thoughts are spiralling, and I'm grateful to Vivi for bringing me back to the present.

'I do, but you can't live in the past. Literally. How long are you going to keep this up? It's nice that you have a new friend, but . . . maybe time to move forward?' she says gently, almost as if she is talking to Kitty.

I can't think of anything I'd like to do less than give up Bea, give up that feeling of acceptance and that glimmer of hope she somehow manifests. Plus, Vivi was all for it not that long ago.

'It's bizarre,' I reply, an anxious knot tightening in my tummy. I don't want to talk about this so soon after a blazing row with my idiotic, unfeeling boyfriend. I'm so aware how ridiculous it sounds to want to hide Bea, the ring, all of it, away. I want to keep my 2022 the same and protect 1989 as my special, hidden space, just for me. I wish I hadn't said anything now. Ever.

'Anyway, never mind your *time travel*.' She says the last two words slowly as though I'm a very silly schoolgirl making things up. 'What are you going to do about David?'

Sidestepping the offence, I'm grateful she's changed the subject. I don't want to make a fuss.

'What do you mean?' I ask, genuinely surprised by the query. I never actually DO anything. He has a go, I seethe, I rant to Vivi, he calms down, everything is back to normal again.

'Well, what I said. What are you going to do?' she repeats. I wish I could be as forthright.

'He'll cool down. So will I. It'll be fine in the end.' I feel daft for ringing her now. I thought she was on board with the current programme of 'row, call, calm'. Suddenly she's added a new element to the regular routine, and I can feel that knot really squeezing. God, I hope I don't throw up. That's the last thing I bloody need.

'You don't have to live like this, you know. You deserve a lot more,' she says, softer now. She knows me well. Knot loosens.

'Viv, that's so nice of you, but it's not true. He's good to me. I love him. Everyone has arguments.' As with most things, I just want to take a deep breath and push this aside.

'Babes, I think he's misguided and stupid, but if you think you can re-educate him then I'm here for you. You'll make him a true feminist, I know it. You're a good woman, and I love you, you'll be golden,' she finishes with such conviction I'm sure she's silently fist-pumped the air on the other end of the line. Vivi is wasted at home. She needs to be a motivational speaker or one of those life coach people.

'I don't feel too golden. I feel like the least shiny thing ever. Like a blob of meh.' I flump down onto the bed, realising I have been pacing the landing the whole time.

'Wow, OK. Well, lucky for you, I've got a surprise!' Vivi changes the tone, into something decidedly more positive.

'Have you? What?' I sit up on the bed, instantly cheered and glad to move on.

'I'm not telling you over the phone. I'll pop into the shop tomorrow lunch and tell you face to face. You'll love it!' she trills with so much enthusiasm in her voice that I know I should be excited.

Instead, that unwelcome knot is very much back. I know I'm going to have to explain this.

'Oh. Could you come tomorrow just before I close up?' I ask, trying to sound breezy.

'No can do, *mon amie*, Kitty has a birthday party. What's wrong with lunchtime?'

'Nothing's wrong, I was just hoping to go and see Bea, that's all,' I say tightly, knowing Vivi won't like this.

'Tabitha Burnley, newsflash! I am real, I am your best friend, I am coming over. See you at one.' She hangs up, like she's in a movie.

God, I wish I had half as much confidence.

Chapter Fourteen

I T TOOK A BATH, two medicinal white wine spritzers (went in hard, not even rosé), a good night's sleep in the spare room (that'll show him. That's doing something, isn't it?), an early-morning coffee sitting on the back step looking out at my garden and watching a sparrow hop about in the flower beds and a second cup of coffee at the shop once I'd opened up, to bring me back to normal.

I say 'normal', but I'm starting to question what that is. If normal is being OK with my boyfriend thinking it's the 1950s and my best friend thinking I'm delusional and my other new but quite good friend living in nineteen-bloody-eighty-nine, I'm not sure I want to be normal.

In fact, quite subconsciously, I seem not to have dressed

'normally' either. Since I slept in the spare room, I decided to raid its wardrobe this morning. I keep all my vintage items in there. Some I hang carefully on felt-coated hangers, cloth bags full of clutches sit on the top shelf, and tucked into shoeboxes and wicker baskets below I have all my special accessories, nestled like treasure waiting to be unwrapped. Worn leather belts with ornate buckles; silver lockets on every length of chain you could want; two or three pairs of lace gloves that I need to sell; the most beautiful hand-rolled silk scarves and, right at the back, a few pairs of shoes – though I'm fussy with those. Shoes have to be in immaculate condition and, lucky for me, today I picked out just the pair. Brown carved-leather cowboy boots circa 1994.

I've paired the boots with denim shorts (from ASOS 2019 – not exactly collectables yet) and a 1980s floaty silk blouse. I picked it up from a little pre-loved boutique by the seaside, pre-pandemic (which seems like a lifetime ago in its own right) when David and I had a few days away. It was lovely. We should do that again soon, now that life is a bit more open.

Anyway, less David, more blouse: it's cream silk with a very polka dot pattern embedded in the fabric, and the threads create a delicate matt contrast to set off the pattern that you can only see if the light shines on it just right.

The sleeves are billowy to the wrists, and a generous pussy bow ties at the neck, but I've left it really loose, with a few buttons open to keep it breezy. I've kept my jewellery simple with the pearl studs I fell asleep in (mostly because I didn't want to rustle about in our bedroom for more, beyond grabbing clean socks and knickers), and a long chain gold necklace Dad gave me a few birthdays ago. The shirt floats over the shorts which show off my really not-too-bad legs and I feel, dare I say it, good. Not 'incredible', but 'better than average', which is an achievement, right? I'm excited to show Bea.

Her advice about doing what makes you most happy is ringing in my ears. Apart from today's part-vintage outfit, I don't know what makes me most happy. I just thought being in a relationship is what made people happy. That's what I grew up with. I'm an adult and I should be OK about this. Deep breaths.

I'm forcing myself not to think about Vivienne's words. *I am real, I am your best friend.* She was so on board for 'testing' the ring out, and now I have discovered something so magical and astonishing, she's not OK with it. She's always been like this. A bit jealous.

Once when we were about thirteen, a stall on the market was selling denim jackets for a fiver. I'd been excited that my pocket money could stretch to it and suggested we buy a matching pair. Vivi had scoffed saying she wouldn't be seen dead in anything 'off Ottleswan Market' and I remember feeling so stung. That night I told Mum and she was incensed. 'I'm not having some little madam have you feel less than!' Mum loved Vivi, and she too was pretty snobby about shops and brands, but this went above that. Her protective mother instincts kicked in.

The next morning Mum marched me down to the market and bought me a denim jacket. 'You keep that five pounds and put it towards something else,' she said, giving me a little squeeze (not like Mum to show affection in public, so I knew this was extra special). We walked round the market to the haberdashery stall where I picked out metres of cheap cream lace, dusky-pink velvet ribbons, shiny beads in mauve, purple and cobalt and little glass Czech crystals that twinkled as the light caught them.

We took our loot home and Mum, who'd been taught to sew by her own mother, showed me how to trim the cuffs, collar and pockets with the lace and overlay the ribbon for the most wonderful thick luxe effect and then, in just the right spots, add all the colourful beads, like scattering jewels. I was so proud of that jacket. 'You look the bee's knees, Tabs!' Dad said as I twirled around the lounge to be admired that evening. 'Very exclusive, isn't she, Tony?' Mum cooed, proud as could be.

My school friends were in awe of my 'exclusive' jacket. 'Oh my God, is it designer?' Shaznay asked loudly, drawing all the attention towards me.

'People round here don't go to school in designer jackets!' Vivi piped up from nearby. 'She bought it on the market and tarted it up.' I shot her a hurt look. 'It's nice. I love it,' she quickly added.

We never really spoke again about the jacket, good or bad, and I wore it till I grew too big for it. Vivi never scoffed at a shop or market stall again. I must dig that jacket out of Mum's attic at some point. Bloody loved that thing.

Anyway, back to the present, can't live in the past! Perhaps she didn't mean to sound jealous. I don't like to cause a stir, and I'd rather just keep everyone happy. Plus I want to see what she has to say. Hopefully this surprise is quite nice. Even a coffee delivery would be nice. I never sleep well in the spare room.

While I serve customers, I can see the display case with the ring from the corner of my eye and I'm sure it's glinting at me just a tiny bit more than usual. She might be five years younger than me, but Bea seems so self-assured, and

I just know she'd have some sound advice about what to do with David. About my slightly monotonous life.

'Yoo-hooo!' Vivi calls as she pushes the door wide open and steps in, dramatically wafting a piece of paper around.

'Hello, you! What have we here?' I coo, playing along with the performance I'm being treated to today. You can't help but be swept along by Vivienne's energy. She's like walking sunshine. Well, 99 per cent of the time.

'I come bearing good news!' She swishes in wearing tight black skinny jeans that show off her beautifully toned thighs, a bottle-green floaty chiffon top that moves so gracefully as she walks, huge silver hoop earrings and, as always, a plethora of stunning gold jewellery. I've never managed the layered metal thing, but Vivienne is the expert. Even in flip-flops and a topknot, Vivi wows. Comparing myself to her, I don't feel as 'above average' in my cowboy boots.

'Have I won the lottery?' I tease, pushing aside the forever niggling feels of inadequacy.

'Yes, you have me as your bestie,' she smiles, eyes sparkling with anticipation. This must be special.

'Very good.' I laugh, rolling my eyes. 'What is it, really?'

'OK . . . don't be cross at me,' she says, holding the

piece of paper in both hands and taking a very actressy step closer to the till that I'm standing, quite nervously now, behind.

'Oh, God! Nothing good ever comes from someone who starts with that,' I say, instantly worried.

'Shhhh!'

'Last time you said that was when you cut "layers" into my hair,' I say, thankful we stopped before she cut the 'edgy fringe' in.

'No, we sorted that out. It was very "Rachel from *Friends*",' she protests indignantly.

'It absolutely was not. It was very "Boris Johnson", and you know it!' I pout, shuddering at the memory.

'OK, it wasn't, though it looked fine when we put a bit of texture spray in, but this is not the point. I'm not here to defend my hairdressing skills,' she says, flourishing the paper again.

'Of which you have none,' I quip before she has a chance to start another sentence.

'Of which I have plenty! Once it grew out a bit it was *very* Rachel from *Friends*. *Aaany*way, I'm not here to discuss the past – you're too focused on that as it is.'

I let the little jab go as she quickly carries on.

'I'm here to tell you that I've entered you into something

. . . exciting.' She does a little shimmy on 'exciting' to really ramp up the drama. Very Vivi.

'Jesus, not the fashion show?' I wince. There's no way I'm going down a catwalk, hair grown out or not!

'No. Earlier this year I nominated Pearls and Doodles for the Indie Shop of the Year Award. The Vintage Fashion category. AND you've been longlisted!' she squeals, slamming the confirmation letter onto the desk in front of me.

I stand stock-still.

'Oh,' is all I can manage.

'Is that it?' Vivi says, clearly expecting a matching level of enthusiasm.

'It's not my shop, Viv.' I think of Julia. If she saw this, she'd think I was taking liberties somehow. I feel a bit sick. Maybe it's the two coffees. Good job she didn't surprise me with another.

'Yeah, but you run it,' she says, her brow creasing in mild annoyance.

'Mmm,' I say nervously.

'Look, when you win, do you seriously think Julia's going to be annoyed, or is she going to be thrilled that you've just won her this incredible title and some great publicity? You do realise this is a *national* award? Like, the whole country?' Credit to Vivi for knowing what's worried me without me having to explain. That really is the mark of a true best friend. I must remember to give her a hug and tell her how much I love her when I'm not feeling so frozen with fear.

She has a point, though.

'It's sponsored by the Association for Excellence in Independent Business. Everyone is rooting for independent businesses these days, and this shop is so fab. You make it so nice! You could definitely win this, and when you do, Julia is going to be THRILLED,' Vivi says as though she's thought of everything already. She probably has, to be fair. She's usually right.

I don't know what to say.

'OK, cards on the table. Julia's onside. I ran it all by her first, asked her to let me in to film the shop and take some pictures for the nomination. She's cool with it. She told me she more or less leaves you to it, doing the displays, all that, getting to know customers, and you've done a brilliant job so far. So no biggie.'

I can't believe it. I start to feel a fizz of excitement at the prospect. I love this little shop, and I'd be over the moon if we won. The more people that know about this treasure trove, the better. Maybe this is really cool!

Vivienne steps back from the counter and waves her hand animatedly in the air.

'I'll help you. I've been sent an info letter, as your nominator. I've already submitted the pictures, videos, of the shop I took along with the entry form. But you'll need to complete a fuller questionnaire. Goals for the business, forward social media marketing strategy. It'll be fun! I can help you fill that out this weekend. Even better, Tabs, and I know you'll love this, you are booked onto a two-day business course in social media marketing as a bonus for reaching the longlist. In a hotel, in London, no less! Also, the judging panel want to see the shop for themselves, and some kind of presentation of goods, which will also be used as a decider in case there's a tie at the final award stage. Plus I thought we could model some of the shop's vintage pieces at the fashion show, as the presentation! A kind of grand finale. We'll need to ask Julia. What do you think?' She winks, forever my cheerleader. Her enthusiasm is definitely contagious.

'Oh my God, yes! This is so amazing. Thank you, Vivi, you really are the best,' I squeal, racing round the counter to scoop her up in a big squeeze.

'I know, I know, someone's gotta do it! Right, I'll confirm that we're happy to work towards the next round, you keep your eye on the post for the finalists' confirmation letter, which comes to you and will have all the info about the award ceremony, which I think is in September. Or October. Right, I've gotta dash to get Kitty ready for her friend's birthday party.'

'Are you around tonight afterwards?' I call as she heads to the door. I feel so bad for not spending much time with her lately. 'I could pop round for a cuppa?'

'Sorry! I'm at the community centre, production meeting for the fashion show. It's all go! Love you! Text me when the finalists' letter comes through,' she shouts back, leaving the shop in a waft of perfume and exhilaration.

My entire afternoon is taken up by thinking about the award. I spend some time googling it and getting to grips with what it might take to win. Apparently first prize is a six-page spread in a major women's mag and a feature on *Lorraine*. This is big.

The shop has always been immaculate, but I'm looking around it with fresh eyes now, racking my brains for ways we can give it an edge above all the other nominations. I was going to pop in on Bea this afternoon, but instead I busy myself refreshing the window displays. On one side of the big double-fronted window I weave soft, twinkling lights in between the open drawers of the antique dresser from which I arrange vintage silk scarves, dry-cleaned and fresh, to look as if they're spilling out, inviting you to touch and buy them. On the other side, we always feature an old-fashioned tailor's dummy in a vintage outfit, changed every three weeks, and today I dress the dummy in a beautiful 1930s pale rose pink silk evening dress with a long pearl necklace. I pin a corsage of silk flowers to one of the dress straps: creamy orchids.

Bea won't mind if I miss today, because we have next Wednesday booked in for our lunch date.

By home time, the shop looks stunning. I've given everywhere a good dust, rummaged around in the stockroom for anything new and enticing, and taken a couple of snaps to put on my Instagram Stories. Maybe David will realise how hard I work if he sees how gleaming the shop is – at least I know he looks at my account now!

Speaking of whom, I leave the shop ten minutes early (sorry, Julia), pop into the Co-op for supplies and I'm through the door before he's finished at the garage. I set to work peeling spuds, pan-frying meat and laying the table so that when he walks in, his favourite steak, peppercorn sauce and dauphinoise potatoes are sitting waiting for him to tuck in.

'Wow, babe! You didn't have to do all this,' he says, eyes wide.

'I know, but I wanted you to see that I can do it,' I say, raising a freshly poured glass of his favourite red wine in his direction.

'I know you can cook, though.' He smiles, pulling out a chair to sit down and I mirror him. He's right; I can cook, and this smells incredible. I serve myself a spoonful of green beans to accompany the steak.

'Yes, but did you know I can be a wonder-woman career lady AND a good cook?' I ask, grinning, about to raise a forkful.

'Look, I didn't mean to be nasty last night. I know you have customers in the shop,' he says through a mouthful of beef.

'Thanks, love. It does get busy in there,' I agree as he nods in return.

We eat in silence for a few seconds. I wipe the palms of my hands on my shorts.

'I had some good news at work today, babe,' I say casually, nervous with excitement.

'Julia's given you a massive pay rise and says you can work part-time for it too?' he laughs, cutting up his steak.

'Er, no.' I grimace, uneasy at the idea of Julia hearing him say that.

'Ha, OK, what is it then?' He smiles, his eyes twinkling

like they did when I first met him. He's a pain, but he's an attractive pain.

'Well, Vivienne's nominated me for a business award, so that's cool, isn't it?' I say quickly, as though that'll make the news less of a shock to him. Why I'm worried about him being shocked, I don't know.

'Eh?' he sort of says, mouth open, eyes a lot less twinkly now. Yuck.

'Independent Shop of the Year. We've already made the longlist. And they've offered me two days of training in social media marketing!' I say, scooping up some more potato as excitedly as I can, that worry knot re-forming in my tummy.

'It's not even your shop though, is it? What do you wanna do all that for?' he asks bluntly.

'Well . . . yes, but . . . Julia already knows, and she's cool with it.' I look down at my fork. I really don't want to have to battle this with him. I'm only just on board with it myself.

'Mmm. I'd be pleased too if someone did all the work for me and I could take the credit,' he chortles to himself, making me feel idiotic for getting so excited this afternoon.

'She's not like that. She's always been a good boss. She leaves me to it, pretty much. And I want to do it, for me,'

I say, lifting my wine glass to take a big slug for Dutch courage.

David looks at me, utterly lost.

'To feel that I've achieved something,' I say with more authority than I expected, putting my glass back down a bit harder than I'd planned to, splashing red wine on the tablecloth. Vivi would be proud. Not of the wine bit. The confidence.

'Well, you've achieved this,' he says, stabbing his fork into a green bean. 'You've achieved cooking me a bloody lovely dinner. Thank you, Tabs, you're the best,' he says happily.

Not one to rock the boat, I don't go on about the award. After our row last night, this makes a welcome change. Much like Bea and my resale side hustle, the award will just have to be a 'me thing', and I'm fine with that. I'm used to it.

We enjoy the rest of the meal, wash up, watch a film where heroes in New York save the world, have some pretty vanilla sex and go to sleep.

Is it this? Is this what makes me MOST happy?

Chapter Fifteen

'MUM, YOUR ROASTS MAKE me the MOST happy,' I say so enthusiastically I nearly surprise myself.

Even though it's Saturday, mum's done a full roast and we're back round the table with the linen cloth and the old heated hostess trolley, and I couldn't be happier. I've just come from brunch at Dad's flat. Dad even tried avocado, I nearly fell off my chair. It was touching to see Bernie fuss about Dad's cholesterol, and how their hands lingered as they passed the orange juice between them. I stuck to toast and fruit and now I'm almost drooling for Mum's roast.

The weather is warm but the important thing is that

Mum is once again cooking her routine comfort food. We might have been through a lot of change lately, but my mum is never going to be a barbecue gal. And I'm OK with that. There is nothing I love more than Mum's home cooking.

'Ahhh, thank you, Tabitha, it's good to be doing this again, isn't it?' she says, opening the trolley to reveal a freshly baked apple crumble.

'Yep. Ooohhh, my faaavourite.' I smile.

'This was my sister's favourite too,' Mum says with more tenderness in her voice than I've heard in a while.

'Oh, Mum. I didn't know that. It's nice that you're talking about her.' This is new, and lovely. I feel a little squeeze in my heart at the idea of hearing more about Auntie Bridget.

Mum had always told me that her sister died in a car accident many years ago, but has never wanted to expand on that. As a kid I saw some photos in an album, but mum's tucked that away. We never spoke much about her because every time she tried, Mum would end up in tears; obviously it was all too painful and I didn't like to push.

'Yes. Times are changing,' she says with a sigh.

'You can say that again,' I say, thinking about my own escapades with time. I take a moment to appreciate how utterly ridiculous it is that I'm sitting at Mum's table having my standard Sunday roast and casually considering the fact that I can literally travel through time. What the eff is that about? I'm scared to experiment further with the ring, but how long am I going to live like this for? Keeping a scientific impossibility that I found in a piece of jewellery a secret? My head whirs with the madness of it, and I realise I'm staring into space.

'. . . and he liked her too,' Mum adds casually. Shit. Hard to pay attention when you're contemplating the logistics of telling the world you have DISCOVERED TIME TRAVEL. Ironically, no time for that now: Mum's opening up and this isn't to be missed.

'Sorry? Who?' I say, trying to be a bit more on it.

'Michael Parker. My friend – well, ex-fiancé, you remember – I've reconnected with him on Facebook. He knew her. We met up last week, and he spoke so fondly of her. Brought it all back up, maybe,' she says quietly, not looking up from her bowl.

I didn't know she'd been meeting up with anyone.

'Oh nice. Is he . . . local now?' I ask, trying to sound really relaxed that my mum is meeting up with the man she was in love with before she met Dad, and talking about my aunt I never hear of. And trying to stop thinking about the insanity of having a time-travelling ring.

'Lives about an hour away now. He used to live round here, of course, then moved away, moved all over really.' Mum pauses, visibly reminiscing. 'And now he's back.'

'Oh right. Busy guy then. Has he come back to woo you again?' I ask, a tiny bit more strained than I'd like.

'No, no,' Mum replies dismissively, completely oblivious to my discomfort (which I know, as a twenty-six-year-old woman, I should absolutely not have). 'He came back a good fifteen or so years ago, married and then divorced. I think,' Mum adds, her turn to try and sound casual.

'So your old friend from years ago, your *ex-fiancé*, who lived here but moved away, now lives sort of near and is just a Facebook friend?' I ask slowly as if to clarify it to myself.

'Well, not just a friend on Facebook, a friend friend,' Mum offers.

'A friend friend or a *friend* friend?' I ask, raising my eyebrows.

'Tabitha! What are you trying to imply with that face?' Mum exclaims, attempting to hide the flush on her own face by busying herself with folding her napkin neatly on the table.

'I'm not trying to imply anything,' I say smiling, my initial discomfort waning. 'I'm just trying to work out if the sexy Ruth Langsford-style pencil skirt was for your "new woman" vibes or for Michael, or Parker, or whatever name it is he's using these days.' I keep eye contact with her. I know Mum. She'll put on a good show but then she'll crumble.

We look at each other for a short while. It's not like me to be so forthright, if you can call it that, but maybe Mum's not the only person having a 'new woman' moment these days.

'We were very close once,' she begins.

'Ooohhh,' I tease lovingly, almost victoriously.

'Stop it! Neither of us is a spring chicken. We've been through the mill, and if we can find a little bit of happiness in each other, I think we'd be content with that,' Mum says, quite firmly. 'And I'm still dealing with your dad leaving me, so it's very early days.'

'I'm happy for you, Mum. I want you to be happy,' I reassure her. 'You deserve to be happy, and as he's an old flame, maybe you can reignite something.'

She smiles as she starts piling up our plates to clear away. Not wanting to miss the chance to hear about my auntie, I quickly ask another question.

'So he knew your sister, and you've been talking about her? That's nice.' I smile at her.

'He did, and we did. It was nice to hear someone

else's memories of her, but now I feel quite wobbly for it. Dragged up all the pain, I expect. I told him all about what happened,' she says quietly.

'About the accident?' I ask gently.

'About everything,' she pauses. 'I told him about you, that I have you. He was pleased for me.'

'Mm-hmm.' Neutral sounds seem better than questions. I don't want to influence what she wants to share; I just want to let her express herself.

'We talked about the accident, and then the family dynamics changing so much, all of that. I think I was so focused on carrying on and giving you a good, happy life that I didn't really take the time to let it all sink in,' she says, blinking hard a few times, I think trying not to cry.

'It must have been so awful for you, Mum,' I say, wishing we were the kind of people who hugged, because I'd love to walk round the table right now and wrap my arms around her. But I think she'd find that super-awkward, so I decide to stay in my chair.

'It was awful for everyone. Awful for you, awful for all of us.' She takes a sharp inhale remembering such difficult times.

'Well, it's really sad, but it's not been awful for me because I've had a lovely life. I've had you and Dad, and all these fabulous puddings,' I say, smiling, trying to lift the mood a bit.

'Aha. Yes. Bridget loved all the puddings too! I'd say, "Have a quick bowl before you go gallivanting off to wherever," she gently laughs. 'She was always planning her next adventure.'

An image of Bea suddenly flashes into my mind, of her turning to me after we've eaten our lunchtime toasties from Jane's bakery and saying, *Wish I'd bought a pudding now. It's not really a full meal without a pudding.* I get a strange flush that rises from my chest to my face, my heart beating fast. What's going on?

'She sounds like a wonderful woman,' I add, feeling very bad for Mum. I don't have any siblings, but I can't imagine what it would be like to have one and then experience such a loss.

'She was.' Mum takes a deep breath in. 'But now we're here and we have each other, don't we?' I can tell she's worked hard to pull herself back together and don't want to spoil the moment. Time to move on.

'Yes. And now you have maybe a newww ... opportunity?' I pry mischievously, wanting to know more about Auntie Bridget but also keen to hear about Parker.

'Oh dear! I knew you'd have more questions.' She smiles, pouring custard onto her crumble.

'Well, of course I do! You want to find happiness again. Are you going to get married, and shall I be the bridesmaid?' I prod with a little laugh.

Mum pretends to lean over and whack me with her crumpled napkin. Michael Parker, she tells me again, was her first love. It didn't work out. She wanted domestic bliss; he wanted something more wild. Now he's fairly domestic and she's a wild woman. 'Or at least, a bit wild!' She nearly giggles as I try not to laugh through a mouthful of crumble. I'm all for supporting her, but here we are back in 'mum has sex' territory and I'm not up for that. No thank you.

'He's coming to the fashion show, too!' Mum says, raising her eyebrows as though this is the most scintillating bit of news she's ever shared.

'Oh! Why?' I mean, nice to support the town, but a bit niche.

'Because I'm in it! I've been accepted by the planning committee and I'm leading the "Overs", Mum announces, scooping a big mouthful of pudding onto her spoon.

'Oh my God! Are you?' I almost choke on my last bite. This is the least 'Mum' thing she's ever done.

'Yes! Sequinned pencil skirt, satin pussy bow shirt, they've hired a make-up artist, the full works!' Mum says, finishing her crumble and looking gleefully at me. 'You should speak to Vivienne about being in it, your outfit is fab today. I love the blousy thing, reminds me of my younger days! You've always been a fashionable little thing.' She smiles. Honestly, I could wear a plastic bag and she'd tell me I look lovely.

Never one to accept a compliment well, I use my anyway-back-to-you superpower.

'Wow! OK, well, good for you. I'd never have thought it was your thing, but I love it!' I can't keep up with this year. First Dad leaves Mum for Bernard, then the ring, then Parker, then this.

'It probably wasn't, but that's one of the beauties of life, isn't it?' she says, beaming.

'What is?' I'm struggling to keep up.

'You can change your mind, change your path, change your life!' she announces with more passion than I'd expect from her, waving her dessert spoon in triumph.

'Wow, you're really getting there, Mum, you're like a new woman!' I say, super-pleased for her but definitely in need of some time to let this all settle in. Since when was my sixty-year-old mum more exciting than me?

'I am, and I love it! I'll need some help finding some shoes, and maybe some dangly earrings. They're providing the outfit, but I said I'd put my own touch on the extras,' she chimes happily.

'Oh, wow! Course I'll help you.' Mum has come so far since Dad left, so this is a welcome turn.

'Brilliant! Maybe you could ask Julia for Wednesday off? It's the only day I'm not either helping at the Rotary, attending Jazzercize with Debs or taking in my online shop. It's all go these days! We could go to London and have a girls' day out. Haven't done that in a while.'

We clear the plates away, excitedly chatting about the fashion show and how bossy Vivienne is with it all and how Mum loves it. I tell her about the shop being nominated for the award, and the fashion show finale presentation, and Mum is thrilled for me, says they'd be crazy not to make me the winner, even though she hasn't seen a single one of the other nominees.

You can have the best boyfriend, the most amazing friends and all the material possessions in the world, but sometimes all you need is your mum. There's no one you'll ever be closer to, not really; your mum has literally carried you inside her, she's been there for every trauma, every naff moment of your life. Unless you've had a terrible mum, or lost her young – and I can't even begin to imagine what that must be like – your mum will always love you, come what may.

It's funny, isn't it? I've not lived in this house for years, but I still feel properly *home* home when I'm here, nattering with my mum. It's like when you get ill and all you want is your mum, even if you know she won't be that helpful – Mum doesn't approve of anyone wearing their PJs after 9 a.m., no matter how poorly they are. It has been an unreal couple of months, but I can feel my shoulders relaxing and I just feel . . . content here with my lovely mum.

Chapter Sixteen

SITTING DOWN ON OUR chintzy, flowery sofa (one of my best local finds from a dear old lady who was moving into a home, and had the sofa barely used in her conservatory) next to David that evening, I give him a big squish. We'd had a nice afternoon, been for a big food shop, popped in on his parents on the way home for a cup of tea, and then David had tidied up the minuscule front garden for a bit while I'd quietly sold the nesting tables for £80, and now we're about to have an hour watching TV and vegging out. Quiet but content. I think I like it.

'Glad your mum plated me up some grub today,' he says, patting his tummy and giving my head a little kiss. I cringe a tiny bit, not sure quite why, but smile and nod.

'I'll tell her you liked it. I'm going into London with Mum on Wednesday, I think. Just need to check with Julia tomorrow that she'll give me the day off,' I tell him.

'What for?' he asks.

'Mum wants new earrings, new shoes and one of those really cool manicures, the ones where they use crushed shells. I showed her a video on Insta and she was amazed. She's in Vivi's fashion show!' I reveal, looking up at him with a little smile.

'What? Your mum is?' He laughs, squeezing me for more of a cuddle. 'Never thought I'd see the day Barbara Burnley strutted down a catwalk.'

'Nor did I,' I laugh, wriggling out of his embrace. 'And she's actually leading the older women.'

'Bloody hell, so the front runner of the thing.' David laughs in surprise.

'Yes! How cool is that?' I'm so proud of her for putting herself out there like this.

'Isn't she about sixty?' he says, still laughing.

'Yes. And your point is?' I say, sitting up fully from the cuddle, cross that he's brought her age into this.

'Nothing. Didn't realise it was that sort of show,' he says, smiling infuriatingly.

'What sort of show?' I'm really starting to feel angry now. Why is he spoiling such a nice evening?

'Don't get upset, I think it's nice she's in it,' he backtracks.

'I'm not upset. I'm glad she's in it. She's a stunning woman, and will make a very worthy model,' I say with a silent *humph* as I cross my arms.

I don't really know what else to say, and David has already turned the TV up, so I sit absently watching it for a while and think. I love how cosy the lounge is. It's teeny-tiny but with the real log fire, the charming little windows with thick sills for me to display knick-knacks, our cute sofas (that David still moans about, but he isn't ever going to go out and buy the 'cool modern corner ones' he likes, so I'm safe, ha ha), the TV standing on the slimmest console table known to man (literally no floor space), a coffee table of well-read books and our shabby-chic upcycled display case (containing a selection of my finest vintage glassware, all ready for socialising and parties), it is perfect. When you picture a chocolate-box cottage with cosy interiors, this is it.

It may be small but it's the ideal place to entertain, too. Vivi and I could spend hours giggling in here with a bottle of wine, and it is lovely when Dad comes in after doing the garden for a cup of tea and slice of sponge.

As the TV programme – three men racing old bangers across Scotland – plays on, my mind drifts to next year and how I'd like to entertain more. Maybe throw a party. Possibly even something for New Year's Eve, vintage-themed for the 'roaring twenties'. I could wear a real vintage flapper dress and some of the silver filigree bracelets I have squirrelled away in little velvet bags upstairs.

I instantly want to tell Bea about my 1920s party idea! I'll have to share it with her on Wednesday.

'Shit!' I say in horror.

'Oh my God, what?' David jumps violently. Wow, I wasn't expecting that.

'Sorry. I've just realised I've doubled-booked Mum and my friend next week, on Wednesday.' I try to sidestep his dramatic response and work out what I'm going to do.

'Jesus Christ, Tabs! I thought it was something important,' he complains, turning back to the TV.

Anger bubbles again.

'It IS important! I'm helping Mum shop for the show, but I was meant to see my friend Bea,' I say indignantly.

'Just cancel one then,' David says with his eyes firmly fixed on the screen.

'Huh! Yes, thank you, so helpful. You'll be coming to Mum's show, won't you? In three weeks?' I check.

'No can do. I'm down to Brighton to see the lads.' Still he doesn't look away from the TV.

This is the first I've heard of any trip. The lads comprise four guys David met through his motorcross events. They get together, sit in pubs, show each other pictures of cars and guffaw about 'the old times'. Sometimes some of the wives and girlfriends go, so I wait a second to see if he's inviting me.

'Oh. I didn't know about that,' I say, still waiting.

'Just decided yesterday, love. Tommo booked it in,' David replies, still not looking at me.

All the 'lads' have 'fun' names for each other, generally with 'o' or 'y' at the end. Davo, Tommo, Marky and Kevsy. I can't say I'm gutted not to be going, but it stings that he didn't even think to invite me.

'Well, good, I'm glad you're going away. I'll be able to focus on Mum and making sure she has a great weekend,' I say, as if I'm not just a tad hurt that he didn't speak to me about this.

'Ahh, that's the spirit. She'll be fantastic,' he says, squeezing my knee but still not really paying attention.

'Yes, and so will I. I'm in the show too,' I add.

'Amazing.' Deep breaths, deep breaths.

'Yes, I'm in the show, and the judging panel for the

independent business award I'm longlisted for will be there, because models dressed in vintage from the shop, including me, will be doing a finale presentation.'

Without any response from my devoted and loving boyfriend, I take myself upstairs for a hot bath and a long think. Bea's words *do what makes you MOST happy* swirl round my head. I don't know what makes me most happy, but I'm starting to realise it's almost definitely not David.

Shopping in London with Mum is by far and away the best trip I've ever had with her. It's not that hard because we haven't had a lot of girlie shopping trips to compare it to. Mum has never been the frivolous type. She's definitely not tight-fisted, she loves 'something a bit nice' and the house is essentially a living showroom for John Lewis, but she's never been one to 'splash out'. She's the type of woman who makes very considered and well-planned purchases. It took her three months and four carpet book samples to choose the flooring for the landing one year. 'It's a big choice to get wrong,' she'd say when Dad and I pointed out that 'biscuit' and 'oatmeal' were practically identical shades.

This time, it's like shopping with a woman who isn't even my mum! We potter around Covent Garden, enjoying all the boutiques and market stalls. I cast a knowing eye over some of the trinkets and note how astronomically they're marked up compared to Pearls and Doodles. We work our way up Oxford Street, Regent Street and Bond Street, window-shopping outside the stores we definitely can't afford and admiring all the window displays.

As the day turns to evening, the lights sparkle all around and our arms are heavy with our new treasures in their bags. Mum found two pairs of Louboutin dupe killer heels which are totally unlike her but 'so Ruth Langsford' that she had to buy them, tonnes and tonnes of dangly earrings, bangles, delicate necklaces, chunky necklaces and a bejewelled headband. She faltered on the headband, protesting, 'I've got a greying bob and a turkey neck, I can't wear this!' But remembering how ridiculous David had been the other night, I pushed: 'Mum, your hair is lovely and you don't have a turkey neck. To me you are far more beautiful than the headband. Get it and wear it proudly.' 'I'll do it for the over-sixties!' she cheered, throwing it in her little netted basket we'd been carrying around for forty minutes.

I love this new Mum. Aside from the wavering over the headwear, she was so bold. She kept commenting that life is for living, and that we have to live every day with gusto. She was far removed from the 'is the oatmeal shade a tad too warm, Tony?' mum of the past. I don't know whether it was Dad leaving, this old flame Parker reconnecting, Vivi's encouragement for the fashion show or some other mysterious power (you start to believe anything is possible when you have a time-travelling ring, for goodness' sake) but I loved it.

My feet hurt and my debit card hurts more, but when I come in, climb the stairs (before heading in to see David because I want to hide a couple of bags, as I may have treated myself too) and flump down onto the bed, I feel the happiest I have in a long time. Motivated by Mum's new-found confidence, I open my phone, find an old photo of one of my best window displays at the shop, load it into Instagram Stories and type, 'Can't believe our little vintage shop has been longlisted for Indie Shop of the Year! Waiting to see if we've been shortlisted. So excited!'

It feels liberating and wrong in equal measure to 'show off' about something, but I am my mother's daughter and if she can loosen the reins a bit, so can I. Plus, it's only Stories, so it'll vanish in twenty-four hours. Even I can show off for that long!

I give an affirming fist pump, screenshot it and send it to Vivi, just to make sure it is OK. We filled out the big award questionnaire on Sunday, in a password-protected section of the award website, and I'm still buzzing with the confidence and ambition it inspired in me as we went through the questions. Most of it was about what my goals are for Pearls and Doodles, which for me is all about setting up a website – with online shop – and social media accounts for the shop. Vivi was great – she really knows her stuff, from handling the social media for some of the groups she's involved with, and I learnt so much. I feel like my dream is within reach now.

Chapter Seventeen

DESPITE HAVING A LOAD of restocking to do after my day off yesterday, today I can't help but shut up shop for twenty minutes to visit Bea.

'And what time do you call this?' Bea asks jokingly when I stroll in.

'Erm, about twenty past nine?' Shit – does the ring change the hours as well as the years?

'And what day?' she asks, arms folded across her orange blouse as she sits professionally at her desk, surrounded by brochures and booking forms.

'Er . . .' Is this a trick question?

'What happened to our "date" yesterday? Here I was, thinking it was your round on the toasties, but nooo, just sitting on my own, Billy No Mates, and buying my own lunch. Talking to nobody!' Bea mock-pouts.

'Oh, God! I'm *sorry*! I was going to text you but I don't have your number,' I say, hoping that will get me out of things.

'Text me? I don't think the fax has that,' she says, leaning to the sideboard unit behind her to peer at the functions on the fax machine.

'Yeah, no, sorry, fax, text, they all sound the same, don't they, these days,' I cover myself. She must think I'm so weird.

'Aha, yeah! Don't worry, really. I ended up having the afternoon off myself. Spent it with my sister,' she grins.

Relief washes over me that she isn't really cross. 'Oh yes? What did you get up to?' I ask, happy to be moving on from questions about what the date is.

'She wanted me to help her go shopping for some new outfits. Wants to have a "more mature" style now she's seeing this new fella. I said she should treat herself to something sexy, heels and a silky blouse or whatever, but she wants to be "demure".'

'Ooohh demuuure,' I say, smiling, interested to hear what they bought, pulling up the plastic brown seat opposite her desk and sitting myself down.

'Yeah, *demuuure*. She bought two skirt suits from BHS with really firm pads in the shoulders, so I think they'll hold well – hate it when you get those ones that go all peculiar in the tumble dryer,' she gabbles.

'Mmm, me too,' I nod, as if I'd ever let a shoulder-padded item of clothing in my vintage wardrobe near a tumble dryer.

'She can wear the suit to work and then just take the jacket off if she goes out for dinner or to a wine bar after, you know?' Bea moves some brochures around her desk absently-mindedly.

'Hope she's got something on under the jacket!' I giggle.

'Well, I suggested she treats her new fella and doesn't wear anything, but obviously she wasn't up for that. Bought a few boring shirts from C&A, but then, at the last minute, I forced her to buy this gorgeous satin shirt with a massive Princess Di bow on it!' she says with delight.

How I wish I was wearing my cream silky blouse with the bow. I find myself wanting to impress Bea. Today I'm just wearing a loose Indian cotton smock dress with mirror embroidery because the temperature was set to be soaring after a colder spell we've had lately. There's no way I could've donned boots!

'Ohh, a pussy bow? Lovely! What colour?' If her sister

is anything like her, with her huge permed hair and big dazzling eyes, a pussy bow will look fabulously over the top, and I love it.

'Sunshine yellow. Looks mega-cool with the grey pinstripes. Just hope she bloody wears it!' Bea says firmly.

'Sounds so nice,' I lie, imagining Bea's poor sister looking like banana custard in a suit.

'Funnily enough, I went shopping yesterday too. My mum wanted to do the opposite with her stuff, loosen up a bit. It was super-fun,' I offer.

'That does sound more fun than shopping with my fuddy-duddy sister. Hopefully the shirt will perk up her look, though.'

I catch myself. The less I say about that the better.

'Yep, I'm sure it will. Anyway, I come bearing good news and bad news,' I say, excited to get everything off my chest.

'Oh! I hope it's juicy.' She rubs her hands together with glee.

'Sort of. The good news is, anyway,' I say, smiling already.

'Fire away,' Bea says eagerly, leaning forward a little to listen all the more intently.

'You know my shop?' I begin.

'No, but yes. Why have I not visited you there yet?' Shit. Need to deflect.

'Um . . . I don't know,' I stutter, thrown off. 'We'll arrange something.'

Bea nods encouragingly.

'Anyway, Vivienne, my best friend, she nominated it for Indie Shop of the Year—' again, I stop myself from saying 2022, noting how exhausting it is to keep self-editing, 'and it was longlisted! She's submitted all the bits they need, and I had to fill out a detailed business questionnaire, and now we wait to see if I've made the shortlist. I should hear any day,' I nearly squeal, the most excited I've been to tell anyone.

'Oh my God, that's *awesome*! Imagine this little town winning something like that. Bet you'll be in the paper. Maybe even on the news!' Bea squeaks. I absolutely love how much confidence she shows in me.

'Wow, well, I'm not going to win, but it's still cool.' Never one to allow a compliment.

'You might. Will you let me do your make-up for the TV? You can wear a cute denim jacket, I could do you a toner hair colour, you could even borrow the Princess Di blouse if you want!' Bea says with such energy I can't help but go along with it.

'Aha! OK. I'm not sure a banana-yellow shirt and an acid-wash jacket are a good combo, but yes.'

'Are you joking? That sounds like a great combo! You're happy to wear all your funny tight jeans and super-flat hair, but not the best shirt in Debenhams?' she goads.

'Oi! My hair isn't flat, it's sleek!' I try to defend myself. Twenty fifteen me who spent over a hundred quid on GHDs would be totally horrified to hear her hair called *flat*.

'Yeah, lovely and sleek . . . and flat!' We descend into giggles as we discuss my new life of fame and fortune which Bea thinks I'll have after I definitely win the award and feature on that night's news in the yellow shirt. 'You can tell them you've been styled by me,' she insists.

In between a couple of phone enquiries and someone popping in for a brochure (in a vivid purple shell suit that is everything you think of when someone says 'the 1980s') for a Mediterranean trip, we laugh about what we'll do when Pearls and Doodles propels the town into the spotlight.

Once we've settled down a smidgen, Bea changes her tone to something a lot more motherly and gentle. I love this side of her; she can be very nurturing when she's not bouncing off the walls. 'What was the bad news then?'

My stomach drops.

'Bad news is, I had another fight with David.' I sort of

wish I'd never mentioned the bad news. We were having so much fun.

'Ahh, the anti-travel boyfriend.' She shuffles some fax papers around mindlessly, not impressed with even the idea of David.

'He's not anti-travel, he just doesn't like going anywhere,' I correct. Why do I always leap to his defence like this?

'Um, OK. Not anti-travel then.' Bea purses her lips and furrows her brow at me.

'Anyway, we had a non-fight. He riled me, I didn't stand up for myself, just went upstairs, as per,' I say, my disappointment at myself all coming out now I'm here.

'Oh dear, not good.' She shakes her head and offers a kind look.

'I keep thinking about what you said. "What makes you most happy?" I still don't know, but I'm trying to work it out. My little Insta side hustle thing makes me happy, Vivi does, you do, Mum and Dad too, maybe being longlisted does. David's not on the list, though.' I flop my hands into my lap and let out an exaggerated sigh, looking at Bea as though she'll have all the answers.

'Well, it's good your instant hustle makes you happy. Is that the antique painting and clothes thing? Good that you can turn it round so quickly – that's what you want in business these days. Instant profits, instant cash, you know?' Bea says, looking for me to validate her sweet guess. Maybe she looks up to me as I look up to her. No. Silly thought!

'Yes. Yep. That's it.' I let one slip through the self-edit there.

'And it's even better that you have so many people that DO make you happy. I wish I did,' she adds, surprising me that she feels that way. She's always so chipper.

'Thank you. I'd never really thought of it like that. Also, just so you know, you've got me.' I put my hand on hers but go to pull it back immediately after. Don't want to seem overkeen.

She clasps her hand firmly over mine, gives it a squeeze and says, 'I don't know what the answer is with David, but I think we should always trust our instincts and follow our heart. You'll know what to do when the time is right.' She looks into my eyes with so much conviction I almost want to cry. I am a mess in 1989!

'Bea, you are very wise, do you know that?' I say, gratefully giving her hand a return squeeze.

'Yes, I do.' She takes her hand back and fluffs her hair with it, smiling. 'I tell my sister every bloody day, but she just rolls her eyes. You should meet her and tell her for me.'

'I'd love to! Don't think I could miss the banana shirt.'

I laugh, moving away from the tense knot I get in my stomach when I think of making a big choice about David.

'Aha, definitely not! I'll tell you what I'm going to miss, though.' Bea has a twinkle in her eye as she leans across the desk.

'Huh?' I say, confused by the jump. I need another coffee.

'These chats. Time is of the essence,' Bea says, grinning mysteriously.

For a split second that old panic wave washes over me. Does she know about the ring? Has she worked it all out?

'I . . . erm . . . it's just . . .' I falter.

'I've been saving for so *long*! Went into the bank the other day, had them check my account and I've got enough in there for my tickets if I book them in the end-of-summer sale!' she says, standing up, dashing over to the big grey filing cabinets, pulling out a large paper envelope and showing me some documents inside. 'Look! Mrs Fletcher's running a sale at the end of the month to squeeze out the last few holidaymakers. It just came through – not even on the shelves yet. I could book and go!'

'Oh my God! So amazing,' I say, jumping up to look. 'You're actually off!'

'That's right. Twelve months of sun, sand and—'

'Culture!' I say. I have no idea why I interrupted there.

I knew where she was going and felt very weird about it. I think because Bea is younger than me. That'll be it. I'm being motherly.

'Aha-ha, yes, OK, culture!' Bea sings, swinging round on her swivel chair. 'I thought I'd be waiting ages, but the price is great, my sister seems to be settling with her new beau, so it's time. With Mum dying, I don't take life for granted – you've got to seize every opportunity.'

'Oh Bea, I didn't know you'd lost your mum,' I say, feeling a real pang of sadness for her.

'Yeah, a few years ago now. The Big C. That's why I live with my sister,' she says matter-of-factly, in that way people do when they don't want to go too deep.

'Is your dad about?' I ask before I can stop myself. I don't know why I'm being so nosy.

'Nope. He buggered off when I was a baby. Don't even remember him. I think my sister does though, and that's why she's so keen to have a proper family – stable, I mean.' She smiles sadly.

'Well, hooray for your sister, eh? Bet you'll miss her when you go.' I smile back, almost wanting to get up and give her a massive hug.

'I will, but that's about it. Not much else stopping me jetting off.' She laughs, wafting a stray brochure in the air.

'Um, me?' I say, laughing, feeling a teeny-tiny sliver of sadness that she's going.

'You'll be here when I get back. Anyway, right now we need to CELEBRATE!' Bea throws her arms up in the air with such delight I mirror her body language and cheer 'Yeeaaahhh!'

'Tomorrow night, after work, you and me, wine bar. Let's paint the town red!'

'Ha ha, ha ha ha,' I laugh, silently freaking out because I've never been much of an out-out party girl, and adding that in with a whole different time zone, that's so far beyond my comfort zone I can't even *see* my comfort zone anymore.

'Your little knick-knack shop is straight up the high street, right? But going away from town? In that little row of old-school shops? Is it the bright pink one?'

'Mm-hmm,' I nod, my throat too tight to say much more but a forced smile still plastered across my face.

'So odd, I never really go that way. I'll make an exception! I'll lock up here at five, come to yours, we can get ready there. Just dress up a bit for work and then I'll tease your hair and do your eyes, yours is all smudged. Where did you learn to do your make-up?' Bea gabbles excitedly.

I try to tell myself the smoky eye look wasn't big in the 1980s and ignore the accidental insult.

'Uh-huh, ha ha, just watched a lot of tutorials,' I say, trying to match her enthusiasm.

'At college? Babs wanted me to go there after my O levels. I did think about hair and beauty,' she says, fluffing up her bobbed perm.

'Yeahh,' I trail off, twisting the ring round my finger, running through a million logistical worries like taking the ring out of the shop after closing, not going home to David straightaway, drinking wine and forgetting to self-edit (I'm bad enough sober), and spending too much time wearing the ring.

'Bloody hell, we've been gassing for an hour! Mrs Fletcher will be furious if I don't put these bookings through,' Bea says, now mirroring my panic but over much more typical concerns.

'Shit! I was only supposed to pop in for twenty minutes. Argh,' I squawk, grabbing my bag (just Dorothy Perkins circa 2017 today, sadly not vintage glamour) and heading out the door. 'Bye, Bea!' I call.

'Byeee! See you tomorrow niiight,' she calls back, waving.

Chapter Eighteen

'ARE YOU ALL RIGHT, Tabitha? You're looking a bit peaky,' Julia says on Friday morning as I help her sort through some new merchandise for one of the displays. One of the vendors has dropped off a box of miniature gilded frames with tiny oil paintings of little girls in bonnets and little boys in blue jackets playing with fluffy dogs, and a box of floral china all wrapped carefully in old newspaper. The china will sell quickly, I think; always does.

'Mmm, sorry, yes. Just a bit tired, maybe,' I lie, pulling out another trio of vintage Moss Rose china pieces and putting them gently on the table.

'Are you sure?' Julia pushes. She's known me a long time; she's not stupid.

'You'll think I'm foolish if I tell you,' I smile, privately glad of the opportunity to let it all out. Well, most of it.

'I bet I won't.' She smiles back, putting some newspaper in the recycling pile and pulling more china out of the box.

'Well, I'm going out tonight,' I begin, 'to a wine bar.'

'Ah, that's why you're all dressed up. I haven't seen a skirt like that for a long time!' she exclaims, nodding at my rara skirt. 'I bet you'll have a nice time. Are you going with David?'

'No, I'm going with a girlfriend of mine,' I say, not making eye contact in case she has superhuman detection skills and can tell that my friend is either from 1989 via a magical crystal ring, or that I'm having a fully delusional relationship with a woman in my head.

'Right, so far this all sounds very above board. What's with the pained face then?' She stops emptying the boxes, stands up straight and forces me to look at her.

'Just . . . I'm not really the . . . the out-out type,' I mumble.

Julia smiles kindly. 'This is 2022, Tabitha. You can love whoever you like and be as in or out as you feel best. I didn't know it was over with David, but good for you, and this girlfriend, well, you're only young once, aren't you?'

'Oh no! No, no. Um, no,' I stutter, realising how wrong she's got it.

'No?' Julia repeats, obviously baffled.

'I'm with David. My friend is a girl called Bea. Just my friend. "Out-out" means going out for a big night out. Sorry. I'm just not the type for that, I mean. Sorry. Aha-ha,' I trail off awkwardly, wishing I hadn't begun.

'Ha ha, oh Tabitha! Sorry. Ha ha! What am I like?' Julia gabbles. 'You're young and lovely. Of course you're the type. I'm not sure they call them wine bars anymore, but whatever they are, they're made for you and your friend. You'll have a lovely time!' she cheers me along, shaking my arm with her warm hand.

I cringe that I said 'wine bars'. Turns out I need to self-edit in every time zone.

'I'm just a bit nervous. She wants to go after work. I hope you don't mind, but I said we could get ready here. In the loo, I mean. After I've closed up. Not in the shop or anything,' I say, starting to worry that even that part is a bad idea.

'No, I don't mind at all! I think it's lovely you're doing something nice with a gal pal. You deserve a bit of fun. Why don't you take the keys to the flat upstairs? Trevor hasn't been in for over a month, and won't mind if you just use the bathroom and lounge. I'll tell him I nipped up for a sit-down. Just clean up after yourselves.'

She smiles, giving my upper arm another little squeeze of encouragement.

'Wow, thanks, Julia, that's so nice. Too nice of you, really. We won't make any mess or touch any of his stuff,' I say, somewhat taken aback.

'You're a good girl, and a tremendous help to me. I've been meaning to say, I'm delighted about the shop nomination. Even if we don't win, it'll be great publicity. Anyway, your friend – give her a call and tell her. I'll finish up these,' she says, gently dismissing me.

I wander back into the shop, knowing I can't call Bea, obvs, and still nervy about the evening ahead. What would Vivi do? I know she'd be up for it. I feel a slight pang of guilt for not spending a lot of time with her lately.

There's no time to fret over the evening's plans, though, because it's Friday and the shop is bustling with customers. Julia stays all day to keep things going and there are definitely no gaps to pop out for a break, let alone off to 1989.

'Haven't you got anything bright, like a blue?' Bea says, assessing my slightly feeble make-up bag of neutral tones and warm browns.

'I think there's a goldish sort of colour in there, that

looks nice,' I suggest as she opens all three of my ages-old eyeshadow palettes in despair.

'I know, but we want to look extra WOW,' she says, despairing at my shabby collection of shadows. 'Don't worry! I have a reaaally nice frosty white. We'll do that on the lids and brow bones, loads and loads of mascara and my candy-pink lipstick. It's brand new from Boots! It's called "Sugar Frost",' she says, cheerily applying another swirl of blusher to my already heavily blushed cheeks. 'Do you not even have any good eyeliner colours? Like a turquoise blue would be sooo cool!' I pretend to have a rummage, knowing full well anything beyond a black eyeliner is laughable in my collection.

When Bea first arrived at the shop twenty minutes ago, she loved it. Before heading up to Trevor's never-used lounge, she walked round every nook and cranny, saying it was like a treasure trove, picking little ornaments up and holding sparkly jewellery to the light.

I wasn't sure when would be the best time to start wearing the ring, let alone the fact that I might actually be mad and none of this was real. So as soon as Julia left around 4 p.m., I put it on and waited. And fretted. What if Bea never showed? What if the ring only worked on a one-way travel basis? What if she never even *existed*? But I *knew* it wasn't all in my head, and that was confirmed when a customer walked in with a shopping trolley and asked if we sold cassettes for her grandson's 'new Walkman thingummy'.

I never wear a lot of make-up when I go out. I guess I'm too worried about drawing attention to myself, even though I love practising vintage looks at home – Vivi says I'm queen of the winged eyeliner flick, and I've even enjoyed experimenting with a 1950s-style beauty spot. I'm about to protest and tell Bea that I don't want to look too over the top, but then I remember where – or when – I am. I've travelled back in time and am about to go on a full night out in the 1980s with someone I barely know. I'm not sure too much blusher is the biggest thing to fret about here. Besides, this is the 1980s: if ever there were a time to go OTT it would be now – then. God, I'm so confused, and we haven't even started drinking yet. Before I have a chance to have a freak-out, I'm given a thick coating of Barbie-pink lip gloss over my 'Sugar Frost' lipstick and there's a backcombing brush in my fringe. My fringe! I'm coated in Elnett (finally, something I recognise) – don't let me near a naked flame this evening. I've dared to stick on some false eyelashes, despite Mum's warning about the glue so close to my eyes. And now, emboldened, I pick up Bea's tube of blue mascara. When in Rome . . .

'Wow. You. Look. Stellar!' Bea says, stepping back from her artistry with pride.

I look in the mirror and my jaw drops. I barely recognise myself. My fringe looks like I've stuck my fingers in a plug socket and my make-up is very reminiscent of the play sets I had when I was little. It is not exactly the look I've been practising at home, and you'd definitely never see Taylor Swift sporting it on a red carpet, but it is fun to see me looking so different and there's no denying what decade I'm in. I try to find something complimentary to say as Bea watches me expectantly. 'It's lucky we both have the same skin tone and hair colour,' I try. 'Good that we can share make-up, I mean.' If I pretend I'm at a fancy-dress party, I can get on board with this 'lewk'.

'Pink lipstick and white shadow goes well on everyone,' Bea says earnestly, gathering up all our make-up, chucking it unceremoniously into its bags and pulling her Doc Martens back on.

'Right. I'm ready!' she says, standing up and giving me a little twirl, which I smile at in approval. 'Thanks for helping with my make-up. Feel like I'm in *Dynasty* or something glam! Just call me Alexis,' she jokes. Thank God for the new Netflix version, so I get the reference. 'As you can see, I changed at the agency. Wasn't about to be seen dead in that uniform for a second longer than needed.' She laughs. 'You're so lucky you can wear whatever you like to work!'

I smile, inwardly quite pleased with my outfit. All those times I've been too afraid to wear some of my special vintage pieces and left them languishing in the spare room wardrobe and now, here I am, rocking them! I knew I was saving them for something special, but I'd never in my wildest dreams have imagined it was this.

I picked up my genuine 1980s black rara skirt, with its layer of frothy tulle, at a vintage flea market in Manchester three years ago, and have teamed it with a tucked-in sleeveless black polo neck that isn't really vintage (unless ASOS from last year counts), along with those fishnet tights that I had stashed away for a fancy-dress party David and I were meant to go to (I was going to be Madonna in her 1980s onstage leotard and tights days, not the fishnet legs stuck out from under the bed Insta days, I might add), but which we missed, as he ended up staying late at the garage on an emergency engine repair. And, my pièce de résistance, my real vintage Chanel handbag that I secretly bought six months ago with some of the money I've been making from my Instagram sales. It's a beige lambskin small double flap 1 series. As the influencers would say, it's 'buttery soft'. Gold hardware, a few little scuffs underneath (that you'd never really see), a couple of leather indentations from the chain strap (which I think just add a little character) and one mark on the inside, but for a 1991 Chanel, I'm not complaining. It cost a small fortune even in its pre-loved condition (I've told David it's a fake, and I daren't let Mum ever see it, far too extravagant for her approval), but on the next-to-never occasions I wear it, I feel a million bucks. Tonight felt like the perfect night.

'I know, my boss is really great,' I smile, swinging the bag onto my acid-wash denim jacket-clad shoulder with vigour.

'Oh. My. God. Is that a real Chanel handbag?' Bea says in awe.

I'm about to say it's a fake and diminish the grandeur of it, but stop myself. It's just a bag. I deserve to have a special bag. There's nothing wrong with that. I straighten up my posture, reach down and hold it out. 'Yep! The real deal. I've wanted a Chanel for years, and when I saw this for a fantastic price – well, for Chanel, ha ha – I just knew I had to have her.' I smile with a confidence I didn't know I even had.

'Wooow,' Bea whispers, running her fingers over the soft leather. 'You're such a whizz, finding all these fashion-able treasures,' she says, beaming at my beautiful handbag-of-dreams.

'Yes, I'm basically the best site scourer you'll ever find for bargain vintage,' I say, taking the bag off and handing it to her.

'You say such wacky things, I love it.' Bea laughs, stroking the soft leather. 'What the hell is a site scourer?'

'Aha-ha, you know, looking round shops, flea markets,' I add, thinking that was quite a good edit, in fact. I'm getting used to it now.

'One of your antiques terms?' she says, still besotted with the bag.

'Yes, exactly,' I say, relieved that she can't date bags and work out that for her, this bag isn't vintage at all. It's a 1991, so technically it's from the future. Sort of. Wow, tonight is going to be tricky!

Chapter Nineteen

THE WINE BAR IS BUSY, bodies squashed up against each other, or maybe it's just that there are so many shoulder pads and such giant hair, it feels crowded. The air is thick with the smell of cigarettes, and it seems like everyone is smoking. It feels completely alien to me – where's the designated outside area, with the nice heaters and people borrowing lighters, just to chat someone up? I'm busy thinking about how different it is until something jolts me back to the present. Or the 1989 present, at least.

'Oh my God!' I scream over the music.

'What?' Bea spins round, wide-eyed.

'Someone just groped me!' I yell, whipping my head back and forth to see who the culprit might have been.

'What?' she shouts, clearly struggling to hear over George Michael's 'Faith'. What a legend, but no time to focus on that.

'Someone just touched my bum!' I shout, furious.

Bea grins and gives me a thumbs up; I can't work out whether that's because she thinks this is good news (ick), or she just couldn't hear me. I hope the latter. I watch her sashay up to the bar, squeezing in between two men wearing so much aftershave I can smell it over the smoke.

Wow, things really *are* different in 1989.

Before I've had a chance to hunt down the man who really needs an evil stare (because, let's face it, what else was I going to do?) Bea turns round with two huge glasses of white wine and the biggest grin I've ever seen in my life.

'Thank you! How much do I owe you?' I say, taking one out of her hands.

'Zilch! Those guys bought them,' she says, nodding back and giving a little shimmy at the two aftershave-soaked chaps who are now blowing us a kiss. I shudder.

'I never really buy drinks,' Bea confesses as we find a slightly quieter corner with a bistro table and a few chairs. I'm trying to act normal but I can't stop looking around, taking it all in. On the wall there are posters of Madonna in corsets and lace and the kind of volume I'm always trying to 'tame' out of my hair, and so many neon lights and mirrors I barely know which way's up. Although that might be the drinks . . .

'Really?' I say, intrigued and, ashamedly, impressed.

'Nope. I just bat my lashes, say something charming and voila, drinks!' she says, picking up her glass and cheersing mine.

'You really do have the gift of the gab,' I agree.

'Woo-hoo!' she says with her face in her glass.

'I wish I was a bit more . . . out there. My mum's always gone on about what's "sensible" or "appropriate", and now I'm a bit . . . I dunno.' I instantly feel guilty for saying something negative about my lovely mum. She's a great mum, but I can't help thinking her shyness has rubbed off on me.

'Your mum sounds like my sister. Bit prim and proper.' Bea shrugs, taking a huge sip of the wine. More of a gulp than anything. Love that gusto.

'Yes. Not bad, though. She's a brilliant mum,' I add to alleviate my guilt. 'Love her to pieces, obviously.'

'Yeah,' Bea says, looking distracted.

We sit in silence for a moment and I feel a tad worried that the night is going to be very long. What the hell am I doing? Glad of the large, full glass of wine, I take a confidence-boosting glug.

'Do you want to dance?' Bea asks, looking over to the packed dance floor, half her wine already gone. Wow, she's really putting it away.

'Oh God, no, I'm a terrible dancer,' I protest, smiling to mask my state. It's one thing to dress the part, but to dance the part . . . bloody hell.

'No, you're not!' she protests, as Bon Jovi's 'Livin' On A Prayer' starts belting out of the speakers.

'I am, I am!' I laugh, wanting the chair to swallow me up and trap me so I don't have to walk onto that dance floor, despite it being what David would call 'an absolute tune'.

'Right, drink that up and take a deep breath. We're doing it! Your mum's not here, at least I hope not!' We both giggle at the thought – maybe the wine is going to my head.

Bea continues, 'We're two bodacious chicks, and we need to celebrate. I'm going travelling! Your shop is the best shop in the world, probably going to win that award thing. Those boys from the bar are looking at us. Let's go!'

The temptation to stay put is strong but as I twist

the ring on my finger and think of all the times I've sat on the sidelines, something bubbles up inside me. The wine, perhaps.

I knock the rest back (I'm sure I'll regret that in about thirty minutes), leave my jacket on the chair, straighten the strap of my Chanel, brush down the tulle on my skirt and stand up. I'm doing it!

As we approach the dance floor, a really pleasing thought pops into my head. Nobody has phone cameras. Nobody here knows me, nobody has any expectations of me. The phrase 'dance like no one's watching' rings in my ears. Here we go!

'You are Vivienne, none of this matters, what would Vivienne do?' I silently chant as I let my hips move to the music with a smile plastered on my face, one hand protectively on my bag, one swaying about in what I hope is a 'cool move'.

'Woo-*hooo!*' Bea calls as she throws her hands confidently in the air, twirling round in her cerise puffball minidress. 'They don't generally have the music this loud,' she shouts over to me. 'It's usually a bit more upmarket, but they must be trying something new.' She carries on turning and shimmying to the beat. The music feels like we're at a theme night, or one of the many weddings of Mum's pals I went to as a child. It's nostalgic and comforting. I can feel myself relaxing, and I love it. Why has it taken me this long to enjoy a moment here and there?

Bea's carefree attitude is so attractive. Men from every corner of the room are eyeing her up, and women are smiling back when she gives them one of her signature warm grins. Objectively, she's not supermodel stunning but she's pretty and her energy is magnetic. It's her confidence that shines through. She's so thoroughly . . . Bea. She's happy in her skin and everyone in the bar is drawn to it. I bet Vivienne would love her, I muse.

'If I didn't know her, I'd ask if you were sisters,' a man's voice half bellows in my ear, frightening the life out of me.

'Er . . . no . . . what?' I stutter, completely perplexed by that offbeat introduction. Is this how they used to chat people up?

Just as I'm preparing my best 'I have a boyfriend' line, Bea spots the man and, with a squeal, launches herself into his arms for a hug. I wonder if they have a history. Eventually they break apart and Bea tries introducing us, just as everyone screams 'wo-ah' along with Bon Jovi. Of course, I'm way too shy to ask him to repeat his name.

'Hi!' The classically tall, dark and handsome man puts a hand out. I instinctively shake it. Before I know it, the song changes and Bea's off, spinning with her eyes closed. I laugh as people move out of the way, letting her 'dance'. It's 'If I Could Turn Back Time' by Cher, and Bea clearly loves her as much as I do, over thirty years later. It wouldn't even occur to Bea that her dorky shop friend might feel awkward talking to this strange man. Nor should it. I remind myself to channel Vivi again and give him a smile.

'Gets warm on the dance floor, doesn't it?' he says, and I can hear him this time as the music isn't as loud. For a moment I wonder if this is leading up to him asking me to pop outside with him, which reminds me of school discos. But that isn't the vibe he's giving off.

'I could do with a cold drink. Can I get you one?' he asks, and something about him makes me trust him. Bea knows him, after all.

'All right, thanks. A white wine,' I say, and he nods with a grin.

'Better make it a large one.' And he heads off towards the bar, while I go and rescue my jacket. The bass beat of the next song is vaguely familiar. I rack my brains to try to remember and it comes back to me, just as he does. It's that Prince tune, 'Sign O' The Times'. It has to be a crazy coincidence, I think to myself.

'Here.' He hands me a chilly glass and then steers me to a banquette a little way away from the dance floor, where it's quieter. 'At least we can hear ourselves think over here.'

His jacket has shoulder pads, I note.

'So, you're a friend of Bea's.' He has a sip of his own drink – a bottled lager.

'That's right. Tabby,' I say, hoping he reminds me of his name as I didn't catch it thanks to Jon Bon Jovi giving it all to the chorus.

'Mike.' He raises the bottle and chinks it against my wine glass. 'I suppose you could say I'm a friend of hers too.' He pauses. 'Well, not really, or rather, I'm closer to her sister. *Was* closer, I should say.'

'Oh?' I don't want to comment, but he does look older than Bea. Although it is so hard to tell people's ages here – the styling makes everyone look about fifty! He's probably more my age or even a couple of years older. He looks as if he's got something he wants to get off his chest. Normally I'd run a mile from a good-looking man in a club; I have a boyfriend, and I'm bad at flirting anyway, it makes me so awkward. So I'd never sit down away from the crowd, but I'm pretty sure he's not hitting on me, plus nobody knows me here. I've always been a good listener – maybe I can be of help. 'Did something happen?'

He gives a long, deep sigh and shuts his eyes for a second. 'In a way.' He turns the bottle round and round in his hands, scratching a bit at the label, as he makes up his mind whether or not to explain. 'The thing is . . .' He looks at me. 'I can trust you, can't I?'

Usually I'd back away from such a heavy question, but here in 1989 I have nothing to lose. I'll never see him again, and whatever he's about to tell me happened decades ago for me. I swallow, trying not to get overwhelmed by that thought. 'Of course. Absolutely,' I say.

He leans back against the maroon leather back of the banquette. 'I was dating Bea's sister, and she's great,' he begins. 'She's clever, she's pretty, she's funny, although I don't think she knows it, and I thought we'd be together for ever. But she's dumped me. It's over.' He looks down at the bottle in his hands.

I realise this is not his first drink of the evening, and that's probably what's made him confide in a stranger. 'I never cared before, you know, thought it was madness when anyone said their heart was broken. But now I know what it means.' He looks sadly at the floor. 'It's not her fault, it's not my fault. That's the crazy thing. We just want different things. I want to see the world, find out how other people live, what it's like to stay somewhere for longer than two weeks on a summer holiday. I'm not thirty yet. I want to live a bit before I settle down, you know? But Barbara, she wants it all: the house and two-point-four children.'

I nod. I understand how he feels, or part of me does. I think it is so hard to even know what you want; we're always surrounded by this image of the 'ideal' life path – meet someone, marry them, have kids. I suspect the pressure was even greater in the 1980s. And yet a little part of me wonders what it would be like to cast off, go travelling, do something different. Bea's ideas have opened my mind, even if I'm not sure I'd ever act on them.

'I can't give her those things. Not right now. I would if I could.' He lifts the bottle again and I can see it's almost empty, whereas I've barely touched my drink.

'You can't do it if your heart isn't in it. That wouldn't be fair on either of you,' I say. 'You've got to do what makes you happy. What makes you most happy, even.' I smile as I think of how Bea's words have struck a chord with me.

He nods slowly. 'That's very wise . . . Tabby. It is Tabby, isn't it? I never met a Tabby before.' I shrug. Usually this is when a guy would make a crude joke about a cat. I hope that's not where this is heading. 'I know travelling will make me happy, and settling down will make her happy. And so that means we can't be together. There's no way around it, and she saw it before I did. Gave me the push.' He swallows hard. 'Didn't see it coming, to be honest. It's never happened to me before. The hardest thing is, she's right.'

'Then she's very brave, to make that decision,' I venture. I wish I had half the courage of this woman I've never met. Somehow it's easier to have forthright conversations in 1989. I automatically touch the ring, still snug on my middle finger.

'You're right.' He gives another heartfelt sigh, and then looks at his bottle, seemingly surprised that all the beer is gone. 'Can I get you another?'

I raise my glass a little to show him there's plenty left. 'No, I'm all right,' I say. 'But thanks.'

He stands up. 'No, thank you, Tabby. Thanks for listening to me witter on.' He sways a little but holds it together. 'I'll see you around.'

'Bye,' I say to his retreating back. I realise that can't have been easy: men hate to share their feelings, don't they? Or is that just my man? Perhaps it was easier because he doesn't know me, and has no way of knowing if he'll see me here again. Ha, little does he know how true that is.

I stand up as well, but not to go to the bar. It's a heaving mess over there, and there's no chance I'd get across the room to wherever Bea is without spilling my drink all over the place. I feel a bit lost. This is why I don't love going out-out. But I know the rules; if in doubt, head to the ladies'.

I edge carefully around the outside of the room, my elbow brushing against the fake dado rail. I make it as far as the door to the loos, push it open and step inside. The air is cooler in here and the volume of noise drops away, both a relief. For a few moments I stand with my back against the wall, taking in the differences.

The small room is lit by old-fashioned light bulbs, those filament ones, but not the trendy kind I'm used to. The tiles are all diamond-shaped, and a curious shade of somewhere between peach and coral. In the corner is a hand towel on a roller that looks pretty unhygienic. On the other hand, there's a bowl of potpourri on the wide windowsill, so someone's made an effort.

I'm so intrigued by all the details that for a moment I don't notice the faint sound coming from one of the cubicles. But in another gap between the songs back in the bar, I catch what I recognise as a sob. For a moment I am embarrassed for whoever it is. They've shut themselves in there to get away from everybody. I know I'd hate to be overheard if I wanted a good old cry in the loos. And let's be honest, we've all been there.

I pretend to be checking my make-up in the mirror in case anyone comes in. The backcomb needs some attention, for a start. All the while I tell myself that I've just been a shoulder for Mike to cry on and nothing terrible happened. Perhaps I can help this person too. Maybe that's why I'm here?

Before I can rustle up enough courage to knock, the cubicle door swings open and a woman comes out – no, more of a girl. She doesn't really look old enough to be drinking but she's clutching a glass of what seems to be red wine – uh-oh. Good job I'm wearing black, but she's got white jeans on – or they were white once. Now they've got big crimson splodges on them.

She comes across to the sinks and our gazes meet in the mirror. Her mascara has run, and her pretty face is stripy where the mascara has mixed with the (very 'bold') blusher. I just can't let her go out into the bar looking like this. Sisterhood and all that.

'Here,' I say, reaching for the box of peach tissues thoughtfully left by the basins for a crisis such as this.

She hiccups but takes a couple. She blows her nose. 'Thanks,' she says, though it comes out as a squeak. She turns to face me properly. 'I hate men, I hate the lot of them,' she says, and she starts to cry again.

It's obviously my night to play agony aunt. 'What's wrong?' I ask gently.

'Oh, you really don't want to know,' she wails.

'I do,' I tell her. And I do. Right now I can be more useful here than out on the dance floor.

And so the floodgates open and she tells me all about her cheating boyfriend, and I'm outraged on her behalf. Who could deliberately hurt such a sweet girl as this? But somebody clearly has and she pours it all out, his lies and the other girls she's found out that he was seeing at the same time, and how she'd hoped he would be different. I think back to how I was at this age, and what it would have been like if David had betrayed me. My world would have shattered. I know I often think I'm a bit timid and lacking in confidence, but I realise that in comparison I'm far more experienced than her.

'You'll think I'm talking rubbish, but you can do so much better than him,' I reassure her, as she dabs at her face. 'If he treats you like that then he doesn't deserve you.' All Vivi's empowering talk must have sunk in. I channel my best friend some more, in order to help this broken-hearted young woman. 'It's true. You don't need him. You don't need *anyone* – you can just go out there and take the world by storm. A boyfriend like that will only hold you back, and that's not what they're for.' I almost want to shout 'Girl Power!' and then I remember the Spice Girls haven't happened yet.

My positivity seems to have done the trick. My new young friend has revived after throwing cold water on her face and poured the rest of her wine down the plughole. I offer to get my comb out and try to do her hair the way Bea did mine, and by the time a couple of women who look as if they've come straight from the office stagger into the room, we're nearly good to go.

I let her leave first, giving me a moment to process what just took place. Someone who didn't know me from Adam took my advice and was grateful. I don't know how much she'll remember in the morning, but it's done the trick for now. Bea would be proud of me!

Talking of whom, I'd better find her. She'll be wondering where I've got to, although I don't expect she'll be worried. She'll assume that I'm just as happy on my own as she is, mixing with the crowd in the bar. As I come back into the main room I glimpse a flash of vivid cerise across the dance floor, and there she is, arms in the air once more.

Just as I'm about to make a beeline for her, there's one more obstacle to overcome. A tall figure lurches towards me, all sharp lapels and smarmy expression. 'Give us a smile!' he demands, sticking his arm against the wall and blocking my path. Then he smirks as if he's come out with the wittiest comment in the world.

He's much bigger than me and for a moment I feel threatened. But then I find I'm simply fed up. A minute ago I had plenty to smile about. I'd listened to Mike, helped a young stranger and not unnerved at being left to cope alone in an unfamiliar bar – and a whole different decade! I won't let this man ruin my night. I rarely lose my temper, but this is too much.

'Why don't you fuck off!' I shout in his face.

For a second I think I've really messed this up, that he's going to have a proper go at me. I would flinch away – but I'm already against the wall. So I have no choice but to stand my ground. With all the courage I can muster, I meet his gaze and stare him down. Instinctively my fingers find the ring and twist it; just touching it makes me feel safer, bolder.

His eyes widen in surprise. His mouth opens and shuts with nothing coming out. Then he regains his voice. 'All right, keep your hair on!' he says, and he backs away first. I keep glaring at him until I'm sure he really is going. 'Bloody lesbian!' he hisses, and turns a bit drunkenly on his nasty loafers.

I stand up straighter, taking his insult as a compliment. If he means I can cope without a man at my side every minute of my night out, turns out he's right. All the same, it's time to join my new friend on the dance floor, and I shoulder my way through to where Bea is every bit as full of energy as she was earlier.

'Tabitha! Tabby! Woo-hooo!' She's twirling in time to the music. 'Look, some guys just bought us a bottle! Have you still got your glass? Here you go!' And she tops me up, just as a Cyndi Lauper track comes on. 'Hey, this is our song! Let's get up on that stage area!'

I would never in a million years have agreed to do this in 2022, but something about the atmosphere, the adrenaline from standing up to that guy and being with Bea encourages me. Before I know it I'm waving one hand in the air while clutching my glass in the other, shaking my backcombed hair to 'Girls Just Wanna Have Fun'. Because, it turns out, we do.

The rest of the night is a blur. I know we drank all of that bottle, and possibly more glasses kept coming. It didn't matter that lots of the music was new to me – nobody really cared if I knew how to dance to it or not. I kept telling myself that I never had to see any of them again, and if I felt like waving my hands like Bea did, then who was going to notice? My ring glinted down at me and protected me as I danced like there was no tomorrow. After resisting him at first, I may even have flirted back with a nice-looking guy who danced with me on the little stage, who at one point took my hand, the one with the ring on, and asked me if I was with someone. I freaked a bit about the ring, and he eventually melted away. But it felt so good. I let myself be old-fashioned and lapped up the attention, just while it lasted.

I do have a dim recollection of the evening finishing with another Cyndi Lauper number, 'Time After Time', playing as we gathered our jackets and belongings, feeling tired but happy. I was on cloud nine. I'd done things I would not have dreamed possible at the start of the night, and wondered if I could keep this happy glow of optimism alight. How I got home I have no idea, but I do remember waving goodbye to Bea and then carefully slipping the ring off and into my purse, keeping it safe.

Chapter Twenty

I'M NOT ONE FOR hangovers, since it's so unlike me to overindulge, but wow, this is horrid. I feel like all my internal organs have had a massive fight. My mouth didn't get the memo to work normally, and tastes like the inside of a vacuum cleaner. I imagine. All dusty and grim. My eyes feel so crusty. The chemist said my contact lenses are OK being worn for up to sixteen hours, but maybe that doesn't include quick trips back a few decades.

'Ohhh wowww, you are a STATE!' David roars with laughter when he comes back in from the bathroom, pulling the curtains open. I cower from the light like a vampire.

'What the hell have you done to your hair?' He carries on laughing, at an unnecessary volume, I might add.

I tentatively reach up to touch my head and learn very swiftly that backcombing your hair with half a bottle of spray and tossing all night in bed equals not such a good look. Or feel. You know when your Barbie's been dragged around for a few years and her hair becomes a dry, matted mane? That's me, but without any of Barbie's redeeming features.

'Oh-my-gud,' I mumble croakily, trying to flatten down the candyfloss blob of hair that my previously sleek side-swept fringe has become.

'You look like a naked clown, babe!' David says, pulling on a pair of jogging bottoms.

Instinctively I wrap the duvet over myself even more tightly, embarrassed that I've been sprawled here naked with mad hair and – let me just do a touch check – yep, false lashes still on, last night's lurid make-up smeared across my face. I dread to think what 'Sugar Frost' looks like now.

'Mmmnnnooo urgghhh snnnurb,' I manage.

'Cup of tea and a round of toast?' he offers, smiling down at me, his naked clown.

'Yus pls,' I say, pulling the duvet over my head and hoping this will all stop when I re-emerge.

While David is downstairs making me some breakfast (so nice of him), I piece together the night before. The hair, the make-up, the endless free wine, the heartbroken man and the lovely way he spoke about Bea's sister, and the girl in the loos, and standing up to the sleazy man. The whole thing felt like . . . well, how do you describe it? I guess a bit like a holiday – you know, when you're away and you become like a different person? More chill, less worried about what people think of you, more willing to wear bonkers outfits(!).

It's been fun living this double life, and having a secret, special friend, but I don't know how I can keep it up. I feel like I am lying to everyone who is important to me. It's like I am half in 1989 and half in 2022, which means no one is getting my full attention. Myself included. But I also don't want to lose the joy Bea brings me. I don't really want to lose Bea, full stop.

Problem is, so much has been going on here, with my parents separating and me fighting with David, I've not been giving my real life enough time, because I've been fascinated by the ring (I feel like Frodo). I guess I've been using it as a distraction – the most extreme burying my head in the sand! Lying here in bed, my head pounding, I resolve to turn over a new leaf. If I survive this hangover, of course. Life here is what I want. I have a lovely boyfriend (OK, a bit rough around the edges, but he's boiling the kettle for me at this very moment), a job I enjoy, and – if

I let myself be a bit cocky here – one I'm really good at (and could even win an award for!), a brilliant best friend, a loving mum and dad and a lot of opportunity at my feet, if I want it. Mum's walking in the fashion show in a couple of weeks, and it won't be long till I hear if I've been shortlisted for the shop award, and secretly I'm quietly confident about it. Bea and Vivi must be rubbing off on me – confidence! You're new. 'That's it,' I decide. I'm focusing on the now. I need to find a way to keep present but also keep Bea.

'Tea and toast for my beautiful clown,' David says, placing my favourite white wooden tray down on the duvet, laden with hot jammy toast and milky tea.

'Thank you so much.' I smile up at him.

'No worries. I was thinking I might crack on with my new motor today. You don't mind, do you? I thought you'd probably want to chill and sleep it off,' he asks hopefully, like a little boy would his mother.

'So sweet of you to ask, I'll be OK here,' I say, nodding at the hot mug of tea clasped between both my hands.

'Yeah, maybe have a little wash too,' he smirks as I chuck a frilly floral cushion at his head, nearly spilling tea all over the duvet.

'Go and play with your toys!' I call to him as he pounds down the stairs, eager to start on his engine.

I sip my tea in peace and mull over the day ahead. I force myself not to think about the previous night and focus on the now. First things first, I need to sort my hair out. Whatever I do, I can't do it looking like this.

There are few things in life more relaxing than a deep bubble bath. Our cottage may be tiny, but it is definitely mighty. Our bathroom is small but perfectly formed, and somehow we have a claw-foot slipper bath (it's only three-quarter size, but I'm only five foot four so it suits me, though it was pretty hilarious the one time David tried to lie in it, giant limbs spilling out all over) that sits under the window. Today I have the window open wide and am looking out on to the roses in the back garden. The fresh air seems to be helping too.

I make a mental note of things I plan to do today. Place an online shopping order, call Mum, call Dad, pop a couple of things to the post office (made three small sales this week), reply to any direct messages on Instagram, whizz through my emails (I barely get any, but I like to keep my inbox orderly) and maybe make a start on some food prep. The perfect chill day.

Legs shaved, hair washed (and detangled – oh my God, how did girls in the 1980s cope with that much knotting?

I've used almost all of my conditioner!), fresh clothes on (have made good use of 2020's loungewear splurge and feel like I'm basically still in my PJs), and I'm back in bed checking my phone. Oops.

It doesn't take me long to reply to everything on Instagram and check my emails. I was half expecting there to be something in my inbox about the shop – but nothing. I was so sure we were supposed to have an answer by now. Vivi said they'd send details about the awards night, but maybe it's digital? Maybe my secret hopefulness was misplaced. Snail mail or virtual, it would be nice for them to let us know, rather than leave me hanging.

Text to Vivi: *Hey! Have you had anything through about the award ceremony yet? Are we shortlisted? Not bothered either way (obvs) but just wondering xxx*

Dot-dot-dots appear before I've even closed my screen. Feel like my heart has jumped into my throat as I wait for her reply. Obviously, *obviously* not at all bothered.

Reply from Vivi: *Hey bae! Nope, all sent to your address. Should be with you by now x*

Hmm. Digging a bit deeper, I go onto the award website for more information. Just like Vivi said in her text, I should have it. The website states:

ARE YOU READY TO SKYROCKET YOUR INDEPENDENT BUSINESS TO SUCCESS?

Thank you, everyone, for your nominations!

This year the Association for Excellence in Independent Business has been inundated with entries of an exceptionally high standard for the Independent Shop of the Year Award 2022.

All nominees have been notified, by post, of their award shortlist status, and we greatly look forward to our esteemed Blue Ribbon panel review of the finalists. Year on year the standard of entries increases and we are certain this year will be no different.

Please keep an eye on our social media platforms and website for details of the Independent Shop of the Year Award 2022 Award Ceremony in October! Shortlisted nominees will also receive details by post.

I read and reread the blurb on the awards landing page. 'All nominees have been notified.' I'm a nominee. I've not been notified. I read it again. And no, they've only notified the people who made it onto the shortlist, and I haven't. It's absolutely fine that I haven't made it through, I wasn't expecting to win and it's not even like I own the shop, so it's not that I'm hugely let down, it's just that ... well ... yes, OK, I'm hugely let down.

There's no way I can go on the social media business training course now. Not that I need to, anyway. I'm good with Insta, and how hard can it be to get a website designed for the shop, open Twitter and Facebook accounts and post some videos on TikTok to drive the traffic? Wow, I think to myself. You see, you already know how it all works. But still.

I'm close to tears. I sit down on the edge of the bed, my hair still wet, and give in to my emotions for a minute. Thank God I scrubbed all the make-up off, or I'd be staining my face blue with running mascara right now. After a few minutes, I decide misery likes company. I thrust my feet into my sliders with more gusto than I intended, stomp down the stairs, fling the back door open, power down the garden path and almost rip the summer house door off its hinges.

'Jesus Christ!' David welcomes me.

I don't say anything, just stand there and burst into tears.

'Oh my God! Babe! What the hell's happened?' he says, putting down his spanner (or whatever it is), walking round his workbench and coming over to cuddle me. I don't care that his hands are filthy and his hoodie smells of oil, I'm just glad of the embrace.

'I didn't get through,' I sob into his warm neck.

'Through what, my love?' he asks sympathetically.

'The shop award. I'm out of it,' I try to say through big, heaving tears. 'They didn't like my stuff.'

'Nooo, that's not it, that's not true at all. Maybe there were just better entries than you, that's what it'll be,' he soothes, holding me tighter.

'Exactly!' I cry, irritated and slightly offended.

He puts both hands firmly on my shoulders and forces me to look up at him. His brown stubble cradles his sharp jaw so well, I note through my despair. 'Tabitha, the shop is amazing. You are amazing. You didn't need this poxy award,' he tells me.

I stand there, looking up at him, trying to swallow my sobs and making wet little hiccuping snorts. From the highs of last night to the lows of today, I can't believe how far I've fallen.

'I know you're upset, but that's probably the hangover as much as anything. The award would have taken up so much time, and you'd have been way too busy with it all,' he reassures me. I'm not sure I agree, but I know he's just trying to make me feel better, and I appreciate it.

'Yeah,' I mumble, using both hands to wipe tears off my face, calming the snorting down a little.

'You don't want to be mucking around with all that social media rubbish. You want to be here, cosy, near your mum and dad, making your gorgeous boyfriend a cup of tea while he slaves over this motor,' he smiles cheekily.

'Oh, I see!' I laugh weakly.

'Go and put the kettle on and I'll be in in a minute. Maybe we could pop to the shops and do a barbecue later?' He gives me a tight squeeze and goes back to his workbench.

I know what Mum and Dad think of David, but I'm glad he's here today, I think as I plod around the kitchen. I fill the kettle, flip the switch and ping a quick text to Vivi.

Text to Vivi: *Didn't get through to the shortlist. Not bothered. Might do a BBQ. Do you and Kitty fancy joining, or busy with the show? x*

I expect she'll be busy and I don't want to say I'm upset, but deep down I'd love her here. Kitty brings such a lovely energy to the house, and I want Vivi to tell me my shop window displays were the best, not that the other entrants were better – even if it's probably true.

'Ohhh a cuppa will cure what ails you, even in summer,' David says, coming through the door and wiping his hands on my nice tea towel. I bought that last year from an antiques emporium with Mum. I hang it on the cooker handle more for show, but David takes no notice of things like that. I open my mouth to tell him but he pips me to the post.

'I've packed my tools away. Whatever you want to do this afternoon, we can do,' he smiles, chucking the embroidered towel onto the worktop behind him.

Wow. It's not like David to put me above a car. Maybe I won't moan about the tea towel after all.

'Ohhh, David! Thank you,' I coo, walking over and nuzzling into him again. I feel so needy hanging off him like this, but I don't care. This is what boyfriends are for, isn't it? Even independent women need support sometimes.

'Maybe we could go and visit Dad and Bernie? Feels like we haven't seen them in ages,' I suggest.

'We saw them a few weeks ago, didn't we?' David cuddles me back.

'Not properly. They came into the Weathered Oak as we were finishing our meal. We didn't spend proper time with Dad, did we?' I protest.

'Why don't you see if your dad wants to come over then, join us for the barbecue.' David smiles, squeezing me and stroking my hair.

'Good idea. With Bernie too, though?' I add, just to make sure we're on the same page.

'Why are you so desperate to have Gay Bernard over?'

David asks, pulling away to make his tea now the kettle I put on has boiled.

'Er, I'm not? It's just, they are a couple, and that's the nice thing to do,' I say, recoiling at him referring to Bernie as 'Gay Bernard'.

'It is, but I don't need to see all that in my own back garden,' he says casually, reaching for a mug off the stand.

'All what?' I ask, feeling instantly defensive on Dad's behalf.

'You know all what.' He smiles, trying to get me onside.

'I think you're referring to their sexuality, and I'm not going to have it. You're being an actual homophobe! It's 2022. What the fuck's wrong with you?' I say, with a lot more force than I expected.

We're both taken aback, and David looks immediately affronted.

'No, no, no! Absolutely not! Keith at the garage is gay, and I don't have any issues with him,' he backtracks.

'But you do have an issue with my dad, don't you?' I challenge.

'You're buzzing,' David says, pointing at me.

'I'm bloody what?' I start to shout, all my emotions from earlier added to the excitement of last night bubbling up and almost over.

'Your phone is ringing in your pocket and vibrating,' he says matter-of-factly, like he hasn't just been a disgusting pig.

'Right, well, we'll leave this here, shall we?' I say, rummaging to reach my phone in time but missing it. 'I'm going upstairs to call Vivienne back,' I say, livid but managing to squish it all back down safely in its box. We'll tackle the Dad and Bernie situation later. I let a lot slide, but I'm not letting that one go.

Chapter Twenty-One

VIVI KNOWS HOW OUT of character a night of wine and talking to strange men, even if innocently, would be for me, so hangs on my every word as I regale her with what happened.

'So the ring worked further than just the travel agent's?' Vivi asks.

'Yep,' I say, biting my thumbnail, still churned up from David's comments a moment ago.

'In-ter-est-ing,' she says, enunciating every syllable.

'Why? Did you think it wouldn't?' I wonder if she has any insight on what the hell is going on.

'Well, it just means that if you are imagining it

all, you're really imagining hard if you can make up multiple locations.'

'I'm not imagining it, Vivienne! Last night I went out to a 1989 wine bar, danced with my arms in the air, and felt freer than I've ever felt in my life.'

A quick spill of my last twenty-four hours later, and Vivi is coming over. 'Pals before charity fashion shows,' she says, agreeing that we probably need to work on something a bit more catchy. 'I need a full debrief on all this before you zoom back to your new best friend again!' She laughs. I really need to give her more of my love and attention. It's so hard splitting your time, especially between eras.

Ninety minutes' pottering upstairs organising my stash of Victorian jewellery to sell, David watching TV in ignorant bliss that I'm at all wound up, and things have calmed down. I don't agree with what he says but I don't have the energy to fight him – or at least, not yet. I check out the window to see if Vivi's walking down yet, my knight in shining armour.

Happily, I was right; Kitty fills the house with a joy only children can bring. She's ecstatic to be helping me pick some roses to make pretty bouquets with. 'I'm actually a flower expert,' she tells David as she directs him on which blooms she'd like snipping with the secateurs, and I roll out (shop bought, shhh) pastry to make a feta tartlet. 'Are you?' I hear him ask. 'Yep, I was on the gardening committee at school, and we grew loads and then put them in vases in the dining room and I chose which ones went where. It's because I have design flair,' she says with a self-assurance I'd kill for.

The apple doesn't fall far from the tree, I muse as I trim the pastry and Vivi picks at the offcuts from her seat across the table.

'I've been trying to think of ways I can make more money,' Vivi announces out of nowhere.

'Haven't we all?' I quip back, thinking of my ever-growing Insta nest egg.

'Not for me, but for the charity. To boost the fashion show ticket sales,' she adds.

'Yes! Sorry! God, I sound so greedy now.' I laugh nervously, reaching for my egg-wash brush, wishing I hadn't said that.

'Nothing greedy about a woman earning some cold hard cash! You get those pounds in the bank,' Vivi asserts with a floury flourish of her hand.

'Ha, I'm trying,' I say. 'Not that I need to. I'm happy with what I have, but you know, nice to have savings,' I add, almost tripping over my words.

'Again, there's no shame in you wanting to have your own stash, whatever it's for,' Vivienne reassures me, rolling a pea-sized ball of pastry between her thumb and forefinger.

'Yes. Absolutely. Anyway, you want to raise money for charity?'

'Mm-hmm. Just want to give as much time and energy as I can, and with all the focus on your shop and the award—'

'That I lost,' I can't help interjecting bitterly.

'That you didn't lose, and did very well to go as far as you did—'

'Which was because you put me up for it. I did nothing.' It's crazy to be this upset over something I didn't even know I wanted, but I can't help myself. I didn't realise how good it would feel to stand tall, and the prospect of that was a taste of what I could have had all the time if I'd made it through.

'Stop it! You're not having a pity party on this!' Vivi squashes the ball of pastry with her forefinger onto the table. 'And we are absolutely still going to feature your Pearls and Doodles vintage outfits, which you will style, in our fashion show finale. Don't even think we won't.'

'Yeah, but—' I try.

'ANYWAY.' She cuts me off with a smile. Years of practice have shown Vivi it is best not to let me spiral.

'I'm taking a leaf out of your book and I'm going to find valuable things, sell them for a profit and raise a tonne of cash! What do you think?' she asks as though she's just come up with the plan of her life.

'I love it, obviously. Very up my street.' I'm distracted from my loss and feel a sense of fizzy excitement at the idea of helping my friend do something I love so much. I'm not sure how helpful or patient Kitty will be at car boot sales, but I'm excited to have a buddy (or two) for them.

'I know! You've made thousands,' she says, so much louder than she needed to.

'Shhh,' I panic. I've not deliberately kept it from him, but I still haven't told David how much I've made. It's not that I wouldn't share it with him, but something's always made me feel like I should have my own little back-up. For what I'm not sure, but you know when you have that niggle? It's been like that.

'Sorry, sorry,' Vivi whispers, theatrically crouching in her chair.

'I have made thousands, but it's been over the years. Takes ages to find the good gems. I don't just come across them all at once,' I tell her, looking over both my shoulders as if David's crept up behind me and is about to yell, 'Aha!'

'Oh yeah, hadn't thought of that.' She sits back in her chair, deflated.

'You could ask people to help, though! Bet there's loads of old biddies round here with all kinds of junk in their attic they'd love to donate.' I didn't mean to put her off the idea, just wanted her to shut up. This is all getting a bit stressful!

'Any in yours?' she asks with a knowing smile.

'This is why you came round, isn't it?' I grin back.

'Nooo. Definitely not. You had a big night last night on the wine . . . *in 1989*,' she adds a bit pointedly. Maybe she's sick of my tales. 'And you've had a row with Dicky out there. You need a friend,' she soothes.

'First of all, I don't like your tone on the 1989 bit, but the less said about that the better. Don't call him "Dicky", and I always need a friend. I'm glad you're here.' I flick a little bit of feta over at her as I drizzle more oil onto our delicious creation.

I pass Vivi the little glass jar of Italian herbs to sprinkle on the tartlet and pop my head round the back door. Kitty is bossing David round the garden while he gracefully obliges her in cutting roses and laying them in a little wicker tray she must have found in the shed. He's so good with her. As per, I can't help but imagine him as a dad.

'Babe?' I call gently.

'Mmm?' He turns round smiling, rose in hand.

'I'm just going to pop up in the attic to find some bits for Vivi,' I call.

David looks horrified.

'No, babe, that'll make such a mess! I've got it all organised up there,' he protests as Kitty huffs at the interruption.

'Eh? I'm literally going to have a quick look through those boxes at the back and be down again.' I start to feel frustrated.

His cheeks flush the same colour as the rose in his hand. 'No! I know what you're like, you'll be rummaging around for ages, stuff everywhere. I'll go for you when we're done here, OK?' Kitty smiles eagerly, willing us to finish so she can carry on with her selection process.

'All right. No need to be so stressy about it!' I say, a bit taken aback at how rude he's been. He's right; I would have a good rummage, but who cares if the attic is messy, it's not like anyone sees up there, anyway. I live here and I haven't been up in about six bloody months!

I turn back into the kitchen from the back door. 'David says I can't—'

'I heard him,' she says, rolling her eyes hard. 'Can I have a rummage in the spare room wardrobe? All your vintage bits? I PROMISE NOT TO MAKE A BIG MESS.' She adds the last sentence just for David's benefit, and I can't say I mind, even though realistically he won't hear her out there. Petty but satisfying.

'Why yes, Vivienne, you can. I'm glad you won't make a giant mess or we won't be allowed in there again by Sir David,' I semi-shout, again just to make sure he hears.

We run up the stairs, half giggling at the cheek of it, and fling open the spare bedroom wardrobe. Vivi starts flicking through, asking if I want this and this and this and this. It doesn't take long to ascertain that I do in fact want to keep everything. I've managed to part with one very small silk coin purse, but anything else feels like giving up precious offspring.

'You can't possibly feel emotionally attached to every single thing in here!' Vivienne exclaims. 'You don't even wear any of it out the house. You just don't need it.' She leans back on the bedroom wall. It's so hot up here; digging through the wardrobe has taken it out of us.

I'm slightly stung that she's suggested I don't wear my vintage clothes, when I do. I've worn a few pieces out when visiting Bea. I feel OK there. Free. But now's not the time to delve into all that with Vivi.

'My dear, lovely Vivi, you are a minimalist. You can

never understand the sublime joy of having fifteen beaded clutch bags, all lined up and sparkling away. You can't grasp the feeling of finding another hand-rolled silk scarf and bringing it home to your collection, washing it meticulously in the bathroom sink so it's fresh as new. You can't wallow gleefully in the glory of hand-sewing for hours to restore something to its former glory. You can never—'

'Yeah, OK, I get it. You love them, you work hard on them. Can we go in the loft then? You surely can't get "sublime joy" from your dusty old boxes, can you?' she huffs playfully.

'Aha, no, but David said we can't.' I struggle to make eye contact; I feel like a silly little girl.

'So is David your dad now?' Vivi goads, hitting that sore spot perfectly.

'No, obviously not, but he's worried about the mess, and . . .' I trail off. I'm not sure who I want to argue with here. David or Vivienne.

'Good job I'm the tidy minimalist then! What he doesn't know won't hurt him,' Vivienne says with mischief all over her face.

I can feel my heart quicken and my palms are sweating. This is absurd. I can go into my own loft if I want to! We walk out onto the landing and gaze up at the hatch.

'Just . . . don't want to cause an argument,' I say, looking at the carpet, embarrassed at how ridiculously weak I must sound.

'Baaabe.' I know Vivi means business when she brings out the 'babe' talk. 'You're not doing anything wrong, you aren't owned or controlled by your boyfriend, you are entitled to make as much mess as you like, but we're not going to anyway. Plus, surely he's starting the argument by banning you?' She looks straight into my eyes and I feel my willpower dissolve.

I nod submissively, glad to have her take control, feeling exceptionally stupid but completely relieved.

She continues. 'Look, we don't need to talk about this right now because we're going to go in the loft, but maybe, at some point, when we're totally alone, we should talk about you and David. I'll support you whatever you do in life, I'm your bestie forever, but I hate seeing you like this. You're better than this.' For a moment, I feel frozen. But then, without saying another word, Vivi steps forward and wraps her arms right round me, the same way you do for worked up little toddlers who need a mummy cuddle.

We stand on the landing and hug. Vivienne holds me for longer than any normal hug and I let her, even though she's a bit sweaty. I'll perhaps not spoil the moment by asking if she wants a squirt of perfume. I know she's right. I know I need to be stronger; it's just so hard. I know I can do it. If I can dance on a stage with my arms in the air wearing a rara skirt and fishnets, I can do anything. It's just, right now I don't have it in me. Shame is what I think I have in me. Shame at being so weak and allowing a man to make me feel controlled like this. To my horror, tears trickle down my cheeks, making two little dark patches on Vivi's grey cotton top.

Anticipating how much I hate showing any kind of emotion to anyone, Vivi says, 'I'm a mum. I'm used to a few tears. It's all right. I'm glad you're having a cry, it reminds me you're human,' she soothes, still hugging me. 'Been a funny twenty-four hours, eh?'

'Mmm-hmm. Just feel so stupid,' I sniffle, pulling away.

'You know what would be even more stupid?' she asks, putting her hands up on my shoulders and giving me a little shake.

'What?' I struggle to think of something more stupid than this.

'If we didn't wipe your face, dust you off and get up there.' She gives me one last extra-tight squeeze, pushes the tears off my face with her palms and smiles in that way only mums do.

'Thank you,' I manage.

'I love you. I've got your back. Now, where's your big pole?' She looks round expectantly.

'What?' I splutter.

'For the loft, to pull the hatch down.'

Back to business. I've got this.

Chapter Twenty-Two

I HARDLY EVER COME UP here. As with everything in our house, it's teeny-tiny. The floor space spans the map of the two bedrooms and bathroom below it but the roof slants in, making the standing space very snug indeed.

To our left is a big heap of boxes where the Christmas decorations are kept; to the right are all the old boxes of treasure I've found over the years and not quite had a home for, things from Granny Maeve on Dad's side (he knew I'd love all her old bits and pieces), and a few from David's side that I'll be extra careful not to touch. Above the stacked-up boxes is a tiny little window which is encrusted in cobwebs but lets in a beam of sunshine, highlighting the dust and adding to the stuffiness.

'Oh my God, if there are rats up here I'm going to scream!' Vivi states, a slight change of tune from her empowering chat five minutes earlier.

'I don't have rats in my house, thank you very much,' I quip back, not definitely sure that we don't.

'Mice then,' she says, wiping what I'd expect are sweaty palms down her sides. It was hot enough before, but up here it's sweltering.

'The most you'll be bothered by is a family of friendly spiders,' I say, making scuttling actions with my hand and climbing over an old upturned armchair to the boxes we want. I really must have that chair upholstered soon.

'Right, this is them. Shall we take one each?' I suggest, gingerly picking up a box, not wanting to wipe dust all over my clothes, even if they are just my lockdown loungewear.

'Yep,' she says, squeezing past the chair to join me, grimacing. One day, when I've done every other job, I'll bring the vacuum up here and sort it out. I'll put everything in matching clear containers with little labels on like the organised vloggers do. I drift off into a happy daydream thinking about how satisfying that day will be.

'Argh!' Vivi squeals, snapping me back. 'I swear to God, if I get caught up in all these bloody webs I'm gonna— Arrrgghhh!'

'Shh-shh-shhh,' I giggle. 'David will hear you. He's only outside!' I gesture towards the back of the building, trying not to laugh even louder at how ridiculous my usually bolder-than-bold friend looks, all flinching and squirming near one of the eaves of the house.

'I don't bloody care! Get that thing away from me.' Vivi bats her hands about. There is an envelope hanging off the windowsill and I pick it up, swirling an old web round like some kind of horrible arachnid candyfloss and wiggling it at her.

'Ha! Sorry, couldn't resist,' I say, wiping the webs off onto the beam next to me.

It takes me a second, but I notice the envelope isn't as old as I'd expect, and it isn't empty, plus it's addressed to me.

'This is mine, I think,' I say, turning it over in my hands, noticing it's been neatly opened but with the letter left in.

'I'd hope so, since we're in your house,' Vivi says, crouching to open her first dusty box and pulling out some yellowing scrunched-up newspaper.

'No, I mean, this is a letter addressed to me that I've not opened. Someone has, but I wouldn't have brought it up here. Think it's a bill, it's official. How weird is this?' I say, looking at Vivi.

'Why would you put a bill in the loft? Just read it. Maybe you forgot,' she says, still not really paying much attention to me.

My heart is pounding. Something about this makes me feel really uneasy. I slide my finger into the white paper envelope and pull out my letter. I read it out loud:

'Dear Miss Burnley, we are delighted to have received Ms Vivienne Hawkins' nomination of your independent shop for the Independent Shop of the Year Award 2022.

'The Association for Excellence in Independent Business are pleased to inform you that your shop has been shortlisted by our esteemed Blue Ribbon panel. Your independent shop Pearls and Doodles has, along with nine other enterprises, made it through to the finalists of this year's award.'

'What?' Vivi says slowly, stopping mid-riffle through the box, looking up and paying full attention now.

'So . . . the shop . . . our entry . . . it . . . it made it,' I say slowly as all the information trickles through my brain.

'Why is it up here though?' Vivi is as confused as I am.

'Well, I think it's fair to say that I didn't pick the post up off the mat, take it upstairs, climb a ladder and file it away on the attic windowsill,' I say, rage starting to fire through my veins.

Vivienne, still kneeling by her box, gazes up at me open-mouthed. In all the years we've known each other I don't think I've seen her speechless.

'That bastard!' I whisper, almost shaking with anger now.

'OK, maybe there's a reason, let's not fly off the handle,' Vivi reasons uncharacteristically.

'There is a reason, and it's that he's a fucking *bastard*!' I say a bit louder now, not wincing at the swearing like I usually would. 'Earlier, when I thought he was being *so* kind, he said I didn't need all that extra fuss. More like he didn't want me focused on something that wasn't him!' I fume. 'I'm so *stupid*!'

'First off, you're not stupid. Don't ever say that,' Vivi says, coming back to life and standing up as best she can in the tight space, trying to avoid the webs.

'Secondly, I'm going to pack up my stuff and take Kitty home. I think you guys need to talk,' she says, purposely not giving an opinion, scrambling to put the crushed paper back in the box. 'We'll do this another day, yeah?'

'Yeah,' I say, breathing hard, the letter clutched tightly in my hand.

'You're better than this rubbish, Tabs. So much better,' she says, gesturing at the letter in my hand, a soft sadness in her voice that I wasn't expecting.

'I bloody am,' I say, bolder than I've ever felt before.

'You off, Viv?' David says as he clocks her picking up Kitty's little straw sun hat from the hook by the door. He's come into the kitchen now, secateurs left on the side, pink and cream roses strewn all over the table and the feta tartlet cooling on the side for later.

'Yep. Kitty, come here please. We've got to get going,' she says tightly with no elaboration at all.

'But I've not had any tart yet. David took it out of the oven because you were taking ages with Tabitha! I've been waiting to have some,' she protests as she climbs down off the kitchen chair.

'Don't worry, sweetie, I'll put some in a special takeaway box,' I say, my voice quivering a little, knowing I'm about to explode.

'Yay! Can I have two slices then?' she says with glee. Only Vivienne's daughter would have a taste for feta tart with balsamic glaze.

'Yes, yes! Two slices coming up.' I squeeze past David in the kitchen, who makes room by moving into the lounge. Passing her the box, I say my goodbyes, trying to sound as cool and collected as possible.

'Love you lots, have a good night with Mummy and I'll

see you soon.' I usher them out, giving Vivi a quick squeeze. We don't need to say anything to each other.

'Don't I get a goodbye then?' David calls from his spot on the sofa.

The nanosecond the door is shut I spin round in my socks and stride over to him, standing right in front of his eyeline.

'Gorg, you're in the way of the telly,' he says, looking bemused.

'David, you know I don't like confrontation, but I need to tell you something,' I begin, legs secretly trembling in my jersey joggers.

'OK, cool, but could you tell me out of the way of the TV, please?' he asks, moving his head to the side to see past me.

I keep my composure as best I can.

'This won't take long. I went up in the—'

'Could it not take long away from the telly, please, love? It's a good bit.' He smiles up at me, completely oblivious to the anger radiating from every fibre of my being.

'David.' I draw a breath to steady myself. 'Unfortunately—'

'Tabitha, honestly, get out of the way of the TV!' David interrupts, losing his patience.

It was almost palpable. I think I actually felt myself snap. It was sensational.

'Fuck your fucking TV!' I scream at the top of my lungs as I reach round, grab the top of the flat screen off its little stand and rip it down, watching it smash onto the corner of the coffee table and then go completely silent.

'Fuck you, and fuck your TV you sly, lying bastard!' I continue, so loudly I almost scare myself.

David, as you'd expect, is utterly stunned. He doesn't speak, he doesn't move, I'd wager he doesn't even breathe for a couple of seconds either.

'Didn't want me to make a mess?' I rage, shaking the somewhat crumpled letter at him, broken bits of TV plastic round my feet.

'I . . . I . . . it was . . .' he trails off, clocking the letter in my hand for the first time and looking horrified. Even more horrified than a man who has just watched his beloved TV get smashed to smithereens.

'No! Absolutely not! You read my letter, took something I really wanted, something I deserved, that's all about the work I love! You didn't even have the balls to destroy it. You just hid it like the pathetic little coward you are.' I'm so past filtering myself that I couldn't do it now even if I tried. It's all coming out, and I feel magnificent for it. Why have I held every tiny thing in for all this time?

'No, it wasn't . . . I . . . you've got it wrong . . . I was protecting you from not winning in the end,' he tries, falling over his words.

'No, you weren't. You couldn't bear for me to have something of my own, to experience a sliver of success that didn't revolve round you,' I spit. More and more tumbles out.

'Gorgeous, you're working yourself up, you're being all emotional,' he weasels.

'Do you know what, David?' I say, this time a bit calmer, a bit more in control, feeling more powerful than I ever have in my whole life.

'You realise how insane you're being?' he says, becoming bolder now I'm not shouting and have taken a small step back from looming over him on the sofa.

'No. I realise it is normal to be emotional when your supposed partner has screwed you over. Your controlling, narcissistic, Stone Age partner. Maybe *you're* not being emotional enough!' I say, throwing my hands in the air to labour the point.

We both pause, neither of us really knowing where to go now, this is such uncharted territory.

'I think you might be overreacting. Has Vivienne worked you up to this? Plotted for you to have your little hissy fit?' He's clearly feeling brave, sensing I've run out of steam, knowing how unlike me this all is.

'No, David, I've decided to do this all by myself. Isn't it something? Shall I tell you what else I'm going to do all by myself as well?' I half-smile.

David blinks at me.

'Leave you.' I raise my eyebrows a fraction and stand stock-still.

'Tabithaaa,' David says, shifting on his sofa spot, wringing his hands, obviously a little panicked now. 'You don't mean this. Let's calm down and talk about it. I'll forgive you for breaking the TV, and we can talk things through and make up, eh?' He pats the sofa next to him, beckoning me over. As if I'm going to sit down and get cosy now. The lazy git hasn't even had the decency to stand up and fight for this, hasn't begged me to stay. Underwhelming in the relationship and underwhelming in the break-up. No thank you.

'Forgive this!' I say, stamping my foot so hard into the remains of the TV that a few shards of casing fly off, leaving David dramatically cowering with his arms over his face.

I leave the room (trying not to wince as I feel the blood from my newly cut foot coming through my sliders; apparently they're not built for TV stomping), run upstairs, pack a bag (not forgetting the ring, which I still haven't returned to the shop but will the second I get the chance), grab the car keys and drive straight to my mum's house where she opens the door and I promptly burst into huge, heaving sobs for the third time today. Bloody hell.

Chapter Twenty-Three

'THEY ALWAYS SAY THEY didn't see the red flags, but Mum, I did! I saw them and ignored them. What's wrong with me?' I sob, my head in her lap on the lounge sofa while she strokes my hair lovingly.

Mum has been brilliant. She rang Julia and said I wouldn't be in work for the whole week. At first I was silently concerned because I still have the ring and Julia might think I've stolen it, while Bea will be wondering where I am and, to be honest, I just want to see her and tell her what's happened. She always seems to know just what to say to make things better.

I quickly let it go, though, because in times of need, Mum is what you want most so I focus on mine again. She's cooked me all my favourite dinners and served me all my most-loved puddings. She didn't moan when I spent the first three days lying on the sofa with my duvet, watching trash TV about women trying to find love by interviewing men blindfolded, or the ones where two families swap homes and realise that the true meaning of life isn't money. When she noticed I hadn't washed my hair in four days, she ran me a bath, I got in and she washed it for me. She drove over to my cottage and took all my clothes out of the bedroom wardrobe and carefully folded up all my precious vintage bits from the guest room wardrobe and put them in a huge wicker hamper to bring home.

'There's nothing wrong with you, sweetheart. You wanted it to work, and so you tried your best to make it what you wanted,' she says ever so kindly.

'I wanted to be happy and looked after, but not in the old-fashioned, bad way – I can look after myself – but just in a nice way,' I mumble, fiddling with the frayed drawstring on my pyjama shorts.

'There's nothing wrong with wanting to be looked after, as long as you're prepared to look after him too,' Mum soothes.

'I did look after him! I never strayed. I supported his hobbies. I cooked for him. I watched hours and hours of his fucking stupid car TV programmes!' I say, feeling the heat rise in me again.

'Don't let him work you up again, love, he's not worth it. He's nothing and you're everything,' Mum whispers. She used to do this thing when I was very little where she would whisper when everyone else was angry or shouting. It forced us to be quiet to listen, and there's something very calming about her doing it again.

I sit up and look at her, tears running down my face. 'He lied to me, Mum. I can't bear it. If he could hide something that important from me, what else was he hiding?' Fresh tears roll down my cheeks. My face stings from how many times I've cried and wiped, cried and wiped.

'There are things hidden in every relationship,' Mum says, looking at her wedding band and engagement ring, still on her left hand.

'Oh Mum, sorry, I'm being so insensitive.' Guilt washes over me for being so selfish. We watch a little more of the film Mum had put on before I started crying, and then I excuse myself and go to bed.

The next day is Thursday, five days post-TV smash. I wonder if David has replaced it yet. The first night after I left he came to Mum's and she wouldn't let him in. She told him she'd call the police if he didn't get back in his car. When he refused and insisted he was coming in, she shouted, 'If you continue to threaten to enter me I will call the police!'

I wasn't sure if it was the fact that my historically mild-mannered mother was shouting and alerting the attention of the neighbours, or that she messed up and said 'enter me' instead of 'enter my house', but she came inside beetroot red and burst out laughing.

'Oh my giddy aunt! I said "enter me"!' She howled with laughter, reaching out to the wall for support. 'Nigel was out trimming the bushes and I shouted "enter me"!' she roared, having to sit down on the stairs to stop herself keeling over.

'Mum, I can't believe you shouted, never mind yelled about him . . . *entering* . . . you! Who are you, and what have you done with my mother?' I joke.

Suddenly the energy in the air changed. Mum stood up and brushed the invisible dust off her. 'Well, deary me, I wasn't having David coming in here and upsetting you. I'll put the dinner on and we can forget all about it, eh?' and she marched off towards the kitchen, leaving me to peer out of the hall window to check he definitely had left. He had, but Nigel the neighbour was still looking pretty alarmed.

That night I had to turn my phone off. David was ringing incessantly and I didn't have the energy to answer.

I rang Vivienne off the ancient home phone and it felt like old times, sitting on the stairs, winding the curly wire round my fingers as we talked. She said she was proud of me and that I was welcome to stay with her any time. I thought about it and decided to stay where I was. Vivienne is wonderful but I knew Mum would go full mumsy mode, which is exactly what I needed.

By Tuesday I'd managed to turn my phone back on. I think David had sent me more messages in those two days than he had in our entire ten-year relationship. They started off irate, then he calmed down and apologised for everything (repeatedly) and then, when he realised I wasn't responding, sent long irrational rambles, twisting and turning it so things were all my fault.

Tabby Cat, please come home. I'm sorry I was such an arse. I was stupid. I don't even know why I did it. I'm so sorry. It's not the same here without you. I need you. I love you. I'm so sorry things went wrong. Let's forget it and start fresh. Come home tonight please xxxx

Tabby let's start again. I'm sorry you were so upset but we can sort it out. I miss you and love you and want you back xxxxx

Tabs this is so stupid. I've said I'm sorry and will keep s aying it but it's time to sort this out now. Time to come home. I love you xxx

Tabitha I love you and I want this to work. We've both made mistakes and I'm willing to let go of that and make the most of what we have now. I'm sorry you found the letter, I'm sorry I didn't tell you that the shop stuff was getting a bit much for me. I love you and I know you love me but you staying at your mum's isn't helping. How can we be together if we're not together? Like I said, I want this to work and I love you so let's talk xxx

I didn't reply to any of them.

Babe, I'm not having this now, it's all getting a bit silly, isn't it? I don't mind you working longer hours, I don't mind you not really being around much but you ignoring me is out of order. How are we supposed to get anywhere with you being like this? Come home please and I'm willing to let it all go and start fresh. If you're worried about the telly, I've sorted a new one and I'm willing to forgive and forget X

I forwarded this one to Vivi and she offered Neil's mates to go and 'sort him out', but I suggested doorstep violence probably wasn't the answer here.

Then things got worse.

OK then, let's leave it. I've tried my best with you, given you everything but you've done nothing to make this work. You've shown violent behaviour and I'm obviously not safe in my own home. You should be ashamed of yourself. I saw all the stuff your mum took. Bags and bags of jewellery. Clearly you've been hiding more than I ever could have. How are you affording all that? You're obviously doing something extra to pay for it. Disgusting. Good luck, Tabitha, I'm out. I deserve more than your lies and deceit.

Incidentally, the 'bags and bags' were three sandwich bags of broken sterling silver pieces I'd bought in an online auction. I was planning on mending them to sell. I suppose deep down I did know I was keeping them from him.

The next day, another.

Hi Tabitha, I'm a decent man so I'm willing to give you one more chance. I think it's best you look at your life and work out what's really important. Are you really willing to lose everything for a low-level job in retail? I'm willing to put in the time to help you prove yourself as proper wife material. I love you and I'm here to help you. Time to come home now, thank you xx

His messages appalled us all. Mum, Vivi and I were horrified at how far wrong he was going, amazed that he believed this nonsense. I cried till the delicate skin around my eyes felt sore. All this time he'd held these views, he'd had this poison in him, and all this time I'd loved him.

I was glad he sent his vile messages. They helped cement the fact that I'd made the right decision. I didn't regret smashing up his TV and leaving. I regret not smashing up his car parts as well.

But, as much as I hated everything he'd said, I hated even more the time he'd taken from me. Could everyone see his true colours except me? Or maybe, and I'm ashamed this thought slipped into my mind, maybe he was right about some of it. I did keep that jewellery from him. I've kept all the profits I've made from my DIYs from him. I've kept a time-altering ring from him, for goodness' sake!

'I'm just as bad as him, Dad,' I confessed when Dad came over to see me during a particularly low moment. Mum had gone out to M&S for 'a bit of me time', after greeting Dad at the door more warmly than I'd have expected.

'No, love. Squirrelling away some broken necklaces is not the same as hiding someone else's opportunities.' He reaches his hand across the dining room table and gives mine a little squeeze. Mum had laid out the old linen cloth, perfectly ironed of course, and put out a freshly baked lemon drizzle sponge.

'Secrets destroy relationships,' Dad says, looking at our hands. 'Look at me and your mum.'

'Oh, Dad. It's all been such a lot, hasn't it? I feel like I've not been there for you. I've been so self-absorbed. I didn't know what to say.' I prod my fork into my last bit of lemon drizzle.

'Don't think any of us did. I didn't know what to say for years.' Dad smiles kindly.

'Have you always known?' I look up at him, almost afraid of the answer.

'Yes, I think so. I never felt particularly attracted to ladies, but I didn't know if that was "normal". Men didn't talk about their feelings when I was young, and there's a lot of masculine bravado. It wasn't like it is now. Your Granny Maeve knew, but wouldn't have any of it. She pushed and pushed for me to find "the right woman to sort it out", and she was glad when I met your mum.'

I look at the cake, wondering when would be a good time to cut another slice but sensing it's not now.

'I did love your mum, Tabs. Still love her. Just . . . not romantically,' he says, awkwardly.

'You had me, though,' I say, skirting around the fact that there must have been a degree of romance involved.

'Well, yes . . .' He clears his throat. 'You should talk to your mother about that,' Dad says, really uncomfortable discussing anything to do with his sex life, understandably.

We pause and sit in silence, but not the comfortable type. The air is heavy. Dad looks like he's wrestling with himself to say something. It must be so hard for him to share his side after all this time.

'OK. Listen, I know we're not the talking-about-our-feelings sort,' I begin, 'but I want you to know I love you, and will love Bernie too. I can see how happy he makes you, and that's all I want. I'm going to speak to David about him moving out and finding somewhere else to live, and then I'm going to have you both round for afternoon tea in the garden and it'll be lovely.' I realise of course that at some point I'll have to come up with more rent, without David paying half, but don't dwell on that one for the moment. I have my nest egg.

'I see. You just want me to come and do the roses, don't you,' he teases, finally cutting another slice of Mum's sponge.

'Aha! You've got me.' I giggle.

Mum manages to spend over three hours in M&S, which is almost impressive. Dad and I don't discuss his relationship with Bernie anymore but the air feels lighter. I'm glad I told him I loved him, and I think we are both ready to start a new chapter.

When Mum comes back, laden down with bags, she announces she's finally found the 'perfect Ruth Langsford pencil skirt' and asks Dad if he wants to stay for dinner.

Startled, Dad accepts the invite. As if trying to shock us even further, Mum suggests ordering a curry.

'I thought you weren't keen on foreign food, Mum?' I say, flabbergasted. I could count on one hand the number of takeaways I've seen Mum order.

'Live and let live, Tabitha! That's my motto.' Mum takes her bags upstairs, leaving Dad and I speechless.

'Wish I'd known twenty years ago that was her motto,' Dad smirks.

Chapter Twenty-Four

I NEVER WANT TO MAKE a fuss, but coming to Mum's and not going to work is just about the biggest fuss I've ever made – bar smashing up David's telly. I think of the letter, the trashed TV, driving to Mum's with hot tears streaming down my face. Reading the award letter properly at Mum's was another blow. I've not been on the social media business course now, and I rang the award sponsors to apologise. They were fine about it when I explained what had happened, and we've organised for the judging panel to view the shop and take publicity shots, just before the fashion show presentation.

I've cried for days, I've screamed into a pillow ('wonderful relief, but you don't want to overdo it or you'll hurt your throat,' warned ever-practical Mum) and passive-aggressively shared a selection of pretty quotes on Instagram about what 'real love' is and how honesty is so important – obviously all cheered on by Vivi. Might delete those later. The tone is not too in keeping with the vintage aesthetic I was going for.

With all of that, a tonne of Mum's cooking and a lot of doing absolutely nothing, a calm has descended.

For the first time in a while, I feel almost relaxed. I don't feel like I'm working to anyone else's timetable or agenda, I don't have to please anyone, I don't have to be something I'm not. I'm not torn between two time periods. It's as though I was walking round with hundreds of bags hung off my shoulders, and now I've put most of them down.

There's one thing, though, that's been bothering me.

'Mum,' I start as we clear away the breakfast things from the dining table on Saturday. Of course Mum has a full sit-down breakfast ready on the weekend.

'If you're going to ask me why I still like to eat my breakfast at a properly laid table, it's because I have standards, Tabitha,' Mum interjects – she knows me well.

'No, I wasn't going to ask that,' I reply, noting that she might be all sexy skirts and new-old man, but she's the same old Barbara Burnley.

'Apologies. Go on then love,' she says, putting the selection of home-made jams back into the fridge. I mean, does she need to get four different jams out on the table when she's only having one slice of toast? I daren't ask.

'Dad was a bit strange the other day.' I watch Mum's face intently. If she seems upset I'll stop, but so far, no obvious distress at the mention of the man who left her just before she served a spotted dick.

'He's going through a lot, Tabitha. He's probably still processing it all. I expect he felt a bit strange being back in his marital home,' she says, moving into the dining room to retrieve more breakfast paraphernalia.

'Yes. There's definitely that . . . but also something else,' I say tentatively, trailing after her. 'I'm sure I'm being silly and overthinking it, but I just want to tell you and then you can tell me if I am, OK? Being silly,' I ask, picking up the three straw place mats (one for each of us and one for the jams) to put away in the kitchen.

'All right,' Mum says, matter-of-fact, one hand leaning on the back of a dining room chair, the other on her hip. She seems so together and powerful. Definitely an energy I want to note and copy. No time for that, though; it's time to delve into what's been playing on my mind, like when you get a really annoying song stuck in your head for days on end.

'Right. Well, sorry if this is weird or awkward,' I start, not at all together and powerful. 'When he said he thought maybe he'd always known, deep down, you know, about how he feels about men, right? I said that you two had had me, and so there must have been . . . *something* there . . . right?' Wow, it's hard talking about sex to a mum like my mum.

'Right,' Mum says, walking past me to put the plates in the dishwasher. I'm grateful we don't have to make continuous eye contact throughout this.

'And then he said I should speak to you,' I say to her back as she pulls the dishwasher door down. I can see her upper arm muscles tense and she pauses for just a second, long enough for me to know it's hit a nerve.

'Perhaps he didn't like to talk about S-E-X, Tabitha,' Mum says. Not a problem she's had herself recently – I still blush when I think about it. But I get it when it comes to Dad; I certainly don't want to talk about Dad's sex life with Mum – or lack thereof – but I've come this far now, and I feel like something's not being said.

'I know, sorry, I thought that too, but I dunno, there was just a strangeness to it. I know you had me later than you would have liked. I just wondered if, well, maybe I was one of those . . .' I take a deep breath. *Why is this so awkward?*

'Test-tube babies . . . ?' I almost flinch as I say it. I know Mum hates talking about her pregnancy. Once we covered the topic in biology at school and Mum shut down the conversation because 'pregnancy can be very different for different people'. I assumed it had been really traumatic for her so never asked again, and now I feel very uncomfortable, but I do deserve to know.

'Test. Tube. Baby,' Mum repeats in clipped tones.

'You know, like if a couple has . . . trouble . . . conceiving, they can do unbelievable things with science,' I say gently, trying to show how fine I would be with it if this were the case. There's no shame in it, and I'm certainly not going to blame Mum, who's definitely been through the wringer here.

Mum doesn't say anything.

'I don't think there is anything wrong with that at all, Mum, by the way,' I gabble, panicked by her silence. 'I think it's sensational that couples can still have children and live glorious, happy, loving lives, you know? I love it. I love you,' I continue.

Mum turns away, rests her hands on the sink next to the dishwasher and looks out on to the garden. She stays silent a few seconds longer, and I can't bear it.

'Mum?' I nudge, shifting my weight from one foot to

the other, too awkward to go over to her but uncomfortable just standing still.

'Sorry, love.' She turns round, familiar smile on her face, wiping her hands on her apron that she always wears to load the dishwasher, though I'm not sure it's that messy a task.

'I'm not trying to upset you, I just wondered if there was a bit more to things, maybe? I don't care if there was. I was just . . . wondering,' I trail off nervously, using all my willpower to stop fidgeting and stand still.

'No, it's all right, we all wonder about these things,' Mum trills with her customary smile back on.

I'm not sure we do all wonder about these things – I never have before. I fiddle anxiously with a bit of skin down the side of my nail and decide to push on.

'So, was I then?' I ask again, quietly this time.

'Yes, love,' Mum says, popping a tablet in the dishwasher and turning it on.

'Something like a test-tube baby?' I press. Feels like I may as well get the full answer now while it's so uncomfortable.

'Something like that, yes. Now, did you want to see if we can get you in at the salon today? You'll feel much better in yourself with a fresh cut and maybe even some highlights. I'll cover the cost. I always think a bit of blonde shakes the blues away,' she adds, presumably quoting Gok Wan or someone as she sprays the countertops with antibac and wipes them vigorously. Very vigorously. She's still not made eye contact.

'Um, yes, that's sounds lovely, thank you. I'm sorry, I just want to quickly ask, um, sorry for banging on about this. But, erm, if you used *science*, which obviously is great, Dad . . . was . . . er . . . involved, was he?' Again, I don't know how to handle this. I realise I haven't actually asked the question, but I'm not sure I can bring myself to.

'Tabitha. I love you, your dad loves you, let's not rehash old ground, all right?' Mum says, weary-voiced.

I feel weary too. I'm tired of letting things go, tired of not making a fuss, tired of trying to please everyone. Walking away from David felt amazing (metaphorically, I mean. The actual walking part was quite tricky, since I'd cut my foot pretty badly on his blasted telly), telling Dad I love him and want him and Bernie in my life felt amazing. It's the constant tiptoeing that feels terrible. It feels like no one in this family had ever had a proper conversation until that moment with the spotted dick. I didn't realise what a can of worms that would open, but now I want to *really* talk. And get some answers.

'Mum, no, I'm not dropping this. I'm tired of brushing

things under the carpet. I'm not cross at you, I'm not judging you, I just want a bit of honesty,' I say boldly and calmly. I'm quite proud of this; mostly I am so nervous of causing a scene that I only ever stand up for myself when it has gone too far, and I end up snapping and regretting it. Still, I do quickly add a 'please'.

We stand in silence for a few seconds, at a strange stalemate. I lean on the worktop, staring down at my mismatched socks (good job Mum hasn't noticed, although that's very unlike her – she likes order, and for me to be 'well-turned-out'. She'd moan, 'What does that say about you? That you can't even sort your socks out?'). I consider how much resolve I have to maintain a silence like this.

I look up at Mum, worried she'll be staring directly at me, but she's not, she's leaning against the sink, quietly crying.

'Mum! Don't cry.' I rush over to hug her – we're not huggers, but then she's not a crier, and I felt it was necessary. 'Whatever it is, I don't mind. There are so many ways people have a family these days. Look at Brianna and Jaylen from Dad's old work. They used her eggs and a surrogate, remember? They're all happy!'

'They got divorced,' Mum sobs.

'OK, not a good example, but I meant they didn't have a

baby the conventional way, and they love the twins so much, don't they?' God, this has not gone well. I hate seeing Mum upset, so much that I've almost forgotten we're talking about my actual life. About who my dad is.

Mum takes her apron off, mindfully folds it back into the drawer under the microwave and walks through to the lounge. Nothing ever changes in here. The coasters are exactly where they should be on the nest of tables, the photos of us all are arranged in the same formation on the mantelpiece, and the faux flowers are in the same cream vase on the windowsill. It's comforting to be somewhere that time seemingly has had no effect on. Especially after the last few weeks I've had.

I follow her through and sit down on the sofa, tucking one of my legs under me and picking up a cushion to cuddle, sensing this is going to be a bit more than one of our usual sofa chats.

Mum sits in the armchair opposite and pulls her pencil skirt down a little closer to her knees. She's meant to be going out for lunch with her new-old friend Parker later, so I notice she's vamped herself up a bit. Probably best not to ask after him right now. I'm possibly about to find out I was grown in a Petri dish.

'You know I don't like causing a fuss,' she starts.

'I know, nor do I. I promise I'm not trying to cause one now, I just—'

'Listen, Tabitha. This is going to be ever such a lot.' She exhales hard.

I squeeze the cushion a fraction tighter.

'I want you to know that I was always going to tell you the whole story, but there never seemed to be a good time, and everything was going so well until . . .' Mum leans down and picks invisible flecks off her tights. She seems lost.

'Until Dad told you he was in love with a man called Bernard and I found a hidden letter, smashed a TV to pieces and left my boyfriend who I thought I would marry?' I offer.

'Well, yes. Ha! When you put it like that, it seems almost comical, doesn't it?' Mum smiles weakly, her eyes still sad and watery.

'Almost,' I agree, wondering if now would be a good time to mention that I have also been travelling in time to 1989 and have a new BFF called Bea. Probably not.

'Well, I don't know if this time is a better one, but I do know, from everything that's gone on, that hiding things isn't the answer.' She gives me a small nod, I think more for her sake, and I nod back, willing her to go on.

'OK. So, are you . . . well, are you hiding something?' I ask, confused. Is she talking about me? Does she know about the ring?

'Yes. And I want you to know that I love you more than any woman could ever love a daughter.' I don't think this is about 1989, but it's getting super-weird.

'I know you do, Mum. I love you more than any daughter could love her mum,' I reassure her, seeing her eyes well up. My stomach starts flipping and I hold onto the cushion like a life raft in a storm.

'Ever since I was little, I wanted to be a mother,' Mum starts, unnecessarily flattening her skirt with the palms of her hands again.

'Yes. I know that bit.' I smile encouragingly.

'When I started stepping out with Michael, not long after I left school, I fell so in love with him. I thought I'd settle down and marry him—'

The blood pulses in my ears. Is this Michael – Parker – guy my biological dad? The man I jokingly call mum's new-old friend?

'But it wasn't to be.' She pauses. 'As I told you before, he was adventurous, he wanted to travel and see the world and felt there was more out there for him than little old Ottleswan.' Another pause. 'Maybe more than me.'

She says that last bit so sadly, it shakes me out of my Tabby-centric panic. 'No, Mum! What a jerk! There wasn't more than you. You're an amazing woman, a real catch.'

'It's all right. I've found a lot of peace since Parker's come back into my life, and we can talk about that later. But for now, I want to answer your question.' She tells me, quite firmly, 'I always wanted to have a child of my own.'

'Yes, OK.' I knew this, I *know* this. I wish she'd get to the point, the anticipation is killing me, as is my overactive imagination.

'Not too long after Michael and I broke up, I met Tony, and he was nice. Very nice. I was feeling a bit lost, my sister had just left home. Did you know Auntie Bridget used to live with me?'

'Yeah.' I nod. 'I know you were only twenty when Granny Aida died, but I've never really thought about what that meant for Auntie Bridget.'

'Well, yes, she was thirteen, my dad was long gone and I was an adult, and so I looked after her. It was that maternal side of me again. I'd always loved her, of course, but suddenly it was just the two of us and I loved her so much, Tabitha, I loved her like she was my own.' Mum takes a breather to steady herself and I give her space, wanting her to carry on talking when she's ready.

'Bridget was what you'd call a "live wire",' Mum says with a sad smile 'She wasn't anything like me, not really. She wasn't worried about what people thought of her, or keen to fit the mould. She wanted to do big things. She was special. She had this energy I could never emulate. People said she had an infectious smile and a twinkle in her eye, and they were right.' Mum smiles at the memory. 'She'd light up a room as soon as she walked into it. If I hadn't loved her so much, I might have been jealous of how easy life seemed for her. She'd meet someone and within seconds you'd think they'd known each other for years. She just got on with everyone.' Mum talks so fondly of her, I start to relax a bit, letting go of the cushion ever so slightly.

'She sounds lovely,' I say. 'I wish I could have met her.'

'Me too, she'd have loved you, I'm sure. When Bridget left school, she knew she wanted to go travelling, so she started saving and then went off. I was with Tony by then, of course, and we were such a match. We wanted the same things from life. He wanted to settle down, and I knew he wouldn't leave me for a big adventure like Michael and Bridget had. He'd not had any partners before me. But I always thought that was romantic, I thought he was just waiting for the right woman.'

'Oh.' I'm stumped for what else to say.

'I know you don't want to hear all this, but it's important to the story,' she says, almost physically wincing. 'Your dad wasn't ever very physical with me. That's the truth, Tabs.'

'Right, yep, understood,' I say, wiggling a loose thread on the cushion, hoping she doesn't carry on.

'When I did try to make things a bit physical, there would be some, er, performance issues,' she carries on, to my horror.

'Yes, completely get it,' I say, blinking a few too many times like I'm having a stress reaction to how much I don't need her to explain further.

'Now I know why, of course, and I don't blame him at all. We did try to have a physical relationship, but it never really worked. We had so many wonderful years together, but I still wish he'd been able to be who he wanted to be, to live life happily as he really wanted to. It's a great shame for him,' she says sincerely.

'Yeah. I know. Poor Dad. I think he loved his life with you though, in so far as he could,' I add.

'With us,' she corrects me. 'Yes, I'd like to think so.' She seems overwhelmed again, before focusing and saying, 'Right, so, making a baby was proving very difficult, as you'd imagine, given the circumstances.'

'And this is where you got science involved?' I question, everything starting to make sense.

'No. This is where fate took over. If you can believe in fate,' Mum says more than asks.

I believe in magical jewellery nowadays, so I can absolutely get on board with a bit of fate, I think to myself.

'I'm going to try and say this all at once, so just bear with me, all right?' she says firmly again.

'Mmm-hmm,' I reply, barely moving a muscle as I brace myself for whatever bombshell she's about to drop.

'It had been almost seven years since Bridget went off on her adventures. She flew out to France, travelled all round Europe, really "found herself", as you young ones say. She met a man in Austria. She was such a free spirit. She was definitely one of those go-with-the-flow types, always happy to see where life might take her.

'Things went well with the Austrian chap for a while, but I think he had a lot of problems. Did a lot of things he shouldn't. Smoked all sorts and lived recklessly, you know?'

Even though I don't know, I nod so she'll carry on.

'Bridget wasn't being careful and before long, she found herself in the family way. Pregnant, I mean.'

'Yep, understood,' I nod, shocked that I have an older

cousin I don't know about, and planning on secretly getting on Facebook to find them the minute Mum is finished.

'Clemens, that's the Austrian, she thought he'd support her, but he didn't. I don't think he was a bad man, just that a baby wasn't on his radar and he had nothing to support her with. He was a free spirit, just like her.'

'So what did she do? Do I have a cousin in Austria?' I want as many clues as possible so I can find them online tonight.

'She did the best thing she could have done, and came home.' Mum looks into my eyes, smiling.

Hmmm . . . perhaps my cousin is in England.

'That day when we picked her up from the airport, she cried and cried. It was relief, I think. She loved the adventure, but she knew I was there for her and she was ready to be home. Properly home.'

Absolute dread washes over me. I know what happened to Bridget. Mum barely speaks about it, but I know about the car accident.

'Oh my God, and then that awful icy day. The accident. Oh, Mum! Was she pregnant when she died?' I gasp, hand over my mouth.

'No, my love,' Mum says much more tenderly than I've ever heard her speak to me. 'She came home and had her baby a few months later, safe and sound. Oh, my goodness, she loved her baby with all her heart.' Tears are running down Mum's cheeks now and she's not even bothering to wipe them away.

'She loved her baby fiercely. All that fire inside her, that spirit, it was all channelled into her love for that little baby. We brought them home, and your dad was happy for them to keep living here. In fact, he insisted on it. She was a beautiful mother. She played and cooed and sang. I loved having a baby in the house. I even loved the nappies and sleepless nights. I loved looking after them both, felt like I finally had a purpose, and my life had meaning.' Mum swallows hard.

I can barely move listening to her.

'One awful, terrible day, she'd gone down to her favourite little sandwich shop we used to have on the high street—'

'Jane's,' I say, my heart racing.

'Yes, that's right! Do you know it? It shut down years and years ago. Anyway, she went out with the pram to buy cheese toasties for us all, she loved those things. I could have made them here but she insisted. Said they were her favourite. I told her to be careful, that it was icy, but I couldn't tell every driver, I couldn't stop what happened.'

Mum is fully choked up, but I need to know the rest.

'She was on the zebra crossing, toasties in the pram basket, and he didn't stop. Or maybe he did, and the ice made him skid – that's what the courts said, but we'll never really know. It was instant. They said she didn't feel a thing, didn't even see him coming but I know she did. Onlookers said that just before he hit her, she pushed the pram with "tremendous strength" and the baby was spared. The very last thing she did was save her baby,' Mum sobs, hands over her face, her chest heaving.

I'm stunned. I have no words of consolation, tears dripping off my cheeks and onto the cushion I'm still gripping.

'So,' I begin tentatively, 'where did Bridget's baby go?' My mind is whirling so fast I feel dizzy; the cream vase of faux flowers on the windowsill opposite looks like it's wobbling.

Mum pulls her hands away from her face and looks at me.

'Who raised the baby?' I ask again, needing to hear it from her.

The pause feels eternal. It's astonishing how many thoughts you can think in only a matter of seconds.

'I did,' she whispers through the tears.

Chapter Twenty-Five

MY HEAD FEELS AS though I've just spun round a thousand times and then had someone crash cymbals next to each of my ears. I don't know what to do, sitting there in the lounge. My eyes start stinging and I feel like the walls are closing in on me. I stand up, gabble about 'needing a minute', walk straight out the door without my shoes on all the way to the postbox at the end of Mum's road and throw up. Mum's road. Barbara's road. Bridget's road. I don't know who my mum is or what bloody road I'm on.

You know when you watch a film and you're just enjoying being given all the pretty scenes, but there comes a point where you go, 'Oh my God!' and all the pieces fall into place? That feels like my life right now, except so much more.

I instinctively reach for my phone to call David but, one: I didn't pick my phone up when I ran out and two: I've left him. I consider walking all the way to Vivienne's house, but it's spitting with rain and I don't think my socks could hold up that long. What I really want is the ring. I want to run away to another time. I want to go and tell Bea about my mum, my biological mum, about the accident and the Austrian and Jane's bakery, and then it hits me like a thousand tonnes of bricks all at once, and I'm sick again. A little bit on my socks this time.

Back home, I lean on the doorbell. Mum opens the front door, looking worse than I've ever seen her, and I see the hallway phone receiver lying on the side table. She picks it up and replaces it.

'Who was that?' I demand, nodding at the phone she was just using. If she was talking about me and my past, I have a right to know.

'It was Parker, love – Michael. He knew Bri— your mum – Bridget – my sister,' she tries.

Still standing panting on the doormat with my own

vomit soaked into my sock, I say, breathless and woozy, 'Mum, did you used to call Michael Mike?'

'What?' she says, completely lost, still taking in the sight of me with sicky socks and a heaving chest.

'Did you?' I demand.

'Some people did. I don't like to shorten names, you know that,' she says, looking all around but not straight at me.

'I know, but did Bridget?' I know she's uncomfortable but we're past being coy now.

'Yes, I suppose so. She shortened everyone's name. Why? Does it matter?' she says, bemused.

'She shortened everyone's name,' I repeat, a million thoughts racing almost as fast as my heart.

'Yes. It always annoyed me. Called you Tabs, Tabby, Tabsy. I think Tabitha is a beautiful name,' Mum smiles, stepping towards me, reaching over to lift the stray hair out of my face.

'But ... Bridge is short for Bridget, isn't it?' I say, knowing exactly what's coming next.

'It is, but she loved to be called "Bea".' Mum brushes a hair off my mouth.

That's when I black out.

Chapter Twenty-Six

I SO BADLY WANTED TO put the ring on – still in my purse, naughty, I know – but I couldn't face Bea. Suddenly it was all too raw. Mum helped me up and into a hot bath, and now I feel so much better. Mum's left now, for lunch with Parker. She seems just as shaky as I am. I wonder if she's told Dad that I know. I'll have to speak to him soon. He obviously wanted to tell me. He nudged all of this.

I do the only thing I can do – text Vivi. In an emergency she's the one person I trust, and I can't wait to see her.

So that's why the evening finds me round at her place, seeking solace. Even though I've had a few hours to calm down and gain some kind of control, I still feel sick.

The shock of it all washes over me in waves. Vivi is fully prepared, with a comforting selection of snacks at the ready. 'Let's get Kitty settled, and then you can tell me all about it,' she greets me. As ever she's in bright colours – today it's sunflower yellow and neon pink, which on anyone else would look weird but on her it's fabulous. Whereas I've retreated into beige, trying to be as invisible as possible. As I keep shivering, I've borrowed a big oatmeal cardigan from Mum – from Barbara. Or whatever I'm meant to call her now.

Kitty's room is all bright colours too, turquoises and purples alongside the taste for bright pink that she's inherited from her mother. She's too distracted by choosing a bedtime story to notice I'm super-quiet. Something about the routine of helping put her to bed helps me feel more myself, and she lets me brush her hair before tucking her in.

I'm tempted to stay in the cocoon of the little room, but Kitty will never go to sleep if I do. So we leave her with her *Frozen* night light on and make our way back downstairs. Settling on the corner sofa (which David loves, but he's never coming in here again), Vivi pulls across the side table with the big bowls of snacks. 'All right,' she says. 'Better tell me what all this is about.'

So I do. I recount the conversation I had with Mum (I can't call her anything else, can I?) in as much detail as I can remember. When I finish, Vivi is at a loss for words.

I reach for my favourite biscuits. 'That means I've never known my birth parents, I'm not related to Dad, and on top of all that, I've been going back to 1989 and, can you believe, meeting my birth mum. We've even been dancing and got drunk together!'

Vivi nods, and if I worried that she might panic as much as I have, I was wrong. Now that she's taken it all in, she's strangely calm. 'Well, that must explain why you go back there,' she said. 'To that particular time and place, I mean. You were meant to get to know your birth mother after all.'

'But it's too weird!' I take another biscuit and break it in two. 'She's younger than I am. I can't get my head around it.'

Vivi raises an eyebrow. 'You're right, it is weird. But kind of fantastic, too. Don't you think? This is such a special chance you've been given. You're meeting your birth mother as an equal, as a friend – you can talk to her about anything.'

Trust Vivi to see the bright side. Slowly her words sink in. Perhaps she has a point, and the Bea I've got to know is nothing like an actual mother would be, with the age gap and the weight of responsibility and everything else that the mother–daughter relationship brings with it. I've got to try to see this as a bonus, a privilege. But at the moment it's so hard.

'Have you spoken to your dad yet?' Vivi asks gently.

I shake my head. 'Not yet. I need more time. At least he's known about this all along. I've got to get used to it all somehow.'

'You will,' Vivi assures me. 'Then you'll see it means they loved you even more than you knew. They chose to keep you, to raise you, and they've been great parents, *are* great parents. You couldn't have wished for better.'

I nod at the truth of this, even as a lone tear sneaks down my cheek. I'm fed up with crying but can't seem to stop completely. 'It's all too much!' I wail. 'First Dad and Bernie, then the ring, then David . . . At least I've got the award to look forward to now, no thanks to him.' And the tears start to flow all over again.

'Don't you go worrying about all that,' Vivi says decisively, and I love how she reacts like that. She's so protective of me when I'm down. 'You concentrate on realising how much your parents love you – and they are still your parents, don't be in any doubt of that.'

'I know,' I sniff. She's right, of course, but all of this has knocked me totally out of kilter.

'I'm going to fetch some rosé.' She gets to her feet and her bracelets jangle, that lovely familiar noise I always associate with her. 'You make sure you speak to your dad soon. He'll want to know you're OK. Doesn't matter that he's not a blood relation, he's done everything a father could possibly do.'

'I know,' I say again. I haven't touched wine since that night out with . . . with my birth mother, but suddenly it seems like a great idea. I won't get drunk, though. I don't think I could cope with all of this news and a hangover like the last one.

Chapter Twenty-Seven

STANDING BEHIND THE TILL on Monday morning, nothing feels the same. Nothing *is* the same. Or everything is the same, but now I know different things about the same stuff. This is what my brain has been like ever since I found out.

'Are you sure you're all right, hon? You look peaky to me,' Julia asks worriedly. She's in the shop today, doing a stock inventory and contacting vendors with figures. 'Barbara told me you'd fainted the other day. No man is worth that!'

'No, I'm fine, I'm OK to work, honestly. It's nice to keep busy,' I say, probably trying to convince myself more than her, brushing my little cardigan down over the top of my floaty floral skirt that was originally from Debenhams but which I found on eBay and thought had a nice vintage vibe to it. Mum suggested I 'gussy up' a bit for work. 'A nice blouse, perhaps,' she said, but I've opted for a cream cami, dusty-pink cardi and this super-long flowing skirt that I can almost hide away in, like a turtle in its shell. I've added a vintage brooch to make it look a bit more 'work appropriate', but it's a flimsy effort. Good job Julia is relaxed about these things.

'You've had a terrible time, I know,' Julia says, not moving out of the way of the till so I have no choice but to chat, when all I really want to do is open my purse and get the ring out. I'm worried she's going to notice it's missing from the case any minute now. 'Your mum told me about the break-up, of course.' Ah, the joys of living in a small town – everyone knows everyone. Mum and Julia have become firm gossip buddies in the years I've worked here. She continues, unfazed, 'I never liked David. Always thought he was dull, and a bit controlling with you. Bit limited. You deserve far better. I don't think it'll be long before Prince Charming comes riding in, ready to sweep you—'

'Thanks, Julia,' I say with as natural a smile as I can muster. 'I appreciate that.'

'Are you sure you'll be all right here today?' she asks again.

'Yes. One hundred per cent sure,' I tell her with a nod, much more confidently than I feel. 'I'm glad to be here. I need to begin to put the past behind me,' I say, feeling the familiar burning in my throat and tears behind my eyes that have been there all weekend. I've had so much to process, and my mind has been racing for the past forty-eight hours solid. Mum and Dad, Bea and my birth father, David – they've completely consumed every single thought. I've not slept. 'If I feel really terrible, I'll lock up and maybe just sit down in the back room for a minute. I won't overdo it,' I reassure her.

'No, no, go upstairs. Trevor's handed in his tenancy notice. He picked up all his stuff last week, so the flat's empty if you need a rest. He's working from home permanently now, and doesn't need the space. The back room's a bit chaotic. I had bit of a restock last week. The floral phone case lady is dropping off at ten, and then it should just be a very normal Monday, all righty?' she says, unaware that it will be far from normal for me, obvs.

'Yep. Upstairs free, phone cases at ten, serve customers, try not to cry,' I joke with a weak smile.

'Oh, love. You'll find another one,' she soothes, as though a boyfriend will fix all my problems, and passes me over the inventory book she's been holding, pulling her sunglasses off their perch, popping them on her face ready for the late-summer sun and leaving the shop.

It's 9.35 a.m. If I could, I would shove the ring on and sprint down to the travel agent's. I'd snatch the tickets from Bea, rip them into a thousand tiny pieces and tell her never to leave, to stay at Mum's forever and be here with us all for years and years and years. Except if I do that, how will she meet Clemens? If she doesn't meet Clemens, how will she have me? How will Mum raise me, and have the motherhood experience she so desperately craved? Maybe she'd have been happier without me in the end. Free to reconnect and travel with Parker even. So many outcomes swirl round my head. None of them good.

Mum said Bridget had reached out to Clemens but that he 'wasn't in a good state. Not well.' She meant drugs, I'm sure. How dare he not move heaven and earth to support Bea when she needed him most? Anger courses through my veins the more I let my thoughts spiral into the whys and what ifs. What if he'd been there for her and she'd stayed over in Austria, far from icy roads? Did Mum and Dad stay together just to raise me, and was Dad unhappy all those years – trapped – out of duty? So many lives affected. I feel almost frozen to the spot, overwhelmed with what I should do with all this new information.

'Yoo-hooo, I'm here with my box of goodies, Lavender Lovelies?' I'm startled to find the phone case lady standing right in front of me, wearing another totally unique and stunning outfit.

'You were in a world of your own there, lovey, weren't you?' she says. And then:

'I'm so sorry, I didn't even hear the bell ring. Sorry! Yes. Hello. Your products. Right, yes, let me take them, no problem, OK!' I waffle in a fluster.

'Oh lovey, you're not all right at all, are you?' the kind lady asks.

Her warmth breaks me. Why does being asked if you're all right always set you off? I'm mortified to find myself crying again, for maybe the thousandth time in a week. I hastily brush the tears from my face, but it's too late.

'Nooo, no, no, nothing's all that bad,' she says sympathetically, leaning over the counter to give me the most awkward embrace of my life.

We pull away and she carries on smiling so tenderly that I blurt it out. 'My mum told me she was my mum, but really I'm her sister's, who died seconds after saving my life. My biological dad is from Austria and I think is a drug user who doesn't care about me or my dead mum. The dad I thought was my dad is actually not my dad, and has left the woman I thought was my mum for a man called Bernard from the pub,' I say flatly, blinking at the insanity of it all. Wondering what on earth this poor woman is going to say in response. But goodness, it feels great to say it all out loud.

She doesn't move a muscle. Probably no idea what on earth to say. And then:

'When I was very young, I had a beautiful little girl called Eleanor. My mother made me put her up for adoption because I wasn't married and it wasn't the done thing in those days. My heart broke for her every single day. I only found her three years ago after I had a meltdown in New York City, of all places, and my lovely niece found her on the internet. She'd had two daughters, and all of a sudden I had three new members of my family to introduce to my new husband Colin,' she replies.

'Oh,' I say. I thought I was stumped by Mum's revelation, but the fact that this woman is practically a stranger and we have just revealed such personal things to each other is exceptionally awkward. For me, anyway.

'What I'm saying is, nobody on earth has it easy or perfect. Time after time I've learnt things about people that have surprised me. We never know what someone is going through but we all have secrets, we all have twists and turns.

Nobody's life runs that smoothly. Sounds to me like you're a very lucky girl,' she muses, hands on the counter, all her fabulous vintage rings aglitter under the lights.

'Lucky?' I whisper, regaining some control over the crying.

'Your biological mum saved your life, so she surely loved you with all her heart. Her sister, your mum, adopted you and loved you so much you didn't even know you weren't hers, biologically. Two women pouring all that love into one little girl, I'd call that lucky. Wouldn't you?' She smiles.

I am overwhelmed. 'I just wish I'd known sooner,' I say, still processing her comments.

'Time is a funny old thing, lovey. It always knows what's best for us. It doesn't work against us, only with us, even though we sometimes struggle to believe that. It offers us the things we need, when we need them, even though we can't always feel it. You just have to trust it.'

'Oh,' I manage, not really knowing how to respond. Imagine if she knew I had a time-travelling ring. Would she trust time then?

'Time is a great healer,' she says earnestly, head tilted to one side.

'Yes, you're right,' I say, not really sure how or if I should continue the conversation.

'And one of my favourites, "What's meant for you won't pass you by".'

'I like that one,' I say, smiling weakly back, but completely drained by all the thoughts and feelings filling my mind. Was the ring meant for me, so Bea didn't pass me by?

'Well, I only wanted to drop off these cases,' she says, pushing the box towards me an inch, possibly picking up on my readiness to end our interaction, 'but I've ended up baring my soul and giving you my best pearls of wisdom! Maybe now you can pass them on to someone else,' she suggests, reaching into her bag to check her phone. 'All that time chatting, and now I'm late!'

'God, I'm sorry – I've kept you. I didn't mean to blurt all that out. So sorry, I'm not usually like this, usually I'm really, um, really—'

'Really human,' the lady replies, once again bringing a calmer energy to the shop. 'My number is on the inventory slip. If you want to call, I won't mind. I have a daughter, two nieces and a couple of granddaughters – I'm used to chatting things through, I can tell you.'

'Thank you,' I say, tears threatening again. 'You've said all the right things, just when I needed them.'

'You see? Perfect timing!' She smiles and heads towards the door.

With trembling fingers, I fish my purse from my bag, unzip the little pocket and pull out the crystal and amethyst ring. The familiar fizz of excitement I feel at putting it on is replaced completely by an anxious desperation.

I wish I had a plan. I wish I knew how to handle this.

Ring on, shop door open, and the sunshine hits my squinting eyes like a cruel slap. Of course I didn't bring sunglasses on a day like this. It's far too hot to be wearing a cardigan, but the thought of taking it off makes me feel vulnerable and I need every bit of armour I've got right now, even if it's a flimsy bit of knitwear.

As I walk the five hundred yards down the high street, I try to concoct a plan. Maybe with the ring on, being in the right time, I can work out what to do.

'Cheer up, love, might never happen!' a middle-aged man in a high-vis vest and hard hat shouts at me from some nearby scaffolding. Imagine if I stopped and explained the last couple of months to him. How would he feel if I said, 'Well, I live in 2022 and the death of my mother has already happened because I'm somehow in a fucked-up time vortex that I have no idea what to do about.' I want to scream up at him to fuck off, like I did with David, but instead, ever the mild-mannered Brit, I look up, force a smile and keep going towards the travel agency. I've got bigger fish to fry today.

'Ooohhh what a sight for sore eyes you are! Thought I'd never see you again,' Bea says with a slight edge to her tone as I walk in.

'Hellooo,' I try to say, as relaxed as possible, but it comes out more as a squawk than a greeting.

'Bloody hell, are you all right?' she asks, turning from the ancient (or I suppose modern) fax machine in the corner. 'You look like you've seen a ghost.'

I fight back tears. Every emotion I have ever or could ever feel seems to have risen up and traffic-jammed in my throat. I don't know if I'm going to choke or throw up.

'Tabitha, sit down. I'll get you some water.' She hurries out to the back room.

I take a few deep breaths and compose myself in time for her to come back with the tepid tap water.

'Sorry,' I whisper. 'It's been . . . well . . . I've . . .'

'Oh God, it's that awful David, isn't it?' she says, walking over and putting her arm round me.

The feel of her arm, the tenderness in her voice, the fact that I did just break up with my boyfriend of almost ten years – it's all too much. Fresh tears well up and pour down my cheeks. Huge heaving sobs rack through me as I sit on that familiar orange chair in the travel agency.

'Yes,' I sob. 'How did you know?'

'I know you, Tabs, I can just tell. Maybe we're connected, eh?' she soothes with a gentle smile.

'What? What do you mean, "connected"?' I say, wildly hoping she is somehow in on all this.

'I dunno. You know when you just click with someone? Maybe we knew each other in another life, or we're soul sisters somehow?' She looks at me so sweetly.

I look back at her, blink and cry again.

'Or maybe I'm just being extra nice to you because you're sitting in my work crying like a baby over a dud, and I feel sorry for you! Come on. You'll be all right,' she says, squeezing me hard and giving me a little shake. 'He obviously wasn't the one for you, eh?'

I'm lost for words. I hoped something would just magically come out of my mouth but instead, I'm a total snivelling wreck!

This couldn't be going more wrong. I physically shake myself.

Circling the ring round and round my finger, I decide just to launch into it.

'Bea,' I begin, as she gives me one last squeeze and heads back over to her desk to listen. I wipe my eyes with my cardi cuffs (glad I wore this now). 'I found something out.'

'Oh God, do I want to know?' she says, pretending to

wince. I try to step around how poignant her question is.

'Do you remember me mentioning that my friend Vivienne nominated Pearls and Doodles for an award?' I start.

'Yep, think so,' Bea nods, listening very carefully.

'So I got onto the shortlist but David hid the letter they sent me,' I let it tumble out of my mouth all in one breath.

'*Whaaaat*? What a git!' Bea says indignantly.

'I know. I smashed the TV up.' I can't help but smile at that bit.

'Jesus Christ!' Bea looks pretty impressed and laughs at my wry smile. This is getting easier.

'It was part of a bigger thing. We had a row, I went to Mum's, I've been staying there. Didn't go to work for a week, just couldn't face it,' I say. The smile is waning, and now I'm having to wipe more tears roughly off my face as Bea passes tissues over the desk.

'You poor thing. I wish I'd known. I went up to the shop a few times but saw you weren't in through the window. I was worried I wouldn't see you again for a long while. My flight is next week, but Babs is driving me down to near Gatwick tonight. I'm going to stay with some mates and have a bit of a laugh before I head off. So I'm glad you've come by today.'

'Oh. I thought ... I didn't realise you were going so soon.' That traffic jam of feelings in my throat seems to be back.

'I just bought the best deal. For next week, like I said. The beginning of September, a week or so after the kids go back to school, so nobody's booking flights for then. They'll all be back from their jollies, and mine will be about to start! Can't wait,' Bea says with her typical infectious enthusiasm.

'I'm going to miss you,' I say quietly, not caring how simpering I sound.

'I'll miss you too, but we'll see each other again, definitely definitely!' she adds at the end.

I smile, knowing how right she is.

'Listen,' I venture, 'I want you to have a brilliant time. Enjoy it. Enjoy every moment of your life.' I've started now, so I just carry on.

'I know it's only been a few weeks, and this will sound a bit intense, but— Urggh, this is so hard to say because I don't want to sound completely weird, but you're really special to me. I think you're a special person – no, Bea – I *know* you're a special person.' All the words are bubbling out, Bea looks happily stunned and I've no intention of stopping.

'I think you put a lot of good out and you deserve a lot of good back, and if I could be just a fraction as brave and spontaneous and exciting as you, I'd be really proud. You're

343

a good woman, Bea, and I'm glad to have had this time with you. I want you to know it's been incredible to have you in my life.' I take a deep breath and let it out slowly. Deciding I've already said far too much, I bravely add, 'And I love you.'

'Ohhh, Tabsy, I don't think anyone has ever said such nice things to me, especially not while I'm sat in this place.' She gestures to her wall of brochures, smiling that signature smile.

'I know that was a bit much, but I wanted you to know it, before you go away, I mean,' I laugh nervously, pulling at my cardi cuffs to hide my hands as though that'll make what I said smaller.

'Thank you. But you'll see me again – I'm not going to the moon, just Europe!' She laughs.

'I know. I wish I was as adventurous. I think now that David's out of the picture, it's time to shake it up a bit and find my wild side.' I wiggle my shoulders a bit on 'wild side', as if that makes me so much wilder.

'You could do! Or, here's a thought, maybe you don't need to be wild like me, maybe we don't all need to be wild women, maybe it's OK just to be who you are. Wild isn't better than mild. Each has their benefits, right?' She nods, encouraging me to nod too.

344

I do, just to see where she's going.

'I've loved your visits, I loved our night out. We'll do more when I'm back! I love your calm "vibes", as you call them, ha ha! I love how you think things through and work out good solid plans. I love how much you take care of things – your vintage bags, your shop, your friends. That Vivienne is lucky to have you, and David is a total dipstick for letting you go!' she says with genuine emotion.

'He is. Can't argue with that,' I half-laugh.

'I'm not being a lesbian,' she starts as I inwardly cringe at how they spoke in 1989, 'but if you were my, um, lover, I'd never let you go. You're rad, Tab! What you said earlier about "I love you", I'm not slushy 'n' mushy either but yeah, I love you too, you daft old thing.'

That's the moment, the 'I'd never let you go' – even though that's not how she meant it – that I think I might crack and tell her. I want to flip a desk and say, *You will let me go! You're going to push that pram with everything in you and let me go and I love you for it! I want to stop it. Stop it all! Stop you going away, stop you getting hurt, stop the ice, stop the car, stop the accident, stop it ALL!* But I can't. If I stop her going, I stop her meeting Clemens, and then what? No me? No years of love with Mum, no laughing with Dad over the roses in my garden, no day out with

Vivienne to the auction house, no baking with Kitty, no nothing at all.

So instead, I just sit there. I stay most of the day, we buy toasties from Jane's, even in the heat (I apologise profusely for not bringing my purse, but Bea doesn't mind: 'It's my treat, you've had a horrid week and it makes me happy to cheer you up. Gotta look after you, eh?'). We both agree that there's no worries about her being fired since she's leaving work today anyway.

Mrs Fletcher, the elusive manager, pops in with a bunch of carnations and a card around 3 p.m. ('Oh, this is Tabitha, she's thinking of booking something tropical, aren't you?' she fibs, to cover up for having a friend in for a chat), and afterwards I know it's time to go. I can hardly bear it.

'Come here, you old softie!' Bea says, seeing me well up again.

We embrace for a long time and I try to imprint the feel of it in my mind and on my heart.

'Go and have the best adventure,' I say at the door, waving as cheerily as my heart can manage. 'You're worth it.'

'I will! You go and have a ball, your way, while I'm gone – and do what makes you MOST happy, remember? I'm rooting for you!' she says, grinning from ear to ear. 'Don't let anything grind you down, you're the best!' she calls as I walk out, smiling back at her.

The air outside is still hot and thick, and I walk a few steps, vision blurring through the tears, and pull the ring off my finger so hard it hurts the skin underneath.

In a blink, she's gone. Everything is gone. People are walking past me with their faces down, lost in their phones; there are twice as many cars whizzing up and down the road and for the second time in a week, I bend over by the nearest dustbin and throw up.

Chapter Twenty-Eight

'TABITHAAA,' MUM WHISPERS FROM my open bedroom door. I squint over at her, blurry in the doorway, and try to work out what she's holding. I need to put my contact lenses in, but my eyes are burning from crying myself to sleep again last night.

'Your glasses are in the top drawer,' Mum says, instinctively knowing why I'm struggling. I find them quickly and see the tray in her hands.

'Oh Mum,' I say croakily.

'I want you to have something proper to eat before you go to work,' she says, walking over to my old bed and pulling my desk chair across the carpet to sit by me. I hitch myself up against the faded pink headboard and smile.

'Buttered toast, scrambled eggs with a little bit of Cheddar and a dollop of ketchup,' she announces, handing me the tray.

'Just how I like it,' I say, looking at the food and realising how very hungry I am. I didn't eat anything last night. I stayed in the shop late, just so that I could be alone with my thoughts, and then went straight to bed when I got home.

'Just how you've always liked it,' Mum agrees.

We both silently note that this is a maternal thing to do. To know how I've always liked my breakfast, to wake up early to make sure I'm fed before work, to lovingly bring it upstairs.

'My sister liked scrambled eggs,' Mum says, trying to bridge the new gap we've found. 'She used to like dippy eggs when she was little. I'd make them for her a lot.'

I smile, thinking of Bea being looked after by Mum.

'I think about her every day, you know,' Mum whispers, blinking very hard at the floor as I take a mouthful of food.

'Why didn't you ever talk about her?' I whisper, the loss of yesterday still so raw.

'I was too scared,' Mum replies simply, as though she's always known it but was just never asked.

'Scared of what? I'd have loved to hear about her.' I want to sound gentle, not judgemental; I want her to spend hours and hours talking about Bea, just to keep her alive with us for a few minutes.

'I suppose scared the secret would slip out, that I'd say something terribly damaging, that I'd do the wrong thing. I never wanted anything to hurt you. After everything that happened, I just wanted to . . . to protect you, really,' Mum says meekly, so unlike her.

'Mum, you'd never have done anything wrong. It's just, I should have known,' I say, wanting to get up and comfort her, but that's quite hard with a plate of scrambled eggs on your lap.

'I know . . . it was . . . bad timing,' she says slowly, this time looking at me at least.

'Time is a funny thing,' I muse, thinking about the last few weeks and what Kath, my phone case vendor said, while taking another bite of breakfast.

Mum looks confused, but can tell this isn't the point in the conversation to question or query me.

'From now on, I'm going to be an open book. If these last few months have taught any of us anything, it's that secrets don't do us any favours. Transparency. Full transparency,' Mum says, with more vigour than she has shown so far this morning, thumping a clenched fist on her knee.

'Yes. Absolutely,' I say, silently noting how non-transparent

I've been. 'I'll be very transparent about this toast – it's excellent.'

'Or do you mean "eggcellent"?' Mum trills, glad of the mood break.

We sit and chit-chat about the week ahead – the charity fashion show is Friday night, and we run through her outfits and the accessories she's planned to go with them.

'Oh my God!' Mum says, making me jump so much I nearly lose my breakfast tray.

'Mum! Bloody hell,' I say, a bit flustered. 'What? What on earth's happened?' I glance round, alarmed, as though danger could be lurking in any corner, about to upend the remains on my breakfast plate.

'I forgot to tell you. That pig of an ex-boyfriend came over yesterday looking for you.'

'WHAT? Yes, Mum, you really should have told me.' I nearly flip the plate myself. I'm outraged that he'd come here again.

'You were at work. I rang you a few times but it went to voicemail.' I suddenly remember my phone buzzing and me ignoring it. To be fair, yesterday was so draining that if he'd turned up on the other side of my till I don't think I'd have even cared. I was absolutely shattered by 4 p.m. Also, it was a Monday – he must have known I'd be at the shop.

He could have come looking for me. (Admittedly, I was in 1989, but he wouldn't have known that.)

'Well, what did he want?' I implore, furious that he barged his way back into my life, but still wanting to know every detail.

'He wanted to say how sorry he was. He said he didn't mind if you didn't pay for the TV because he's sure it was just a lapse of control, and that he can't wait till you calm down and come home,' Mum says, almost physically bracing herself for my reaction.

'Wow,' I say, completely gobsmacked.

'I told him he won't be gaslighting my daughter like this, that you won't be going back until he has vacated the cottage and found somewhere else to live, and that if he doesn't back off and move out, then you'll be smashing up more than just his pathetic little television set.' She nods her head victoriously.

'Wow again! Go Mum,' I say, almost speechless, but proud of her for knowing about gaslighting and for standing so firm.

'Anyway, he left you a few bits of post and buggered off,' she adds.

Mum puts three envelopes on my bed, takes my tray and reminds me I need to leave in twenty minutes if I'm going to be on time for work. Since I skived off most of yesterday, I don't feel like I can be late. I jump in the shower, scrape my wet hair into a bun, pull on my acid-wash jeans and a super-vintage Freddie Mercury concert tee, and head downstairs to find my flip-flops and bag. Once again I thank my lucky stars that Julia's relaxed with workwear and feel a rush of happiness in my tummy that I'm wearing one of my vintage pieces without a shred of self-doubt. Life's too short.

'Anything exciting?' Mum queries as I flap about looking for my car keys.

'Mmm? Just can't find my stuff,' I say, not thinking.

'No, in the letters,' she clarifies.

'Argh! Forgot. Better check.' I'm such a pathetic stickler for things like this; I'll fret all day that there'll be an unpaid bill to sort if I don't open them now.

I was right; one is a reminder to pay off a store card bill, one is junk and one is from the award sponsors, letting me know all the details of when the judges are coming to see the shop and take photos, just before the fashion show and my finale. They're staying in a hotel in Swindon, and will drive over with a team! So exciting. Must text Vivi. And Julia. The fashion show is on Friday, so we need to get organised.

'Thank you, Mum. You always believe in me, and it means a lot,' I say, beaming over at her, suddenly wishing we were huggy people.

'Of course I do! You're very easy to believe in.' She smiles back, taking a step towards me but stopping herself.

'Am I?' I say, a wave of insecurity and imposter syndrome washing over me.

'Yes. You really, really are. You are the apple of my eye, you were the apple of Bridget's eye, you are the apple of your dad's eye,' Mum trails off, obviously taking a moment to think about Bea and perhaps wondering if we should call her Mum or Bridget from now on.

'That's a lot of apples in eyes,' I offer, happy to steer away from the more difficult issues to think about. There's been plenty of those lately. 'I'm very lucky to have, and to have had, both of you,' I say, hopefully sounding reassuring.

'Well, yes. You're wonderful, and we all think so. The fact that your shop—'

'Julia's shop,' I correct her.

'The fact that the shop you run day in, day out could win this global—'

'National,' I correct again.

'Huge award. It's a sizeable accomplishment, and we're going to celebrate it!'

'Oohh, are we? A special present for me, is it?' I chance my arm cheekily.

'Yes, but also, after the fashion show, we'll absolutely have to have a do! Hot and cold buffet, Raj across the close can bring his sound system, everyone can come, all the neighbours, Vivienne, Kitty, your dad, Julia of course, since it's technically her shop.' She adds the last bit nonchalantly.

'And will Parker be coming?' I ask as casually as I possibly can, not wanting to throw her off her game but instantly failing.

The atmosphere suddenly feels a bit less celebratory. Mum pauses, turns round and pretends she has something very interesting in the sink to look at.

'Yes, I should think so. Perhaps your dad could bring Bernard, too?' she says, not turning back round.

'I think that's very gracious of you, Mum.'

'I assume you're not inviting David?' she asks tentatively.

I almost choke. 'Fuck, no!'

'Language! Deary me. Parker, your dad and Bernard will be enough anyway,' she smirks, knowing full well how outlandish this could be.

'More than enough!' I laugh, checking the time, grabbing my keys, shoving the letters in my tote and shouting goodbye as I dash out of the door to work, definitely late now. Gargh!

Chapter Twenty-Nine

'WELL, THIS IS THE MOST exciting Friday morning I've had in a while,' Vivienne says, opening her brand-new notebook from across the little coffee table in the flat above the shop.

'I know! New job, fashion show, party, upcoming award ceremony – what a time to be alive!' I say, shuffling myself along the sofa and handing her the job spec I wrote and printed out last night.

Julia had been thrilled when I told her Pearls and Doodles had been shortlisted for the Independent Shop of the Year Award. And she was so great about having the judging panel come and photograph the shop. We had a brilliant day! They arrived in Swindon on Wednesday evening. It was a huge task, starting very early on Thursday morning, to get everything ready for the shoot – there was a tech team, with a tonne of equipment in a huge van, and a couple of stylists, and a very helpful photographer, Liam. I warmed to him instantly; he had an amazing smile, was so skilled, moving nimbly around the space and finding the very best shots, asking me what I thought, showing me the shots on the back of his camera. Really kind and personable. Also, the fact he was well built, with sandy hair and blue, sparkling eyes was rather appealing . . .

Anyway: Julia is fine with me borrowing some items from the shop to create outfits for the fashion show. Vivi and I spent a happy evening once the team had left deciding how to work an outfit around each piece, for each of our four models. I will wear the 1930s rose-pink evening dress with the pearls; Kitty (she's HYPER-EXCITED about it) will wear a large vintage diamanté necklace as a tiara and her pale blue and lilac tulle *Frozen* dress with some ivory Bonpoint shoes (another eBay find). Mum has agreed to don a long black slip dress and over it, a superb dark green velvet vintage evening coat, plus her bejewelled headband; and Vivi is going to rock the room in a full 1970s purple and orange outfit – rust suede flares, a purple satin shirt with white pearl buttons and a tan leather jacket. Plus all of her fabulous jewellery and make-up! I might try to persuade her to wear a vintage scarf as a belt, too.

Julia has also come round at last to the idea of getting the shop online and using social media. She wants me to photograph everything beautifully (or perhaps I could ask Liam if he could recommend a photographer, it would give me a good excuse to stay in touch with him . . .) for the website and social channels. She's asked me to find someone to help with the postage and packaging logistics too, and take things to the next level. I imagined she'd be unlikely to go for the idea because I'd mentioned it, very lightly, a few times before, with not much response, but I guessed this was a good time to say it again.

'You've picked your timing well, there, Tabitha, and I think you're absolutely right,' she said, beaming, to my shock. 'What do you need to make it happen? Will I need a fleet of staff and a warehouse?' She laughed a little tensely.

'Ummm, nope.' I paused, my brain scrambling to work things out. 'I think I'd just need an assistant either to help me on the till while I fulfil orders or to pack things up, and a bit of money for a web designer. Or we could start off with me giving it a go – I'd need a little space with good lighting to take photos of stock – or hire a photographer – and then just some time to fiddle about with an e-shop and supporting socials,' I finished, proud of myself for coming up with something half-decent.

Julia promised to think on it, and later that day came back into the shop to tell me her plan. She'd convert the flat upstairs into our 'online space'. I could have a photography area, a space to store all the product packaging, a computer, printer, the lot! I could hire someone to help me part-time, and I could decide how to employ them. On top of that, she promoted me to Assistant Director and gave me a small but noteworthy pay rise. She said she'd been shown my Instagram account, @TabbyRoseTreasure, and could see I had a knack for styling and selling things. She hoped the success of the e-shop would pay for the bills upstairs, and that she knew I'd make her proud.

It only took one bottle of rosé and three boxes of Jaffa Cakes to convince Vivi that it was a brilliant idea to come and work with me. Vivi was careful to say that she was coming to work 'with me' and not 'for me', and I got that. She's my BFF first, anything else comes second to that.

'So, no bossing me around, yeah?' She laughs.

'Sure, but I am the Assistant Director and you are the Retail Assistant, *sooo*, sort of different roles there,' I half-joked.

'Yes, but both assistants, so very similar,' Vivi argued.

'Absolutely, completely right. How cool will it be to work together! I just know all those treasures will be flying off the shelves.' I want us to feel equal anyway.

'Or off the websites,' Vivi chimed excitedly.

Fast-forward to Friday, and here we are, sitting in the 'online space' that I think we'll still call 'the flat' so it doesn't sound so obnoxious, planning how we're going to actually put all this into practice. With my sales and styling skills and Vivienne's boundless confidence and drive, plus her social media experience, this will be a whole lot of fun.

'Tabs! This is going to be epic. I can't wait! I want to wear some of your jewellery for the fashion show tonight. I never knew you had so many fabulous pieces in this dusty old place,' she exclaims after we have come back downstairs and I've given her my grand and very detailed tour.

'OK, so first, we don't call our place of work "dusty" or "old", and secondly, as Assistant Director, I'd be happy to make the executive decision to loan you some of our sensational pieces,' I say with a mock flourish of my arms towards the glass display cabinets.

'Oohh, I like this wild and confident side,' Vivienne says in a similar tone.

I smile, noting that I quite like it too. Being called 'wild' makes me think of Bea and how fun-loving she was. Or is. I feel *most* happy, just like she'd want me to.

Vivi leans close to the cabinets, surveying the goodies we have sparkling inside. She picks out some 1970s silver and turquoise bangles, a beautiful Victorian jet mourning necklace and a couple of large cocktail rings.

'Tabithaaa, oh-em-gee. Look at that!' she says, leaning over The Ring. My Ring. My ring that I don't own and can't stop her taking. Does she know it's The Ring? I know I've told her it's here, but she's not letting on.

'Ahhh, sadly that sold. This morning, before you arrived. Over the phone,' I babble in alarm. I can't bear the thought of anyone else having what I had with it. Right now, it still feels like a piece of Bea, a special thing almost, of hers. I want to keep it that way, keep it special.

'Well, as your Retail Assistant, I should know about these things,' she says, moving on to look at something else.

'Absolutely! Roger that,' I say, relieved she's been distracted, making a mental note to perhaps move it somewhere less visible. I'm Assistant Director, after all – I can do those things now, I think confidently.

Five minutes later, after making a careful note of every-thing leaving the store, and her promising a 'huge shout-out' for Pearls and Doodles tonight at the show, I'm alone.

I stand behind the till and breathe out slowly, surveying the shop I love so much. I know every nook and cranny of this place. I belong here. *This* is my adventure, I think.

While it's quiet and I have the courage, I unhook the little key from under the till desk, step silently over to the display cabinet and twist the lock. The ring isn't sparkling at me today; I expect Vivi nudged it so it's not catching the light as much as it usually does.

My heart doesn't race and my breath isn't short. I feel calm and sure and steady. I slide the ring onto my finger and take a breath. And my phone pings with a message.

Text from Mum: *Hello Tabitha! Heading over to the community centre in an hour for rehearsals! Can't wait. See you soon my love, Mum xxxx*

Chapter Thirty

NOT SURE WHY I ever imagined I could simply turn up at the fashion show, take a seat and enjoy the spectacle. Within seconds of stepping through the doors to the community centre, I'm pounced on by Vivi. 'Come on, we need your talents backstage,' she urges, taking my arm and forcibly escorting me through the gathering crowd.

'Backstage' is complete chaos. In the midst of it all stands my mum, glamorous from the waist down in her sequinned pencil skirt, teamed with daring black stiletto-heeled boots, but the top half is . . . a work in progress. 'Tabitha, you have to help me,' she implores. 'Thank God your vintage collection has blouses like these. How do you even begin to tie a pussy bow? Every time I try it looks more like a dead rat.'

It's a lovely satin piece in a fabulous shade of oyster, but the neckline leaves a lot to be desired. I push up the sleeves of my jacket – I've borrowed a fabulous woman's evening tux from the shop that might even be Saint Laurent – and get stuck in. 'It's impossible to do it yourself unless you have a big mirror, and it looks as if all of them are taken,' I tell her firmly. There's no time for self-doubt now. 'Stand with your arms at your sides, please. There, now I'll even it up . . .' I tug gently at the edges of the material to remove the creases from Mum's attempts at tying it. 'Then it's one side over, make a loop, adjust the length, and hey presto.' I stand back to check my work and Vivi exclaims in admiration.

'Anyone would think you've done this before!' She beams. 'Now we just need to sort out the make-up. How about you take your mum over there to one of the chairs in the corner, and I'll send Skye over, the make-up artist? She's just finished with Debs.'

They're chairs meant for kids, but at least that means Mum's at the right level when Skye comes over to do her eyes. Skye makes her hold an old tea towel somebody's found over her precious pussy bow, in case there's any scatter from the face powder and metallic eyeshadow. Then she sets about giving her the most beautiful smoky eyes. She's almost finished – I'm entranced just watching her – when the memory hits me of Bea doing my face before our big night out. I have to take a deep breath. At least Mum won't have to deal with blue mascara, which I think is just as well.

Skye stands back to survey her handiwork, which is flawless, and moves on to do Vivi.

'Look at you. You're catwalk-ready, Mum,' I whisper.

She blinks and I realise she's holding back tears too. Oh no, just when I thought I could keep it together. But she wins the battle and stands up, handing me the tea towel.

Before we can say anything else, Vivi claps her hands. 'Places, please!' she calls, her voice full of authority, and Kitty dashes out from behind her mother to help everybody line up.

Now that my presence is no longer required, I can sneak back into the main hall. I've got a prime spot, next to the award judges, here to see my finale outfits. I'll have a great view of the catwalk, at least until it's my turn to go on. There, near the side aisle, I recognise the back of Dad's head, and if I'm not mistaken the hairstyle is new. He's sitting with Bernie and I smile at how nice it is for them both to have come down to support Mum and I. We've come a long way since that fateful roast dinner.

Then the lights go down, the sound of Lizzo comes on over the speakers, and there, in the one spotlight at the centre of the stage, is my mum. I inhale sharply. She displays not a trace of nerves, but struts down the catwalk as if she owns it. She's rocking that look. She's so poised you'd think she'd spent a lifetime in stilettos, rather than the sensible M&S pumps I know she favours.

I also notice Liam, the photographer, almost invisible in black T-shirt and jeans, taking pictures discreetly, of the catwalk models. Perhaps he's done some fashion photography. He catches sight of me and smiles his ridiculously attractive smile; I feel myself blushing – who even am I?

Following on come the rest of the models, all made-up, hair styled in glossy waves, but none as stunning as my mum. I feel a lump in my throat. I'm so proud of her. When I think of what she's been through this summer . . . and look at her now.

If I'd ever doubted that she's starting a new chapter, the moment she's back down in the hall, she's swept into the arms of the man I'd noticed sitting in the front row, the side nearest the backstage door. He's got greying hair but he's more silver fox than TV pensions ad, and his posture is as straight as could be. Now he turns and I see it's someone I know. Or knew. Like, a few days ago and yet thirty-three years have passed. It's Mike, the broken-hearted friend of Bea's, and here he is, reunited at last with the woman who dumped him.

I have to look away, as it's frankly a bit gross to see your mum smooching someone, even when you know how deeply he felt for her. I am pleased for her though. She really seems to have her life together. I bet she's relegated all her old just-so outfits to the back of the wardrobe, and it'll be nothing but skinny jeans and Ruth Langsford pencil skirts from now on. She'll be learning to tie her own pussy bows at this rate.

Then she's rushing towards me, Mike trailing behind. 'Did you see me? A catwalk model!' she says with the glee of a small child. But before I can even congratulate her, my old mum is back. 'Come on, we've got to sort out your finale!' she says to me, more animated than I've seen her in years. 'Backstage again! Chop chop!' And with a brief kiss for Mike, we bustle backstage, where our vintage-themed outfits are hanging up, ready for the catwalk and the award judges.

In the time I was away from Mum's, working at the shop, the house has been transformed. She must have had a secret army of helpers: trestle tables already laden with food line the garden and the front wall, Raj has set up his speakers, and there's a massive sparkly banner flying from the upstairs window. Squinting up at it I can see it says, CONGRATULATIONS PEARLS AND DOODLES! SHORTLISTED FOR INDIE SHOP AWARD 2022. How she's managed to organise this so fast I can't begin to imagine, and this was meant to be *her* big moment – but she's made it mine as well. Honestly, she is the most special mum in the world.

Even so, she banishes me to the kitchen, with instructions. There's ice to be taken out of the freezer and put into the ice bucket (it's shaped like a pineapple, and we've had it for as long as I can remember). Then there is the food left in the fridge until the last minute, to be put onto platters. If there's any more time before the guests arrive, I'm to make up a big jug of sangria, in case anyone's thirsty. I automatically think I'm glad not to be wearing white jeans – and then recall the girl in the loos. I wonder how they got stains out in 1989?

No time to think about that now, as I chop fruit and mix it into the drink. I'd better do a Ribena version for Kitty, who won't want to be left out. Turning to the cupboard, I suddenly realise that I'm happy. I've been singing that Lizzo number under my breath, wiggling my bum here and there. Lizzo wouldn't take any nonsense and nor will I anymore!

'Tabby! You're in here,' Kitty shrieks, and that's the end of my daydreaming. I show her that I've made her own special summer punch, and she loves that it's purple. 'Matches my *Frozen* dress,' she points out – Vivi's daughter would of course notice that first of all.

She drags me outside, to where the party is getting going. Dad and Bernie stand together, close together in fact; they seem so relaxed, and I think what a relief it must be for them both, to be out in public and not have to hide away anymore. I notice Dad smoothly take Bernie's hand and hold it. They look at each other and smile and I can't help but smile too.

'So you're the famous Tabby.' Mike has come up to me from the side, and I didn't notice.

I nod, a little discombobulated. I was away with the fairies for Dad and Bernie. Michael is so similar to the Mike of all that time ago, and yet he isn't. Different clothes, of course, and that silver fox hair, and some wrinkles around his eyes and mouth. But also, he's brimming with happiness, whereas before he'd been so low. He's still having to shout above the music though.

'It's funny, I don't think I've met many Tabbys,' he goes

on. 'Just the one, in fact . . . and that was many years ago. A lovely lady, really sweet. You look a bit like her . . .'

'Strange coincidence, or what?' I laugh nervously, keeping it light. After all, there's no way I can even begin to explain. I don't want to start our 2022 acquaintance by making him think I'm crazy.

Kitty bumps into him and instead of being embarrassed, starts to introduce herself – typical of her. Mum beckons me over. 'Can I have a hand, please, Tabitha,' she says, ushering me inside, through the front door. 'There are more vegan sausage rolls to bring out of the oven – it'll be easier with two of us.'

Not only can my mum cook a mean Sunday roast, she's now prepared to cater for vegans as well. Things really have turned a corner.

As we step into the hallway, I pause to let my eyes adjust to the light, now we're out of the dazzling late-August sunshine. It strikes me that something else has changed, and I frown, trying to work out what it is.

'Oh, you've noticed.' Mum knows me so well, immediately tuning in to my confusion. 'It's only a few of them, I didn't think you'd mind.'

I see what she's looking at. We've always had a series of framed family photos on the walls, some of big occasions and others snapped on holiday. There were several of Mum and Dad's wedding, but now I register that there is just the one.

'I didn't want to take them all down, it's like pretending we were never married,' Mum carries on. 'Besides, I like that shot – see how young we look.'

'You rock that style!' I grin, noting the crisp perm and big dress, Princess Di style. Then I spot that she has replaced the other wedding photos with a couple of new pictures. Gazing more closely, I recognise the face. My breath catches in my throat: it's Bea. Bea as I knew her, and then a little older; Bea with her big sister, and between them a tiny baby. They're both looking at the child with love.

I *did* know my birth mother. Here's the evidence. It might not have been for long, but I can tell how she felt about me from the expression on her lovely face. And that expression is mirrored on Barbara's face: her love for me shines out of the picture. My two mothers, side by side.

I have been doubly blessed. That's what I have to remember, what I have to hold onto, if all my self-doubt comes back to haunt me: to keep telling myself that I've been loved by two amazing women, right from the very start.

It fills me with that confidence I've longed for. I don't have to see the world; all I need is here. My fulfilment will come from my little shop – no, my potentially award-winning shop! There's a glittering award ceremony in October, at a big hotel in London (I might spend my Insta nest egg on a dress), and it'll be awesome if we win but I won't mind if we don't. I already have everything I want: the shop is going online; Vivi will be working for – I mean, with – me; I'm reaching my flipping goals! I'm a 'goal getter', as Vivi would say! At last, I don't have to pretend to be anything I'm not. Mum's here, finally totally honest with me and all the happier for it, and Dad's happy with Bernie, living his real life with him at last. I can be whoever I want to be – and just being Tabitha Rose Burnley is absolutely bloody fine. Brilliant in fact.

Epilogue

Five years later . . .

'I F THAT BUMP GETS any bigger, I don't think we'll squeeze you behind the till anymore,' Vivienne says as I practically waddle through the front door, ready for another day selling treasure.

'You can talk! If Kaleb gets much bigger you won't be able to fit him in that sling anymore!' I say, nodding at the bouncing baby boy Vivienne has strapped to her front while she walks round the shop picking things off the shelves that have sold online and need posting out to their new homes.

'Aha! Maybe we could find your old magic ring and

travel back to when we could move about easily, and didn't have giant bags under our eyes,' she quips.

'Speak for yourself! My eyes are fine.' I laugh, smiling at the reference. We so rarely talk about the ring these days. Time really is the best healer after all.

'Kitty! If you don't leave now, you're going to be late!' Vivienne shouts towards the back room where her pre-teen is seemingly talking out loud to no one.

'In a minute!' she snaps back.

'Katherine Mabel Hawkins, take those things out of your ears and get moving. Chop-chop!' Vivienne says so firmly even the baby in my belly jumps.

'Right, well, I'll leave you to that, and I'm parking myself on the till stool all day. I'll serve customers but that's about it. This little gem is heeeaavy,' I smile, stroking my eight months pregnant bump lovingly.

It's a slow morning, so I'm glad to have Vivienne and Kaleb pottering about, helping restock (we sell so much online now, thanks to all the coverage after we won the award – yes, we won in the Vintage Fashion category! – that we are constantly trying to fill the shelves), bringing me cold glasses of squash and very lovely cuddles (with Kaleb I mean, not Vivi – that'd be a bit much, but I'm sure she'd oblige if I let her).

Lunchtime rolls around, and Vivi packs up her laptop, bundles Kaleb into his pram and gets ready to leave. 'Why don't you see if you can manage a tiny little walk?' Vivi suggests. 'It's gorgeous out there today, the sun is shining, the ice cream van's out on the square.'

'Oohh, now you've tempted me!' I say, knowing full well there's no way on earth I'm going to want to waddle to the square in this heat with my ankles as swollen as they are and this baby squashing up almost into my lungs. It's not just my ankles; my whole face feels swollen and puffy. I've gained a fair bit of weight throughout this pregnancy, and I'm really feeling it. But ice cream . . . I wrap my hair into a silky turban scarf, apply deep orange lipstick (so unlike the old me!) and throw on some huge 1970s sunglasses. At least if I'm going to look like a whale, I'm going to look like a chic one.

Then I decide a much better use of my time is to go through a bit of paperwork and stay no further than ten inches away from a large electric fan at all times.

We have a few customers in the afternoon, but the heatwave seems to be putting people off rummaging around old antiques – baffling to me, since that's my idea of heaven, but each to their own.

'Excuse me, do you sell vintage bags?' a customer asks sweetly when she comes in just before closing.

'We do, there's a whole wall of them round the corner.' I smile, noticing how young she is, maybe only sixteen or seventeen. She's wearing a short peach chiffon dress with strips of lace hanging off from all different places, gold Doc Marten boots and the most beautiful gold charm bracelet that tinkles as she walks.

She disappears off for a few minutes while I smile, thinking about how much I love her style. I've never seen an outfit like it in my life, but it's great that she's bold enough to wear something so out there. She pops back round.

'Sorry to bother—'

'It's no bother, lovey,' I say, instinctively feeling maternal towards this sweet young girl.

'Do you have any vintage Gucci bags?' she asks.

'Oohh, we don't really specialise in designer, but what sort were you thinking of? Maybe I could look on our e-store, we have a lot more on there,' I trail off, reaching down for my bag (harder than you think when you're the size of a small car) and looking for my phone.

'It's a bit niche, but I wanted to buy the aqua one with gold hardware that they brought out in the 20s. My mum loves vintage bags,' she says confidently.

I give up trying to reach my bag. 'Oh sweetie, I don't think Gucci did bags until the 40s.'

'They definitely did. My dad bought my mum one when I was born as a special present to her, and she lost it,' she says, so sure of herself it's admirable. 'I'm hunting one down.'

'Are you maybe thinking of another bag? It's just that I'm really into bags too. Your dad sounds like he's got good taste, and I know my stuff when it comes to Gucci.' I smile, thinking what an amazing daughter this girl sounds.

'Oh. I thought it was definitely Gucci,' she says, confidence wavering. 'My dad's a fashion photographer, and he looked around for ages for the right bag.'

'Tell you what, leave your details with me and I'll contact you if anything comes in,' I offer from behind my giant fan. 'Wanna shout it out, or just write it down?'

'S'OK, I'll write it,' she says.

As she walks up to the till, holding out a piece of paper, the first thing I see is her name.

'Ohhh, Amethyst is such a beautiful name!' I gush overenthusiastically. Liam and I have been debating names for months now, and this one is stunning. I wonder if I could get him on board.

'Ha, thanks.' She smiles, looking up at me, as I'm half hidden behind the fan and my giant glasses.

She seems to be looking really hard as she pushes her

hair out of her face, maybe to get a better view. That's when I see her rings. One ring in particular.

'Oh. That's a pretty ring,' I say, feeling a little flutter in my tummy.

'Erm, yep, it's cool. It's just an old one. Anyway, I have to go, thanks for the bag. Not the bag. Thanks for the shop,' she flusters.

'It's a pleasure,' I tell her.

As the bell above the door jingles I instinctively add 'Love you,' but she's already out of the door.

Time is a funny old thing.

Acknowledgments

Writing a book is a rollercoaster experience of high-highs (starting that first sentence, reading through your final draft, seeing it on the shelf) and low-lows (that moment at 4am where you're staring at your screen wondering why on earth the publishing house has any faith in you), but one of my favourite moments has to be this – writing the acknowledgments.

Usually, I like to sit in a quiet house with a little snack (packet of Skips goes down a treat for a task like this) to write this but today, I'm in a hotel room in Florida at a safari-themed resort with zebras, giraffes and flamingos outside my bedroom window. So, things feel a little . . .

wild. Ha. Also, it took everything in me not to type 'Wilde' there. If you know, you know.

Writing, editing, publishing, marketing and selling a book takes a lot of effort and a lot of people. I'd like to take a few minutes to give some of these people my most heartfelt thanks for everything they have done.

As ever, I would never be able to do any of the things I do without my amazing management team. First at Gleam Futures and now YMU Social. Their commitment, drive and skill far outweigh anything I have to offer and without them I'd just be a fleshy blob wafting about on the internet. So, thanks guys! Meghan, I regard you MOST highly. #HighRegard (she knows).

A massive, enormous, giant thanks must go to Bonnier Books UK who are *simply the best* (trying hard not to sing the rest of the song). And I'm not just saying that because they put out bowls of Maltesers at meetings. My editorial team Sarah Bauer and Katie Meegan are creative goddesses who always know just what to do in a pickle (like the time I wrote a whole chunk of book whilst I had a fever and it went a bit . . . wonky). I appreciate the loving guidance, and the fact that Sarah gets just as excited as I do for the 80s, ha!

In design and marketing, I would like to thank Jenny

Richards, David Ettridge, Vicky Joss and Holly Milnes. In sales and production, I'd like to thank Mark Williams, Stuart Finglass, Alex May and Eloise Angeline. I love what you have all done and am eternally grateful for your hard work.

I'd also like to give special mentions to the Bonnier PR legends Clare Kelly and Isabel Smith, as well as Charlotte Tobin and her team at Belle PR. Thank you for helping get the book 'out there' to the masses and thank you for all the fun train chats on book tours!

This book has been unusual in every way. It's a new type of book for me to write but also, for the whole team, this book was produced during 'unprecedented times'. Zooms instead of meetings, publication dates delayed, that fever that sent a chapter very wonky, etc. Throughout it all, the team remained positive (of mind, I mean, not . . . you know!), motivated and focused. They have been dedicated in ways I would never have expected and I hold everyone involved in the utmost esteem.

Time after time, this team has been incredible.

From the bottom of my jaded, withered heart, thank you

xxxx

Reading Group Questions

1. Who was your favourite character?

2. We begin with a shock revelation over Sunday dinner. How did this spark the chain of events throughout the book?

3. Tabitha loves picking up a vintage bargain. Have you ever found anything interesting in a jumble sale or second-hand shop?

4. How does this novel discuss the theme of friendship?

5. If you could time travel, what time would you go to and why?

6. Tabitha grows as a character throughout the novel. How was she different from start and at the end?

7. How does the novel look at motherhood?

8. What do you think happens to all the characters after the novel ends?

9. Do you remember the 1980s? Did the time travelling make you nostalgic?

10. How did the ending make you feel?

11. If you could meet any of the characters in real life, who would it be and why?

Join My Readers' Club

Thank you so much for reading my novel!

If you enjoyed *Time After Time*, why not join my Readers' Club* where I will tell life and all the latest news about my novels. Visit www.LouisePentlandNovel.com to sign up!

Louise xxx

* Just so you know, your data is private and confidential and it will never be passed on to a third party. I'll only ever be in touch now and again about book news, and if you want to unsubscribe, you can do that at any time.

**If you loved _Time After Time_,
you'll love Louise Pentland's other novels . . .**

Robin Wilde is an awesome single mum. She's great at
her job. Her best friend Lacey and bonkers Auntie Kath
love her and little Lyla to the moon and back. From the
outside, everything looks just fi ne.

But behind the mask she carefully applies every day,
things sometimes feel . . . grey. And lonely.

So after four years (and two months and twenty-four
days) of single-mum-dom, Robin Wilde has
decided it's time to Change. Her. Life!

With a little courage, creativity and help from the
wonderful women around her, Robin is about to
embark on quite an adventure . . .

Out now

**Follow the story of Robin Wilde
in the next two novels in the series:**

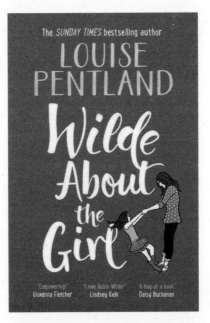

Out now

Discover where it all began with Louise Pentland's own story . . .

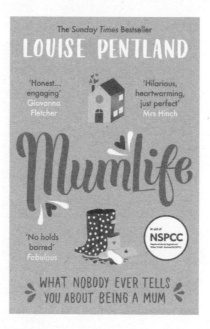

MumLife; noun: the inescapable swirling vortex of love, guilt, joy, annoyance, laughter and boredom that makes up the life of a mum.

Louise Pentland has been through a lot. From a traumatic birth with her first daughter, to single motherhood, to finding love again and having a second child, Louise's parenting journey has been full of surprises.

Discussing the realities most working mums face, plus the impact of maternal mental health, Louise is on a mission to make other mums feel less alone, and very much heard. She beautifully reveals her own imperfect but perfect route to motherhood, as well as the loss of her mum so early in her life, how it shaped her and the mother she became.

Reflective, uplifting and with her signature hilarious wit, *MumLife* will share Louise's ups and downs, reflecting on her route to motherhood and what she has learnt along the way. This is the honest truth, from someone who's been there and experienced it all.